WITHE

DEATH IN THE FOREST

'ł.]   n Division's war-hardened Assault
'ro   ıoves into battle again – as the Nazi
rmȝ   tacks one last time through the
.rde   :s. To carry out their secret
:coɪ   ssance mission, Corrigan and his
ıen   st take on three armies. Between
ıeir ('man objective and the British lines
es a well-armed gang of American
eserters and another army – of escaped
ussian prisoners, crazed with bloodlust
ıd f ɪr – roams the forest attacking
'erma ıs and Allies alike.

DEATH IN THE FOREST

DEATH IN
THE FOREST

by

Ian Harding

Dales Large Print Books
Long Preston, North Yorkshire,
BD23 4ND, England.

British Library Cataloguing in Publication Data.

Harding, Ian
    Death in the forest.

    A catalogue record of this book is
    available from the British Library

    ISBN   1-84262-384-2 pbk

First published in Great Britain by New English Library, 1983

Copyright © 1983 by Ian Harding

Cover illustration © André Leonard by arrangement with
P.W.A. International

The moral right of the author has been asserted

Published in Large Print 2005 by arrangement with
Eskdale Publishing

Dales Large Print is an imprint of Library Magna Books Ltd.

Printed and bound in Great Britain by
T.J. (International) Ltd., Cornwall, PL28 8RW

PRELUDE TO ACTION

'*Messenger:*
Prepare you, generals;
The enemy comes on in gallant show;
Their bloody sign of battle is hung out
And something to be done immediately.'

Shakespeare: *Julius Caesar*

'*Meine Herren, der Führer, Adolf Hitler!*'
As one, the commanders of all the divisions on the Western Front stiffened to attention, the great medieval hall of Schloss Ziegenberg echoing hollowly to the harsh crunch of their highly polished jackboots. All eyes turned to the great door, flanked by enormous SS adjutants with machine-pistols slung across their massive chests, ready for the slightest move. Since the attempt to kill the Führer this July, the guards were under orders to shoot first and ask questions afterwards – and the waiting generals knew it.

Slowly, painfully slowly, the master of National Socialist Germany came through the door, supported by his two chief advisers, Field-Marshal Keitel, tall, erect, wooden-faced, and Colonel-General Jodl, small, pale and cunning.

'*Heil Hitler!*' barked Colonel-General Sepp Dietrich, Commander of the Sixth SS Panzer Army, his voice thick with Schnapps, and flung up his right arm in salute.

'*Heil Hitler!*' roared the others, making the banner-hung, blackened rafters high above their heads in the Gothic gloom tremble.

Adolf Hitler flapped up his right arm

9

weakly and sank down gratefully into the high-backed wooden chair which one of the black-clad adjutants had slid under him. *'Danke, meine Herren,'* he said. *'Bitte, setzen Sie sich.'*

Hastily, these men who commanded the destinies of thousands, hundreds of thousands, of German soldiers fighting in the west, took their seats like chastened schoolboys, anxious not to offend their strict master. From down in the valley below, there drifted up the moan of the air-raid sirens. Evidently the low-flying Allied bombers and fighter-bombers were out again on one of their daily rampages, shooting up the German countryside without let or hindrance.

Adolf's Hitler's lips trembled like those of an old, old man who found it difficult to speak. To those watching him keenly who no longer believed in his star, it seemed impossible that this broken old man should still be entrusted with the fate of the Reich – or rather, what was left of the Reich after five years of total war. But as the presence of the hard-eyed, trigger-happy SS adjutants showed, Hitler still possessed muscle enough to strike terror into the heart of any would-be conspirator. Already in this terrible Winter of 1944, a good score of their former comrades, generals all, had been garrotted to death by chicken wire or hung from butcher's hooks for their supposed treachery. Hitler wouldn't hesitate for one moment to kill his highest-ranking officer here if necessary.

Hitler began to speak, but there was none of the old dramatic fervour in his voice. Instead, it was low and slow and laboured.

'*Meine Herren,*' he announced, 'on December the sixteenth, nineteen forty-four, the German Army in the west will ... will go over on the offensive once more.'

The announcement was totally unexpected. No one there had ever suspected that Germany could ever launch a major attack again. For six solid months, the Allies had chased the beaten Wehrmacht through France, Belgium, Luxembourg and Holland. Now, or so it had seemed to the assembled generals, Germany would have to fight all out just to maintain the defence of its hard-pressed frontier with the west.

Hitler raised his hand, silencing the generals' gasps of astonishment. 'I have decided that I will attack with three armies – Dietrich's Sixth, von Manteuffel's Fifth, and Brandenberger's Seventh. They will attack between Monschau in the north and Echternach in the south. That part of the front is held by four weak Ami divisions. We will go through the Ami gangsters and the Jewish bandits who command them like a hot knife through butter. There will be no stopping our heroic soldiers.'

11

Hitler paused to let the information sink in, before facing Dietrich, the squat, burly bully-boy in charge of the Sixth SS Army. 'You, my dear Sepp, will take our northern flank. Your task will be twofold: to make the decisive breakthrough and to hold the flank against any Ami counter-attack while you head for the River Meuse.'

The SS general's broad, craggy face revealed all too clearly that he was far from pleased with the mission given to his SS armoured divisions, but dutifully enough he clicked his heels together and snapped, '*Zu Befehl, mein Führer!*'

Next, Hitler turned his attention to von Manteuffel, commanding the Fifth Panzer Army. 'Your flank, von Manteuffel, will be protected by the infantry of General Brandenberger. Again your objective will be the River Meuse.'

Von Manteuffel, an undersized, aristocratic gentleman-jockey, bowed stiffly from the waist, but unlike his gross Bavarian rival from the SS, he wasn't completely overawed by the Führer's presence. Boldly he asked, 'And *mein Führer*, what is the final objective of this new counter-offensive?'

'Antwerp!' Hitler answered, with an alacrity that he showed all too rarely these days. It was almost as if he had been waiting all along for that overwhelming question to be asked. 'Antwerp, the Allies' major supply port, *must* be captured before this month is out. Once it is in German hands, the Anglo-American armies will be divided and will be forced to sue for a separate peace. Our Intelligence informs me that the English are scraping the manpower barrel, and I do not need to tell you gentlemen from the front that the Amis have no heart for a real fight. If their tanks and airplanes cannot do the job for them, their infantry will not go into battle. So – once we have Antwerp and the Anglo-American threat is removed, I shall deal with the Bolsheviks – *once and for all!*'

As abruptly as he had started, Adolf Hitler stopped speaking and slumped down in his chair. A silence descended upon the great hall, heavy and brooding, as the generals pondered the Führer's words. For a long time, no one spoke, or moved. In the flickering, fitful light of the candles, the glittering assembly seemed frozen there as if for eternity, the only movement their wavering shadows thrown grotesquely and magnified many times over on the bare walls.

Then Colonel-General Jodl broke the silence.

'*Meine Herren*, could I have your attention, please?' he requested. 'I have a few facts and figures pertaining to the new attack for your information. First, we are feeding seventy-seven thousand replacements into the three armies involved. Each armoured fighting vehicle will have enough fuel for one hundred and twenty kilometres of running time: three million litres of diesel or gas in all. There is enough ammunition stored behind the front for eight days' combat. Three hundred and fifty fighters, mostly the new jets, will support the ground troops, who will total a quarter of a million – opposed by a mere eighty thousand Americans. There will be...'

On and on Jodl droned, in that dry, precise voice of his, never once stopping to refer to his notes, reeling off an endless list of facts and figures concerning the new offensive.

The statistics made the minds of his listeners whirl; Germany had never possessed such strength ever before. The aristocratic, haughty Prussian faces of the generals revealed all-too clearly their puzzlement: where in heaven's name had National Socialist Germany obtained so many men and so much new material, when all the world thought she was about ready to collapse? *Where?*

It was the Führer himself who answered that question for them. Removing the nickel-framed glasses which he had put on to study Jodl's fact sheet, he allowed himself to be helped to his feet by two black-clad giants and stared round the circle of shocked, disbelieving faces, hollowed out to bony death's heads in the flickering yellow light.

'Gentlemen,' he said, hoarse with emotion, 'this great new offensive has only been made possible by the last, superhuman effort of our comrades in the factories and workshops of the Reich – an effort without precedent in the entire history of the German people.'

He paused for a moment to let his words sink in. 'Before you go your separate ways for your briefings, I would like to request you to bear *this* in mind: this battle is to decide whether we live – or die.' Hitler's eyes suddenly flashed fire with a trace of that old magic that had mesmerised them for so long. 'I want my soldiers to fight hard and without pity. The battle to come must be waged with the utmost brutality, and all resistance must be broken with a wave of terror. In this most grave hour in the history of our beloved Fatherland, I expect every one of my soldiers to be courageous – and courageous to the last.'

In his position immediately opposite the Führer, the undersized von Manteuffel, commander of the Fifth Panzer Army, a man long disillusioned with Adolf Hitler, once more felt the full power of that hypnotic gaze. As of old, the small hairs at the back of his shaven skull rose and stood erect. A strange thrill, a compound of fear, pride and foreboding, made him shiver involuntarily. Could this senile madman who had com- manded Germany's destiny for nearly twelve years now and boasted that he would create a Reich that would last a thousand years *really* pull it off again in the eleventh hour?

Adolf Hitler's cheeks flushed a hectic red. His eyes blazed. As in the great days of the old Party rallies at Nuremberg when he had addressed hundreds of thousands of excited, exultant Nazis, his coarse Austrian voice rose to a tremendous, hysterical crescendo, and he roared, 'Comrades, the enemy must be beaten – it is now or never! *Otherwise our Germany dies!*'

BOOK ONE

GOING UP

'If I were fierce and bald and short of breath
I'd live with scarlet majors at the Base
And speed glum heroes up the line to
   death.'

Siegfried Sassoon, '*Base Details*'

ONE

The barn stank of ether, sweat and fear.

On the floor, greasy with blood and urine, the two khaki-clad doctors worked at a furious rate, the orderlies dabbing the sweat from their brows, while more and more wounded men were brought in by the stretcher-bearers.

'...Traumatic amputation, right foot... Compound fracturing of same... Left tibia with massive tissue loss...' someone was saying in a dry voice, leaning over what looked like a broken ivory stick, glistening out of a mass of fig-red flesh.

'Found his boot with the foot inside it, sir,' one of the stretcher-bearers was saying wearily. 'But we left it there... Didn't really know what to do with it, sir.'

Airily, the man bending over the shattered legs waved his hand to indicate all was all right – he didn't need the missing foot.

With a groan, Captain Corrigan, CO of the Iron Division's assault troop, raised himself from the blood-soaked straw that littered the floor. A skewer of excruciating pain dug into his right eye. He bit his bottom lip hard. Carefully, very carefully, he

19

turned his head.

All around him were wounded men in ripped, blood-stained khaki, groaning or moaning, or frighteningly silent, all waiting in long lines while the orderlies sorted out those who were in most urgent need of surgery. There were at least a couple of hundred of them, all wearing the black and red triangle of the Iron Division on their arms.

'No unusual activity on Second Army front... Just routine patrol activity,' commented a cynical voice at his side.

Corrigan turned his head, a lieutenant in the Durhams lay there, face ashen, morphine dosages and other information pencilled on his sweating brow. His right foot – or what was left of it – was swathed in thick shell dressings which were already turning pink. He was smoking a Woodbine slowly and happily, as if determined to enjoy it down to the last drag.

Captain Corrigan laughed softly. 'I suppose you're right. Christ, what a mess!' He indicated the youngster, naked except for his boots, who lay on the operating table immediately in front of them. Under the hissing white incandescent light of the pressure lanterns, a surgeon in blood-splattered rubber apron, his rubber boots deep in blood, was vainly trying to hold a severed artery. But every time he removed his fingers from the slippery mess of raw

20

flesh, blood jetted out in a crimson stream.

'Oh, blast the bloody thing!' he cried. 'Here, orderly, hold him down!'

With two swift slashes, the surgeon cut even deeper into the mangled limbs. Then, dropping the scalpel hastily into the kidney-shaped dish, he grabbed a saw and hurriedly started to hack his way through the gleaming white bone.

'Seen better butchers back in Blighty,' said the drugged Durham, as Corrigan gritted his teeth against the noise. 'Still, at least he's out of it at last. Know the kid. Came over with the regiment on D-Two.' The Durham laughed bitterly. 'Christ, D-Two. It seems bloody light years away now, don't it! Six months since we first tackled old Jerry, and he's still fighting back. Cor, fuck a duck. What a life!'

Corrigan winced as the pain struck him again. In front of him, the surgeon was now tugging away the leg and handing it to the orderly, who took it away and dropped it routinely on a pile of severed limbs next to the door of the Field Dressing Station. For all the world, they looked like the heaps of offal Corrigan remembered seeing outside butchers' shops as a kid before the war.

'Me, I put my stupid foot on a mine. Those bloody Dutch marshes are full of them,' the Durham said. 'You?'

'Eighty-eight. Early this morning,' Corrigan answered, his face suddenly turning bitter at the thought of just how easily the assault troop had ridden into the trap which the Germans had laid for them just across the border with Holland. 'Routine patrol. Spotted a Jerry SP, went after him like rank bloody amateurs – tally-ho, away hounds, the whole ruddy lot. Up beyond the dyke, they were waiting for us with massed eighty-eights. Two Bren-gun carriers and my own White scout-car bought it. Served me right, too. Five of my chaps got the chop.'

'You're lucky, Captain,' said the Durham, still puffing away at his Woodbine. 'My whole ruddy platoon bought it. They must have dropped butterfly bombs into the marshes last night. Christ – five minutes after we walked into them, the place looked like a knacker's yard! My chaps were lying everywhere, screaming their heads off, legs, feet, ballocks, the whole lot gone.' He indicated the surgeon, who was now ripping a yellow, blood-stained wound dressing off what had once been a soldier's genitals, revealing a hideous purple gaping hole with pus oozing out of it. 'He's one of mine. Only seventeen and a half, the poor bugger.' The Durham sighed. 'Thank God, I lost my foot. Otherwise the CO would have court-martialled me for dereliction of duty.'

The boy screamed as the surgeon inserted his probe into the purple hole.

'Captain Corrigan... Captain Corrigan... Assault troop?'

Corrigan turned stiffly and looked up.

A young major wearing the ribbon of the Military Cross and the red band of the staff was staring down at him anxiously, one hand holding an elegant khaki-silk handkerchief to his nostrils to keep out the awful stink.

'Yes, I'm Corrigan... At least, I think I still am.'

Next to him, the Durham laughed hollowly. 'Watch it, friend. The base wallahs are on the prowl.' He looked at the major scornfully, in no way awed by the other officer's rank. His days in the British Army were finished, and he knew it; what had he to be afraid of? The 'Blighty wound', as it was called, solved all problems of that kind. A month or so from now, he would be back in civvy street.

'Kent, Major, Rifle Corps.' The other man introduced himself in a kind of military shorthand, keeping one hand to the side of his mouth as he spoke and staring down at Corrigan's harshly handsome face, marred now by the encrusted bloody at the temple and right cheek. 'The Master would like a word with you, Corrigan, at the earliest possible moment.'

'Master?' Corrigan breathed, a little bewildered at the sudden appearance of the elegant staff officer in the midst of all this dirt, pain and misery.

'Yes–'

'What the devil's going on here?' Suddenly a harsh voice cut into the young major's explanation.

One of the two surgeons, looking dog-tired, with blood splattered all over his apron, stood there, glaring angrily, hypo in his right hand, a bottle of ration cognac in the other.

The major bridled at the interruption. 'I was just attempting–'

'You've no right to attempt *anything* here,' the surgeon fumed, cutting him short again. 'Don't you know this is a ruddy Field Dressing Station? Everything depends on speed. A man's life can be snuffed out just like *that*' – he snapped his fingers – 'by a minute's delay.' He took a hefty swig straight out of the bottle, his cheeks flushing an even more hectic red. 'This officer is suffering from multiple lacerations of the head–'

'*Sir*,' the major interrupted the irate, over-worked surgeon firmly, 'I am from Field-Marshal Montgomery's staff.'

'You mean the Master is ... *Monty?*' asked Corrigan hurriedly.

Next to him, the crippled Durham crossed himself with mock-solemnity and folding his hands, intoned, 'Let us pray...'

'Yes,' replied the Rifle Corps major, 'and I've come all the way from his HQ at Maas-

24

tricht to find you, Captain Corrigan.' He looked from Corrigan to the angry, flushed face of the surgeon. 'So, sir, I suggest that unless Captain Corrigan is totally incapable of being moved, you'd better patch him up as best you can and let us both get under way. Field-Marshal Montgomery, as you perhaps know, doesn't like to be kept waiting...'

Ten minutes later, the young major and Captain Corrigan, his head swathed in bandages and right arm shot full of dope, were on their way.

'What's this all about, Major?' Corrigan asked, his head still feeling as if it was wrapped in thick cotton wool.

Behind the wheel of the jeep, Kent kept his eyes glued to the road. It was pitted with shell-holes, and although the white tapes on the muddy verges to both sides indicated that it had been cleared of mines, you never knew – perhaps the odd one still lay there beneath the oozing mud.

'Can't tell you very much, Corrigan, because quite frankly I don't know too much myself. You see, I'm one of the Master's eyes and ears.'

'Eyes and ears?' Corrigan echoed a little stupidly, as a wrecked British tank, already red with rust and surrounded by a circle of rough graves, flashed by. Another victim of those German 88mm cannon, thought

25

Corrigan grimly.

'Yes – there are about a dozen of us, American and British, all battle-experienced, who make daily trips to our various Allied fronts and report back directly to the Master.'

'Couldn't you just call him Monty? "Master" seems so pompous,' Corrigan objected mildly.

Kent flashed a quizzical look at the tall, bronzed officer with the bitter, down-turned mouth and grinned. 'He likes us to call him that, you know. I think he rather enjoys the schoolmaster-pupil relationship. *Monty*, then, gets his direct reports on what's going on from us. That way, his information isn't filtered and perhaps slightly *distorted* by the gentlemen of the staff.'

'Good idea. But what's all this got to do with me, Major?'

'This. The balloon seems to have gone up on the American front in the Ardennes.'

'South of here?'

'Yes, between Echternach in Luxembourg and Monschau in Germany. The Yanks used that section of the front for resting their combat divisions and training their new troops. There hasn't been any trouble there since last September. The Yanks themselves called it the Ghost Front – that is, until last Saturday, when the Boche attacked the four divisions holding the sixty miles of line there.'

Kent paused and let Corrigan absorb the

information, as he steered his way round a huge crater in the muddy road. In the middle of it lay what looked like a hunk of mouldy green meat. Kent shuddered. It was the shattered leg of a German soldier – he recognised it by the jackboot – attached to a headless and armless trunk. Some joker had attached a crude sign to the horror. It read: '*Don't eat bully beef. This is what they make it from. Kilroy.*'

'But surely, there are no British troops down there with the Yanks?' Corrigan objected.

'I know, I know. But the Master – excuse me, Field-Marshal Montgomery reckons that as soon as the Yanks get themselves into a real pickle in the Ardennes – which he thinks won't be long – we'll soon be asked to bail them out.' He gave a dry chuckle. 'You know what the Yanks have been boasting all along – that if it wasn't for them, we Limeys would have lost the war long ago. They've been saying that in pubs for years.'

'I wouldn't know,' Corrigan said mildly.

'Of course, you've been in foreign parts. Well, now it seems *we're* about to help them out of the mess they've got themselves into. And believe you me, Corrigan, nothing will give Monty more pleasure. Especially if he can rub their big American noses right into the muck, nice and deep, while he's doing so!'

'I see,' Corrigan said, though in fact he didn't.

Now they were approaching Maastricht, Montgomery's HQ – but you didn't need a map to know where you were. Everywhere men in khaki strode back and forth smartly, clean-shaven and fit-looking, their uniforms pressed, the collars done up, their berets set at the correct angle. As the jeep passed, the immaculate Redcaps, their webbing blancoed a brilliant white, swung the two officers a tremendous salute, as if they were back on a UK parade ground.

Corrigan forced a weary grin. 'Bullshit reigns supreme, I see, Major.' And then, as Kent started to follow the signs to Montgomery's 21st Army Group, 'But clue me in before I meet his nibs. What does Monty want the assault troop for, Major?'

Kent's easy grin vanished. Before them, covered with camouflaged nets and surrounded by 37mm Bofors anti-aircraft guns set in sand-bagged pits, was the collection of captured Italian and German caravans which made up Montgomery's HQ, shrouded in the grey afternoon mist which hung perpetually over this part of Holland in Winter.

'A mission, old chap,' Kent answered hurriedly. 'A mission, I don't doubt, of *national importance!*'

The next moment they were rolling to a stop at the barrier, with rigid sentries

28

slapping their rifle butts hard, immaculate NCOs saluting fiercely, officers rapping out orders. In front of them on the steps of his caravan, a small, slight figure buried in an over-large duffle coat with a multi-badged beret pulled down low over his forehead, stared at the new arrivals with undisguised pleasure and impatience...

TWO

'Don't seem the same, Sarge, without the old CO,' said Trooper Wolfers of the assault troop a little sadly, as he fried two looted eggs and some issue tinned bacon on his shovel over the Dutch stove. 'I mean, I know he's a bit of a hard-arsed bugger, but he's fair, and he knows what he's doing. Not like a lot of yer bloody officers.' Impatiently he snatched a piece of half-cooked bacon from the red-hot shovel and swallowed it greedily.

'Not putting yer off yer grub though, I notice,' observed Sergeant Hawkins, as he applied some more cold tea to his dyed hair with an old toothbrush. Since the assault troop had been billeted in the ruined Dutch farm near the German frontier, he'd had more time for his 'ablutions', as he called them – in particular his hair, which had begun to turn snow-white again.

However, irony was wasted on Trooper Wolfers, who, although a giant in appearance, sadly didn't have an intellect to match. 'Yer've got to get summat inside yerself in this weather, Sarge. It stands to reason. A couple of hours of stag out there of a night in yon bloody cold, and yer outside plumbing's froze right up. Yer've got to grease yer innards with *summat.*' He tossed the eggs gently to prevent them sticking to the shovel. 'When do you think he'll be back – the CO, I mean?'

Carefully, his false teeth bulging a little out of his wizened old face, Sergeant Hawkins worked the toothbrush along both sides of his parting, dripping cold tea to left and right. 'Search me, Wolfers,' he said finally. 'But knowing Captain Corrigan, it won't be long. They'll never keep *him* in dock. Besides, by now he'll have heard all about the chinless wonder they've put in his place.' He pointed his toothbrush through the cracked window to the muddy, cobbled farmyard outside, wreathed as always in a grey, dripping, miserable mist. 'Acting Captain de Vere Smythe is one officer yours truly can do without, thank you very much.'

Gingerly, Wolfers started to slide the precious eggs, bubbling and sizzling delightfully now, from the spade and onto a tin plate. 'Yeah, you can say that again, Sarge,' he agreed, eyes sparkling in greedy anticipation. 'He's gonna have a kit inspection at fourteen hundred hours today. A kit inspection in the frigging front line, Sarge! I ask yer!' He shook his head in mock-wonder at man's inhumanity to man, then sighed happily as the two eggs slid onto the plate without breaking. Next he set to work on the curling rolls of tinned bacon, which were

31

spluttering away nicely now, licking his thick wet lips as he did so. As always, Trooper Wolfers was ravenously hungry. 'I mean, Christ, Sarge, if it goes on like this, he'll have us doing frigging close-order drill for the Jerries next.'

'He might well just do that, Wolfers,' Sergeant Hawkins agreed, and started putting away his yellow mug of cold tea and battered toothbrush. 'And by the way, watch it – his nibs is heading straight this way.'

With an oath, Wolfers hastily inserted his jack-knife under the first of the fried eggs, balanced it on the blade momentarily and swallowed it whole.

Outside, Captain Smythe had apparently finished his first inspection of the farm and was marching towards the little kitchen, swinging his left arm rigidly back and forth as if he were back at the depot in Catterick, swagger-stick clasped tightly beneath the right.

Wolfers gave a great sucking motion and the second egg disappeared into his mouth as if it had never existed. Hurriedly he grabbed the bacon, which was still half-cooked, and stuck it into his trouser pocket, while with his free hand he flung the shovel in the corner, along with the rest of the mess of grenades, ammo bandoliers, shell-boxes, towing ropes and the like which littered the floor. Next moment the door was flung open imperiously and Captain de Vere Smythe stood there, all sloping chin and huge black cavalry moustache, and wearing a cheese-cutter of a cap which would have done credit to a guardsman doing sentry-go outside Buckingham Palace.

'What... What a mess!' he cried, his skinny young face flushed angrily. 'Everything absolutely in shit order – *shit order!*' The young replacement officer had, as Hawkins had already noted, a habit of repeating things.

'We've been in the line since June, sir,' Hawkins ventured.

'Absolutely no excuse – no excuse whatsoever,' the captain snapped, thwacking his absurd cane against his leg to drive home the point. 'Back at Catterick, we were out on schemes in all weathers for months on end, but we didn't get ourselves into this sort of shit order! Vehicles looking as if regulation maintenance hasn't been carried out for years. Weapons filthy. Men unshaven. Why,' he cried, appalled, his black moustache bristling, 'the only blanco I can damn well see here is emerald green, when everyone knows that according to BO531/24, it should be khaki green... *Khaki* green!'

'Captain Corrigan didn't go very much on Orders, sir,' Hawkins protested, noting out of the corner of his eye that smoke was issuing out of young Wolfers' pocket as he stood there rigidly to attention, staring at the horizon.

'I am *not* Captain Corrigan,' Smythe said firmly. 'Get that into your thick skulls. *Not* Captain Corrigan. Now, I'm going to cancel the kit inspection for fourteen hundred hours. Instead, I want you to parade this awful shower of yours in full field service marching order, complete with blanket, and properly blancoed in the correct colour. I'm going to show this rabble of an assault troop what *real* soldering is.'

'*Full FSMO, sir!*' Hawkins exclaimed, aghast, his false teeth almost popping out of his mouth with shock. 'But sir, we're only a mile behind the firing line! People are getting killed just up that road! The Jerries have got snipers and FAOs everywhere. They'd just love a target like that.' He gulped hard, trying to ignore the smoke now pouring furiously from Wolfers' pocket as he stood there rigidly to attention. 'You can't have a parade, sir,' he stuttered. 'Not... Not up here–'

'You heard me, Hawkins,' Captain Smythe snapped harshly. 'And by the way, where's that damned new batman of mine? What's his name? Sanders, or something. Have him report to my bunk immediately to get my boots and things bulled up for the parade. Oh, never mind...' Smythe slapped his thigh with his cane in irritation. 'I'll find him myself. He can't be far away.'

Turning, he found himself staring at a crimson-faced Wolfers. 'And you, Trooper – you seem to be on fire or something. Better do something about it at the double... *At the double!*'

With that he was gone. For a moment Hawkins and Wolfers stared at each other in blank incomprehension, the only sound their own heavy, shocked breathing and the hollow boom of the guns in the distance. Then suddenly the giant Yorkshireman with the ugly, spotty face realised that his pocket was on fire from the hot bacon – and that he had a couple of live 36 grenades attached to his webbing belt, only inches away! With a yelp of pain and alarm, he grabbed hastily for Sergeant Hawkins' precious mug of cold tea...

Trooper 'Slim' Sanders sucked his thin lips and looked at the big homely Dutchwoman with cunning eyes. She seemed to be making beckoning movements towards the barn with her red paw, a big grin spread all across her pudding face. What *did* she want? His stomach rumbled suddenly and reminded him that he had only a piece of hard tack and a slab of cold bully for breakfast. Suddenly a vision of six eggs, fried to crisp perfection and washed down with a slug of looted German gin, flashed before his mind's eye.

His stomach growled even more noisily.

'Eggs?' he asked, making a dumb show of flapping wings and crowing like a chicken. '*Oeuf... Uovo... Eier...* You got?'

The big farm woman in her wooden clogs nodded her head eagerly and pointed to the barn once again. '*Ja! Ja!*' she said eagerly. '*Eiern... Komm – komm, Soldat.*' She laughed and rolled her eyes like an idiot.

'Christ!' whispered Slim under his breath. 'What a pig!' But he followed her obediently enough as she clattered across the manure-stained cobbles and began to mount the rickety ladder which led to the top of the barn.

Hastily the little Australian – who was wont to boast to his comrades of the assault troop, 'Mates, I've deserted from more regiments than you bleeders have had hot dinners!' – threw a glance behind him. No one was going to get *his* bleeding eggs. But all was quiet. Most of the other troopers would be inside the half-timbered building, reading the week-old papers from Blighty and drooling over Jane in the *Daily Mirror*. Somewhere, someone was playing a scratchy recording of Bing Crosby, crooning '*I'm Dreaming of a White Christmas.*' The coast was clear.

'*Komm... Schnell!*' the Dutchwoman called eagerly, crooking her small pork sausage of a finger.

'*Ja, ja,*' he answered, 'and cut it down to small roar, willya?'

He began to mount the rickety ladder behind her, her vast buttocks blotting out the grey, misty Winter sky. As she clambered into the loft, he caught a fleeting glimpse of her drawers. They were made of a loose pink woollen mixture and looked as if she might well have knitted them herself. He shuddered with horror. Christ, he thought in disgust, a cobber'd have to be mighty hard up to stick his oar into *that* thing!

He heaved himself over the top onto the straw-covered floor. In the corner the woman was shooing away the chickens roosting there and hastily collecting the still warm eggs and placing them in her apron, clucking away happily to herself like an enormous mother hen.

Sanders let her get on with it, his stomach doing back-flips in greedy anticipation. Cripes, she had at least a dozen in her apron! Wherever would he find a dixie big enough to fry *that* lot in?

Finally she was finished. Still beaming like an idiot, she advanced towards him, her egg-filled apron outstretched, walking on the tips of her toes in her manure-stained clogs as if she were a ballet-dancer. Outside, Hawkins was bellowing something. Sanders didn't care. The silly old shit of a sergeant-major could go and take a running jump.

Whatever the matter was, he was going to have his eggs first.

Suddenly the woman dropped to her heels. Before an astonished Slim could stop her, she took one of the eggs and thrust it deep into his pocket, her face suddenly bearing a look of sheer bovine ecstasy.

'Hey knock it off, Sheilah!' Slim protested, feeling the warmth of the egg penetrating the cloth of his pocket and circle his testicles.

'You like?' asked the woman, breathing hard, lips parted invitingly, giving the Australian the full benefit of her blackened teeth. She grabbed another egg and thrust it into the other pocket. This time her hand penetrated deeper.

Slim jumped back, startled. 'Hey, get yer paws off me!' he yelled in alarm. 'What d'yer think that is, a frigging pump or something? Now–'

But Dutchwoman was not to be stopped. Her massive bosom heaving with blind passion, she released the eggs with her free hand and let them slip into the straw. Next moment she knocked the skinny little soldier over, right on top of them. Her full weight descended upon him, crushing the breath out of him, as she fumbled for the tape which kept up her woollen knickers, chuckling like an idiot and breathing endearments in Dutch. Next moment, they were down around her ankles, and she was sighing in an ecstasy of passion, '*Komm! Komm, Kleiner Soldat... Schnell!*'

'Help,' yelled Sanders, gasping for breath, as the woman bore down on him, legs spread wide apart, skirt thrown up to reveal her enormous naked buttocks. 'Get off me, yer silly cow!'

But the woman was beside herself with passion. She wanted the little Australian with his cocky mouth and bright blue eyes – and she was going to have him. She hadn't had a man since a one-eyed German corporal had jumped her while she had been milking 'Elkse' back in October, and that was nearly three months ago, what's more the German hero hadn't even had the courtesy to take her drawers off. Panting hard, she exerted all her weight, determined to keep the little man pinned down, no matter how hard he struggled. She grinned, her pudding face crimson and greased with sweat. She liked a man who had a bit of fight in him! In the old days, before they'd taken away her husband, old Willem, he used to chase her all over the bedroom of a Saturday night, his salami in one hand and the bottle of *Genever* in the other. Those were the days! The memory of them increased her sexual excitement and freeing one hand, she started to rip open the little man's flies. *Gottverdamme*, wasn't he putting up a good fight! She liked a man with a bit of spirit –

even if he was a little'un!

But the huge sex-starved Dutchwoman was fated never to enjoy Slim Sanders' favours that particular grey, December morning. For suddenly a whistle shrilled urgently, and the plummy, affected tones of Captain De Vere Smythe could be heard calling indignantly, '*Rape! Sergeant Hawkins! At the double, man! One of your damned chaps is trying to have sexual intercourse with one of the native women, the swine! At the double, Sergeant Hawkins… Rape!*'

THREE

Monty fixed him with those pale, hard blue eyes of his, then barked in his high-pitched upper-class voice, 'You look dickey, Corrigan. You'd better sit down.'

Obediently he did so, facing the army commander across the desk in the spartanly furnished caravan, the only decoration on the walls consisting of two portraits of the field-marshal's chief opponents in the west, Field-Marshals Rommel and von Rundstedt, and a couple of maps.

'If you want, you can have a cup of tea.' Monty indicated the Thermos on the desk. 'But I don't want you smoking in here. Now cough. When I start to speak I want no interruptions.'

Corrigan's face remained impassive, but inside he told himself that Monty was running true to form. The man had an ego as big as Everest. 'No, thank you, sir. I don't need any tea.'

'Good, then let's get down to it, shall we? Now I know your reputation, Corrigan, and it's bad. You've always been a bit bolshy. Struck an American colonel at Anzio. Fortunately you won the MC there, or you'd

41

have been cashiered. It wasn't much different in Normandy either, Corrigan. You missed a court-martial sentence there by the skin of your teeth for disobeying a superior officer's order, and if General Horrocks of Thirty Corps hadn't been such a good chap, your remarks to him about the performance of his corps at Arnhem this September would have landed you in serious trouble.' Montgomery sighed and pinched the bridge of his beak-like nose with the air of a man who was tired, very tired. 'You know, Corrigan, you're going nowhere. You're Regular Army, commissioned before the war. By now you should be a colonel. Look at me.'

Corrigan knew he had nothing to lose. Montgomery needed him for something or other, so he was safe; but even assuming he survived the war, there was no future for him in the British Army – and he knew it.

'But you were lucky, sir,' he ventured boldly.

Montgomery shook his head. 'No, Corrigan, you're not quite right there. You have to make your *own* luck, you see. Always have your eye to the main chance. But enough of the lecture. For all your failings, Corrigan, you're the only kind of officer I could entrust this mission to. You're bold, brave – and ruthless. All the qualities I need for the job I'm now going to propose to you.'

Corrigan's heart started to beat faster.

Monty had something for him. At last he was going to bid farewell to that damned, rain-sodden Dutch mud for good. He leaned forward eagerly.

Carefully Montgomery rose to his feet and tapped the big map of the western front pinned to the wall of the caravan, its surface covered with a rash of blue and red pins indicating friendly and enemy positions.

'The Ardennes,' he announced, 'held by the US First Army under General Hodges.'

Corrigan gazed at the mass of red pins which had swept through the Allied line like a blood-red spearhead.

'As you can see, Corrigan, the Boche has broken through there in considerable strength. As far as my Intelligence can discover, three Boche armies are advancing in that region between Monschau in the north to Echternach in the south, in a strength of some sixteen divisions, sweeping the remnants of the four US divisions holding the front there before them. In essence, the American formations there have been beaten and broken. Now, Corrigan, all that General Eisenhower has in the way of reserves to bolster up Hodges' front are his two airborne divisions, the Eighty-second and Hundred-and-first Airborne, which are already on their way to the Ardennes from their rest camps in France. Naturally,' he added matter-of-factly, 'two lightly armed airborne divisions aren't going to stop a German armoured force.'

Monty turned and paused a moment to let his words sink in, staring intently at the young captain with the battered, harshly handsome face and the drooping, bitter lips of a disappointed man; it was almost as if the army commander was trying to find something in those features which would encourage him to continue. Meanwhile, from outside came the harsh voice of a drill-sergeant: *'Come on, you ruddy idle men, open them legs... Nothing'll fall out! Come on now, bags of swank!'* – accompanied by the crisp, precise sound of nailed boots marching by. Montgomery sighed.

Corrigan waited.

'So, Corrigan, what's going to happen up there?' It was a rhetorical question. 'The Americans won't be able to stop the Boche, who are obviously heading for the River Meuse crossings. They'll have to content themselves with holding both sides of the German penetration in the Ardennes. And then what? Whistle in the wind, perhaps? *No.'* Montgomery's high-pitched voice hardened, and suddenly those bright-blue eyes of his gleamed fiercely. 'Once Eisenhower discovers he can't hold the Boche with his two airborne divisions, he's going to call on my Second Army to put a stop to the rot. But by that time, Corrigan,' Montgomery lowered his voice significantly, *'it might well be too late!'*

'I see, sir,' Corrigan said dutifully. Inwardly, however, he was wondering what all this had to do with him and his assault troop. His wounds also, were beginning to throb dully once more, as the morphia shots given him by the harassed front-line doctor started to lose their potency...

'So,' said Montgomery, with sudden jauntiness, a look of almost schoolboyish glee animating his skinny face, 'we shall have to be a little naughty, won't we, and do something slightly illegal, what?'

'Sir?'

Montgomery turned to the map again. 'My chief of intelligence, Brigadier Williams, estimates that the German Army which will make the running is General Manteuffel's Fifth Panzar, which, according to him, is now racing for the Meuse, *here,* and obviously heading for the bridges across the river at Huy, *here* and Dinants, *here...*'

Corrigan followed Montgomery's finger as it stabbed the map, noting that the two Belgian towns were located south of the great industrial city of Liège, with beyond them the great plain of Belgium and northern France – the route the Germans had taken in 1940, when they had raced for the French coast and so ignominiously turfed the British Army out of Europe at Dunkirk.

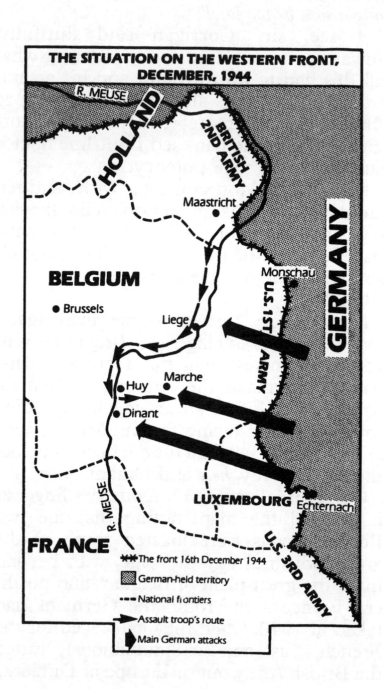

THE SITUATION ON THE WESTERN FRONT, DECEMBER, 1944

R. MEUSE

HOLLAND

BRITISH 2ND ARMY

Maastricht

GERMANY

Monschau

BELGIUM

U.S. 1ST ARMY

Brussels

Liege

Marche

Huy

Dinant

LUXEMBOURG   Echternach

R. MEUSE

FRANCE

U.S. 3RD ARMY

✕✕✕ The front 16th December 1944

▨ German-held territory

--- National frontiers

➤ Assault troop's route

➤ Main German attacks

Montgomery seemed to read his mind, for he said jovially, 'Don't worry, Corrigan – there won't be another Dunkirk this time, because Dunkirk is still in Boche hands. We'll stop him before he ever reaches the Meuse, God willing. Because this is what I'm going to do. I'm going to switch Horrocks's Thirty Corps from the line here in Holland down to the west bank.'

Corrigan gasped. 'But isn't that risky, sir? You'll be exposing your whole front here. What if the Germans attack here?'

'That's a risk I'm prepared to take, Corrigan. You see, I have no alternative. If the Boche *do* cross the Meuse, they'll split the British and American armies, and that'll be the end of our effort in Europe. We'll be cut off from our supply ports, and at best the war in the west will bog down to a stalemate, while our Russian so-called allies are free to walk all over Germany.' Suddenly the little field-marshal in his sloppy pullover and baggy civilian corduroy trousers looked worried. 'Unless we act now, Corrigan, and stop the Boche on the Meuse, the whole future of Europe for the rest of this century will be put at risk. Russia will dominate the post-war continent and we'll have fought this long, bloody war in vain. It's a race against time, *against death!*'

There was a sudden, heavy silence in which could be heard the prissy voice of a headquarters clerk outside: '*Of course, I tried to register as a conchie – I'd have been a fool not to! But I made a balls-up of the interview. The chairman asked me what I'd do if a Jerry tried to rape my sister, and I said, try to interpose myself between the two of them* – gently. *Naturally that wasn't the right answer. So here I am, fighting the war for democracy with my typewriter...*' Corrigan frowned. There were a few too many of *that* kind back in the rear échélons.

Montgomery, however, appeared not to have heard. 'Well, Corrigan, you're probably wondering what all this important, high-level strategic stuff has got to do with you and your little troop. I shall tell you. You're the best reconnaissance officer I've got. I want you to go down to Belgium post-haste – I've laid on a troop train for you – and as soon as you get down beyond Liège, recce a route for Horrocks's Thirty Corps along the west bank of the Meuse as far as the French border.'

'But why a recce, sir? Why not just send the usual advance party?' Corrigan objected.

'Because I don't think it's going to be a simple matter of finding the right roads, Corrigan. According to what Intelligence tells me, the balloon has gone up everywhere. It's nineteen forty all over again. There's panic not only in Hodges' broken divisions, but also among the civilian population. The

48

Belgies are fleeing westwards with the troops. Reports of German spies and saboteurs are flooding in. All hell's been let loose down there, and it's not only the Germans who are taking advantage of it, either: the Belgian communists are, too. Last month we had to disarm the communist resistance in Brussels by force. I had to send in a whole armoured division to do it. Now, I suspect, they're hoping to take a leaf out of the Greek communists' book and attempt to stage some sort of show along the Meuse. You see, at this moment, anything that helps the Germans in the west and ties down our troops, helps the Red Army in the east to grab more of Central Europe. Do you understand, Corrigan?'

Corrigan nodded, his head reeling a little. 'It all sounds very confused, sir. Jerries, refugees, Yanks running away – and now our erstwhile allies turning against us. Bit hard to digest.'

'I know, Corrigan. But that's the way it is – and it's up to you to find a way for Horrocks' chaps to get into position before it's too late. Further' – here Montgomery hesitated, as if unsure whether or not to continue – 'I want you to cross to the east bank of the Meuse, into what is nominally US held territory, heading in the general direction of' – he looked at the map – 'the Belgian town of Marche, *here*... Now, I know it's not quite cricket for one general to invade the territory of another without an invitation. But these are desperate times, and believe me, Corrigan, soon the Yanks'll be only too glad of all the help they can get.'

For the first time since Corrigan had entered the caravan, Montgomery smiled; but there was nothing happy about the look in his eyes – instead they bore an expression of sheer malicious pleasure. 'You see, Corrigan, I've been waiting for this day ever since we landed in Normandy, back in June. All these long months the Yanks have tried to pretend they knew better than I did. And what could I do about it? Nothing – nothing except bellyache. Where I insisted the attack to finish off the Boche should be conducted on a narrow front with our full weight, with myself in command, naturally–'

'*Naturally*, sir,' said Corrigan; but irony was obviously wasted on Field-Marshal Bernard Law Montgomery, for his triumphant, malicious expression didn't change.

'–the Yanks wanted an attack on a broad front, thus spreading our troops all over the place in penny packets. Now they're learning just how wrong they were. They spread their front too thin, and the Boche are taking full advantage of it. So they'll get a bloody nose – and they'll deserve it. And it's up to me to pull their chestnuts out of the fire for them.' He grinned triumphantly. 'But Corrigan,' he added swiftly, waving a warning finger, 'the Yanks mustn't have the faintest inkling of what I'm up to. I want them to crawl first. And if anything goes wrong *before* my people are asked to help out and you're discovered illegally in their theatre of operations, I won't be able to bail you out. If I'm questioned, I shall say that you're well known as an insubordinate young officer and that your whole record in this war proves just how bolshy you are. In other words, if you're found out, you'll be completely on your own. But if you pull it off successfully, it'll be a crown and the DSO. Is that quite clear, now?'

'Yes, sir,' Corrigan answered slowly. Secretly he was amazed at the cold-blooded cunning of the little field-marshal. Clearly he, Corrigan, hadn't been picked solely because he was 'brave and bold'; he had been picked because he had a record. He was regarded as anti-American, too. It would be easy to hand him over to the Yanks on a plate and they would be only too eager to get their own back after what he had done to that American regimental commander in Anzio. He was – what *was* it the Yanks called people like himself? Yes, that was it – a *fall guy!*

'Well, Corrigan,' snapped Montgomery, picking up his little wooden pen, obviously impatient to be rid of Corrigan and all the risks associated with knowing him, 'I

51

suggest you get on with it. Time is of the essence. My chaps will give you full details of the troop train and suchlike.'

'Yes, sir. Thank you, sir.' As best he could, Corrigan flung his commanding general a Regular Army salute.

But Montgomery's head was already bent over his papers, almost as if he was no longer aware of the young captain's presence. From now until he had successfully carried out his mission, he, Corrigan, no longer existed for the 'Master'...

FOUR

Miserable, cold and sick at heart, they stood there, bent under their enormous loads, nostrils assailed by the pungent smell of wet blanco, as the thin, icy Dutch rain beat down upon their helmets and trickled down their pale faces like tears. Slowly their feet were beginning to turn into lumps of ice.

Captain de Vere Smythe let them wait – deliberately. Often enough at the Depot back in Yorkshire he had faced men like this of a cold Winter's morning, and seen the same look of dumb, bovine insolence in their eyes. Always he had broken their spirit sooner or later. So he let them wait.

Standing at his side, and looking smarter now than he had done since they had left Blighty for the Invasion, Sergeant Hawkins frowned hard. He knew the drill. Hadn't he done the same thing to these self-same troopers back in '40 and '41, when they had first come to him as callow eighteen-year-old conscripts?

At first he, too, had been hard on them, very hard, flinging the usual contemptuous drill-sergeant's phrases at them: 'Showers of shit'... 'Nancy-boys'... 'Pregnant ducks' and all the rest – all in a deliberate attempt to break their spirit, to brutalise them, to make them begin to learn to be a soldier, a *British* soldier, the finest in the world.

Slowly he had sweated the puppy fat off them and the city paleness that came from years spent in smoky pubs and offices, until they had begun to exult in the clean, vigorous life of the outdoors. Yes, he had turned them into soldiers, contemptuous of the soft life they had left behind in 'civvy street'. But he, Hawkins, hadn't done it with malice in his heart – he hadn't been motivated by the cheap sadism of many of his fellow 'staffs' at the Depot. He had done it for the sake of the men themselves. Train 'em hard, he had always said, and they would fight easy.

Now the assault troopers were the élite of the division. They had fought their way through France, Belgium and Holland, risking their lives every day to lead the Iron Division to its objectives, often cut off miles behind enemy lines and trying to find a route for the Poor Bloody Infantry. When along came this caricature of an officer with his sodding swagger-stick, trying to treat them like raw recruits instead of the battle-tried veterans they were. Christ Almighty! Why didn't Mr Corrigan come back from that bloody dock and rescue the assault troop from Smythe before it was too damned late?

Captain Smythe made up his mind at last. He turned and looked down at Hawkins, who, like the rest, was buried under a huge back-pack, wrapped round with a blanket, side-pack and other accoutrements at his belt, his helmet gleaming in the rain.

'I shall inspect the men, first, Sergeant,' he announced. 'Then I shall say a few well-chosen words to them before we march off.'

Hawkins opened his mouth to say something, then thought better of it. Perhaps they might strike lucky after all. There might just be a Jerry sniper up ahead in the dripping fir woods that marked the border with Germany; with a bit of luck he might put a bullet through Smythe's silly head.

'Sir!' he barked, and swung round on his heel in a splatter of mud. 'Parade,' he snarled, 'atten-*shun!*'

The assault troop clashed heavily to attention, mud splattering their newly polished ammunition boots as they did so, and sending a great cloud of blanco dust whirling into the air.

Hawkins swung round smartly, hand flashing to his helmet. 'Parade, all present and correct, *sir!*' he barked, his breath fogging on the cold air.

Casually, Captain Smythe touched his absurd cane to his cap. 'Thank you, Sergeant,' he said, and was about to inspect the front rank, standing there in the cold drizzle, when a horrendous fart broke the heavy silence.

The captain stopped dead in his tracks. His face flushed a deep crimson. For a moment, Hawkins thought he was going to faint, for the officer was trembling visibly. Then he screamed, '*Who did that? Who – who broke wind in that disgusting manner?*'

There was no answer. All was silent, save for the steady *drip-drip* of the cold Winter rain.

Gently Hawkins said, 'Is there something wrong, sir?'

Behind him, Slim Sanders said out of the corner of his mouth, 'If I die, Cobbers, willya bury me upside down, so that the whole bleedin' world can kiss me bleedin' arse?'

'Silence in the ranks there!' Sergeant Hawkins commanded without turning round, fighting desperately to keep a straight face, as Captain de Vere Smythe fumed and puffed in front of him. He appeared to be having the greatest of difficulty in giving vent to his pent-up emotions, his head twisted to one side as if he were being strangled.

'*Wrong?*' Smythe exploded finally. 'Someone just farted in the ranks, dammit!' Angrily he brushed Hawkins to one side and bellowed, 'Now who made that obscene noise?'

No one answered.

Smythe slapped his cane against his leg,

eyes glittering with rage. 'All right,' he declared finally, 'if the person concerned isn't man enough to own up, the man *next* to him will admit it.'

Obligingly, Wolfers lifted one foot off the ground and let rip a great explosion of wind, causing the men all around to choke and gasp for air.

Shaking with rage and with little meaning-less sounds bubbling from his lips, Smythe hurled his cane to the ground and barely restrained himself from jumping up and own on it like a small child throwing a tantrum.

Hastily Hawkins stepped in. 'All right,' he barked harshly, 'that's enough of that. Remember, you're on parade. Rifles at the slope! Backs braced! Eyes front... Ready for inspection.'

Touching his hand ceremonially to his rifle butt, Hawkins turned to a gibbering Smythe. 'Parade ready for inspection now – *sir!*'

Like a man in a dream, too choked with rage even to comment on the fact that Slim Sanders was wearing a pair of red silk knickers as a kind of scarf under his tunic, Smythe passed up and down the three rigid ranks of assault troopers, making his final inspection before they marched off. Soon, he promised himself, the sweat trickling down the small of his back in spite of the cold, *soon* he would show the insolent pack.

But it was not to be. For just as Hawkins stood the parade at ease prior to the ten-mile route march through the mud that Smythe had sworn to inflict on the assault troop, the little NCO with the strange-coloured hair said politely, '*Sir,* before we march off, could I just ... er, *show* you something?'

Finally recovering his power of speech, Smythe said, 'Is it important, Sergeant?'

'*I* think it is, sir. After you've seen it, you might understand why the assault troop is like it is, sir. A bit sort of ... well, rough and ready, like.'

For a moment Smythe thought of turning the request down, but the little NCO seemed loyal and respectful enough, and he needed one ally in his new command. 'Oh, all right, if you must. But don't make it too long. I want to get this ill-disciplined shower on the road. Show them what real soldiering is all about.'

'Yes, sir. Of course, sir. This way, sir.'

Behind him, Slim Sanders commented *sotto voce*. 'Crap, said the King, and a thousand arseholes bent and took the strain, for in them days, the word of the King was law!'

Hawkins, however, pretended not to hear.

Briskly, Hawkins led the officer through the mud towards the rear of the barn where most of the troop slept. To the right lay five rigid shapes stretched out beneath a section of wet tarpaulin, big nailed boots protruding from beneath it.

'Ours, sir,' he said briefly. 'Bought it, yesterday. Along with Mr Corrigan. Waiting for burial by the Graves wallahs.'

Smythe nodded, wondering what was coming next. Behind him, he heard the snarl of a jeep in low gear, labouring its way up the muddy trail to the Dutch border farm. Idly he wondered who it might be.

'Over here, sir,' Hawkins said.

Somewhat bemused, Smythe followed the little NCO who was still carrying his rifle ceremonially at the slope. Then he stopped short.

Before him in the brown earth was a ragged shellhole, and in it were four 'things' in ragged, scorched field-grey. Two of them had been flattened against the muddy wall of the hole like gory red cut-outs, still recognisable as human beings but reduced grotesquely to two dimensions, all their bones flattened to pulp. Of the other two, one had his head missing, the other his foot – a blackened, horrifying chunk of ragged meat, with the beginnings of a tourniquet about it. At the bottom of the pit was the missing head. Some joker had placed a damp, drooping cigarette between his lips.

Smythe gasped and fought back the bitter bile that flooded his throat. These were the first dead men he'd ever seen. How ghastly they looked, reduced to hunks of meat like that. He was horribly reminded of a butcher's window.

'That's what it's all about, sir,' Hawkins said quietly, as the noise of the jeep battling up the track in four-wheel drive became even louder. 'The lads – er, the men of the assault troop have got to live with that sort of thing every day.' He looked at the pale-faced young captain.

'That's *no* excuse, Sergeant,' Captain Smythe forced himself to say, vainly trying to drag his gaze away from the hideous head with the cigarette drooping from its bloodless lips.

'But sir,' Hawkins said, 'don't you see? Men go wild after a while, living with things like that. They forget how they stink. They even forget they're human beings. They become animals. They become–'

'*No!*' Smythe interrupted him firmly, finally forcing his eyes from the horrible tableau at his feet. 'They are British soldiers, *not* animals. They'll wash and they'll shave. They'll learn to march again. Captain Corrigan, however brave he may be in action, was obviously too slack.' Smythe straightened himself up proudly. 'This, Sergeant, is the Reconnaissance Corps, RAC. We are the élite of the armoured force, the pathfinders for the infantry. We must behave as an élite, have pride in ourselves, so that others recognise us for what we are – *the best!* Is that clear, Sergeant Hawkins?'

'Clear, sir,' Hawkins answered. But at the back of his mind, a cynical little voice whispered, *'You're all wrong, mate. You won't last five minutes up here. You're a dead 'un...*

'Your orders, sir?'

Smythe stuck his cane firmly under his arm. 'Back to the men, Sergeant. We march off in exactly–'

But Captain de Vere Smythe never finished his sentence. For suddenly from behind the barn on the side where the waiting assault troop was lined up, there came a great cheer, followed by whistles and cries of delight.

'What the devil's going on over there, Sergeant Hawkins?' Smythe cried. 'Isn't there *any* discipline left in this shower?'

Hawkins stared at him in bewilderment. 'I don't ... I don't know, sir,' he gasped.

Suddenly the mud-battered jeep came skidding round the corner, sending up a brown wake behind it as it slithered to a stop. A familiar, if battered-looking face was staring out at Hawkins, its left side covered in purple ointment and yellow plaster.

'What's this, Hawkins?' asked the ragged figure, who bore an ordinary infantryman's rifle and whose dirty khaki tunic carried no badges of rank. 'You planning to mount guard outside Buck House in that gear or something?'

61

Hawkins gave a sigh of relief and lowered his rifle, a happy grin spreading over his wizened little face.

'Who are you? How dare you come bursting in like this?' Smythe cried, enraged.

Captain Corrigan looked the other officer up and own and clearly didn't like what he saw. 'Corrigan's the name, Smythe... And I've come to take back my troop.' Then he raised his voice so that the men on the other side of the barn could hear. 'All right, me lucky lads. Get out of those monkey suits now. Time to stop playing soldiers... At the double now! Monty's given us a job... Come on now, *move it. Assault troop is going to start earning its pay again...*'

FIVE

'The trouble with you, Slim,' Wolfers said slowly, dipping up the oil from a sardine can with a ration biscuit, as the troop train rattled ever southwards, 'is that you don't just hate old Jerry like the rest of us do. Or the Yanks, and maybe the Frogs. You hate *everybody!*'

'... *Tight as a drum, never been done, Queen of all the fairies,*' bawled the troopers at the other end of the long, open, overcrowded coach. '*Isn't it a pity she's only one titty to feed the baby on. Poor little bugger, he's only one udder...*'

'They're all wogs or gooks to me,' Slim agreed, as he squatted there on the hard wooden seat, cleaning his fingernails with the point of his bayonet. 'It wouldn't take much, cobber, for me to go off you Pommies neither.' He took a last slug at his *Amsel* beer, opened the window, took careful aim at a calf being suckled by its doting mother in a rain-sodden field and slung the empty bottle out.

Wolfers shook his head in mock-wonder. 'What did you do *that* for?' he asked. 'I mean, that calf didn't do you any harm, did it?'

63

'Didn't do me any friggin' good though, did it?' said Slim sourly. 'It's dog eat dog in this friggin' world, cobber. I mean what the sweet hell am I doing in this arsehole of the world, freezin' my balls off, when I could be gettin' me knees brown in Aussie?'

Wolfers laughed scornfully. 'Come off it, Slim, pull the other one – it's got bells on. As soon as you hit Australia, they'd have you in the glasshouse – gildy. Yer feet wouldn't touch the ground. I bet yer've got a crime sheet with the Aussie Army as long as my arm.'

Slim seemed not to hear. 'I sometimes ask myself, what the fuck is Mrs Sanders' handsome son *doing* here?'

'Yer liberating the continentals from old Hitler,' someone suggested. 'That's why they call us the British Liberating Army, Slim. We've got a job of work to do here in Europe.'

'*Liberating* – my arse!' Slim sneered. 'These continentals are worse than the Jerries. They'd rob yer bleedin' blind, the lot of 'em – Frogs, Belgies, Cheeseheads.'

'They're all right for screwing,' suggested one trooper. 'A lot randier than our lasses. Lovely cracks they've got, some of them.'

'Slim, here'd screw the crack o' dawn!' chortled another.

They laughed, but Slim Sanders' cunning little bronzed face remained sombre and pensive. 'I hate 'em, the whole bleedin' shower of 'em!' he maintained doggedly.

Wolfers swallowed the last of his cracker and licked his fingers clean of the crumbs, not wanting to waste a bit. 'You know, Slim, it's only a week or so to Christmas, so why don't you give yerself a treat.'

'What d'you mean?'

'Well you could buy yerself an eagle, or a falcon, or something like that, and–'

'Go on,' Slim urged, a little intrigued.

'Well, yer could train it to fly over schools, like.'

'And?'

'It could swoop,' Wolfers went on, a big grin on his ugly, spotty face, *and carry off nippers!* Now wouldn't that be fun? I bet you'd really enjoy that.'

Slim scowled, as the others burst out laughing. 'Yer know what you can do, cobber?' he grunted.

'Can't,' Wolfers replied airily. 'Got a double-decker bus up there already, mate.'

Sitting on the hard wooden bench at the far end of the crowded coach, Sergeant Hawkins grinned. In spite of the hard seats and freezing cold, the lads were in good form again. None of them seemed unduly concerned about the purpose of their unexpected trip southwards.

Hawkins forgot Slim and Wolfers and peered through the narrow square of glass in the boarded-up window. Once more the slow train was chugging past a rusting reminder of the battle that had been fought here the previous September: a wrecked Sherman, its track still trailed out behind it like a broken limb, the usual circle of rough wooden crosses around it, marking the graves of its crew.

Otherwise the countryside, wet, dripping and miserable, was empty. For all Hawkins knew, they could be the last people alive on earth this December day. An hour back they had seen a long trail of refugees, civvies, trudging wearily westwards besides their piled-high ox-carts. Dutch, he guessed. But they hadn't even looked up as the troop train had passed. Nor had the men taken off their caps and the women cheered, as they would have done a week or so before. Even the kids had been down-cast, not even crying out for chocolates and cigarettes 'for Papa', as they usually did when they saw an Allied soldier. Instead they had plodded numbly on their way, gazes fixed doggedly on the ground, as if, now that the Germans were coming again, they wanted nothing more to do with their former 'liberators'.

Hawkins sniffed and started plugging NAAFI tobacco into the bowl of his pipe. Thank God the CO was back anyway! If they were going into action again, he was damned glad the assault troop was being led by him, and not his nibs, Captain de Vere Smythe. Tough and ruthless as he was, Corrigan would at least make sure that the lives of his lads weren't thrown away needlessly, that he would.

Hawkins lit his smelly pipe and sat back as comfortably as he could on the wooden bench. Moodily he puffed away, staring out at the leaden, ominous-looking sky. Before the day was out, he reckoned they would have snow...

In the cramped little compartment reserved for officers just behind the panting engine, Corrigan lectured de Vere Smythe on what was to come, noting that the train was beginning to labour up a steep incline.

'Now get his, Smythe: up there, it'll be totally unlike anything you've learned in training. Rule Number One, therefore: if anything can go wrong, it *will*. Rule Number Two' – he ticked it off on his fingers – 'carelessness costs lives. Think in advance and be prepared for anything. Rule Number Three – and this is the most important rule of all...' He shot the silly-looking, affected officer opposite him a hard, searching glance. 'Your first loyalty is to the assault troop. Now, back at Catterick, they may have told you that you have a loyalty to the Atlantic Charter, Winston Churchill, the British Army, the House of Windsor, whatever.' He grinned cynically. 'But you haven't, Smythe.

The front is a law unto itself, and once there, your first and only loyalty is to the men of the assault troop. We need each other – officers, NCOs, other ranks. At the front it's the only way to survive.'

Outside, the first soft, sad flakes of snow were beginning to drift down aimlessly, as the toiling engine slowed down ever more, trailing a great white cloud of smoke behind it.

Corrigan's face contorted harshly. 'Apart from that, there *are* no rules, Smythe. If you thought there were, forget it. The Marquis of Queensbury is a fairy pub in Shaftesbury Avenue. Got it?'

Smythe, somewhat taken aback by the venom in Corrigan's voice, nodded his head. 'Got it,' he said uncomfortably.

Slowly the train puffed on, the snowflakes beginning to thicken and blot out the un-lovely war-torn countryside outside. Soon, Corrigan told himself as he sat back against the wooden planks, soon it would be dark and he'd have to start posting guards. Out here, you never knew what might happen and it was wise to be prepared. He closed his eyes. Opposite him in the growing dark-ness of the freezing compartment, Captain de Vere Smythe chewed the ends of his big cavalry moustache anxiously. He had been three years in the army, waiting for this day, training for it, month in, month out. Yet at this moment he felt like the rawest recruit: confused, apprehensive, and not a little frightened.

Christ, what if he was a coward after all?

Corrigan woke to a screeching, banging, metallic clamour as the driver applied the brakes. With a banshee howl, they locked, the big steel wheels squealing in protest. The line of coaches and flat cars bearing the assault troop's vehicles clattered and bumped into each other noisily, as, slowly but surely, the train ground to a standstill.

'What is it?' cried Corrigan above the noise, instinctively grabbing for his infantry-man's rifle, instantly on the alert.

'Don't know,' answered Smythe, peering through the square of glass at the whirling white gloom outside. 'It's snowing like the very devil. Can't see a hand before your nose out there.'

'Come on... At the double!' Corrigan commanded, slapping on his cap. To judge by the startled curses and cries of alarm coming from the big coach behind theirs, his men were awake and alert too. He swung open the door, just as the train came finally to rest, and dropped down into the soft new snow beside the track.

For a moment he crouched there, rifle at the ready, trying to make out the dark shapes vaguely glimpsed through the flying snowflakes. Then he relaxed and lowered the weapon. In the ruddy glow cast by the flames from the open door of the engine's fire-box he could see two soldiers standing there next to the footplate. They were wearing American uniforms. They had been stopped, for some reason, by their allies.

'Come on, Smythe,' he cried above the howl of the snow-heavy wind. 'It looks as if those are Yanks up there! We must be inside the US First Army's area of operations already!'

Heads bent against the driving snow, the two officers plodded forward to where the Dutch driver and his fireman were standing on the footplate, peering down, puzzled, at the US soldiers standing there in the ankle-deep snow. Across the track lay a crude log barrier which the driver had evidently spotted just in time.

'Hey,' Corrigan began, 'now what's–'

'Just hold it there, buddy,' ordered a harsh American voice.

By the ruddy light cast by the flames, Corrigan could see a tall figure huddled in a jeep coat, pointing a carbine straight at him.

He stopped in his tracks. He knew of old just how trigger-happy American soldiers could be, especially at times like this. Behind the man in the jeep coat, he could see other Americans, their weapons also trained on him.

'It's all right,' he said, 'I'm a British officer. Now why are you–'

'I'm asking the questions here, buddy,' interrupted the man in the jeep coat.

Out of the corner of his eye, Corrigan could see shadowy figures in the gloom to both sides of the track. Suddenly he was overcome by an uneasy sensation. There was something funny going on. What, he didn't know. Beside him he could hear Smythe swallow hard. Obviously the new boy was experiencing the same uncertain feeling.

'Now then,' said the man in the jeep coat, 'break out some ID, fellah, or I'm showing iron!'

'You mean identification?'

'I sure as hell do! It's outlaw country up here, friend. Kraut parachutists, saboteurs and spies everywhere. You guys *look* like Limeys, you *sound* like Limeys. But what the hell! The Krauts might have Limey-speaking agents. So get your boys out from that train, one by one, and be identified. Okay, let's move!'

A little helplessly, Corrigan turned and started to climb back up the steps to the coach, followed by Smythe. Down below, a cloud of steam enveloped the grim, threatening figure in the jeep coat, as the engine shuddered impatiently.

Inside, Corrigan addressed the troopers.

71

'Now listen here all of you,' he commanded. 'I want you all to come down with your identity discs visible, so that the Yanks can check–'

'Sir!' It was Slim's voice, urgent and imperative. *'Don't* sir! They're looting the bleedin' flat cars to the rear!'

Corrigan thrust his head out of the door.

Shadowy figures, only dimly visible through the white gloom, were crawling all over the vehicles on the flat cars, ripping open the tarpaulins, throwing down boxes of rations and bedrolls into the hands of their waiting comrades below. In a flash Corrigan realised who these mysterious Americans were. They were deserters, living off what they could steal or loot to sell on the black market. These days there were literally thousands of them living by their wits all over the continent, and Corrigan knew they would stop at nothing to survive.

'Stand fast!' he cried.

A dark, wolfish face under a khaki stocking cap appeared out of nowhere. The man had a big forty-five in his hand. Corrigan didn't give him a chance to use it. He raised the brass-shot butt of his rifle and with a harsh grunt, he rammed it with all his strength into the man's face. He went reeling back screaming, his face a blood-red mess.

'The Limeys are wise to us, Cap'n!' a shrill

voice yelled in warning. Suddenly a pistol shot rang out. Two scarlet fireballs exploded just above Corrigan's head. He reeled back, blinded. Wood splintered. Shards of metal hissed through the air, and suddenly he was tumbling back into the coach once more. He heard the driver and fireman struggle vainly to back the train out of danger; steam escaped with a hiss, the wheels chattered impotently. On all sides now the angry snap and crackle of gun-fire could be heard.

With a sinking feeling, Corrigan slammed the door closed with his foot and fumbled for his damned safety catch. Christ – they were in trouble before they had even started to carry out Monty's assignment! Suddenly heavy machine-gun fire started to rake the length of the coach, with a sound like tropical rain clattering down on a tin roof, and Sergeant Hawkins, dependable and unflappable as ever, was yelling, 'Well, go on, you bunch of nancy-boys! What are yer waiting for – a fucking written invitation? *Fire, damn you FIRE!*'

SIX

'Arger, Herr Hauptmann?' asked Martini, as he crouched next to Hartung in the snow-heavy bushes, peering down at the scarlet flashes and hail of lethal white tracer in the cutting below.

'*Für uns nicht*,' replied Captain Hartung, not turning round but aware of his men hidden in the forest all around as they tensed expectantly.

'But we're kilometres away from the front line, sir,' said Sergeant Martini. 'Who could be firing at whom?'

Hartung shrugged his big, muscular shoulders. '*Bin ich Jesus?* How should I know, Martini?' He rubbed the snowflakes from his bold, bearded chin, unshaven these past three days. 'All I know is that this particular shower from the Ninth Parachute Regiment, Greater German Wehrmacht, isn't in trouble – *yet*.' He leaned back on the heels of his jump-boots.

Martini grinned. 'Ninth Para, sir? Hell, this lot are a bunch of wet-tails with the eggshell still behind their spoons! Great crap on the Christmas tree – the Ninth Para vanished years ago, sir!'

Hartung nodded, suddenly looking grim. How right the old Sergeant was. He and Martini were the only ones left of the old gang – the gang who had done their first operational jump back in Holland in '40. Battles from Crete to Monte Cassino had taken their toll. In the whole of the 200,000-strong German Parachute Army there was now only a single company made up of men who had actually done jump training. Still, his greenhorns had tried hard enough these last, terrible days. It wasn't their fault that Fat Hermann's damned flyboys had dropped them in this arsehole of the world, instead of their objective, a hundred kilometres away to the east.

'What do we do, sir – march to the sound of the guns, as usual?' asked Martini. 'Anything's better than freezing our balls off sitting here!'

Hartung turned and saw the frozen, expectant faces of the eighteen-year-olds under their rimless para helmets, and his tough old heart went out to them. *Heaven, arse and cloudburst,* he cursed to himself, *they ought to be back in the Reich, pressing the schoolbank with their skinny arses, instead of being out here in the midst of the enemy, with every man's hand against them. Shit, what a mess!* To Sergeant Martini, however, he said calmly enough, '*Nun langsam, Oberfeld...* Take it easy. Or are you after a bit more tin to hang on yer manly breast?'

'No, sir,' growled Martini, and rubbed a dirty paw over his bearded chin. 'Got a whole drawerful of the crap already. Right now I'd sell the lot for a half-litre of suds and a bite of salami. But we've got to do *something*. We've been on the run for three days now, sir, and those greenbeaks are missing their sugar titty. Anything'd be better than this,' he concluded with a sigh.

'You're right, Martini.' Again, Hartung peered through the flying snow, trying to locate the source of the firefight, and failing once more. 'But I'm not going to waste their lives for nothing. Let's have a look-see at what's going on down there before we make any decisions.'

'All right with me, sir.'

'How noble of you,' Hartung said, rising to his feet.

'I'm all heart, sir.'

'You're all arse, you mean.'

'Just as you say, sir,' said Martini, and raising his right leg, broke wind loudly.

Hartung shuddered. 'My God, Martini, keep that fart cannon of yours down to a low roar, will you! That drunken old sot Churchhill will have heard that in London, I don't doubt.'

'Hope the green gas chokes him then, sir,' Martini answered joyfully, happy to have a scent of the action again, after the aimless wandering and hiding of the last three days. 'What's the drill, sir?'

Hartung made a quick decision. 'I'll go first with One and Two Sections. You follow at a hundred metres with Three and Four.'

Martini nodded his understanding, face grim now; the time for joking was over. 'And?'

'And don't let any of those greenbeaks of yours get taken prisoner. The way things are at the moment, the Amis would shoot them out of hand.'

'Right, sir.' Martini unslung his machine-pistol, which looked like a toy in his big, frozen paws. 'If anybody's gonna do any shooting of prisoners today, it's gonna be Frau Martini's handsome son...'

At that moment, the big German para sergeant didn't know just how right he was going to be.

The back-blast of the American bazooka shook the night with an ear-splitting *cr-aack*. Vicious scarlet flame stabbed the snow-laden air. Next instant the 3.5in rocket slammed into the guard's van. It rocked on its wheels, as if struck by a hurricane. Wood and metal spiralled upwards out of the clouds of thick, choking smoke. The guard's head, complete with blue regulation cap, sailed through the air, slapped wetly against the bullet-shattered window and slithered downwards, leaving behind a red smear that looked like the thick juice of an over-ripe fig.

Captain de Vere Smythe felt the hot, bitter bile flood his throat and he started to vomit noisily.

Next to him, Corrigan snapped off single shots to left and right at the dark, running figures all around. There was no time to concern himself with Smythe and his wretched stomach; the situation was too grave. Already the Yank deserters had seized the loco and wrecked the guard's van, thus trapping the assault troop at both ends. Obviously they were determined to press home their surprise attack – and Corrigan knew why: it wasn't only their compo rations the Yanks were after, it was the petrol too. That would fetch a fortune on the Belgian black market, especially now, when half of Belgium was on the run before the advancing Germans.

Without turning his head, he cried, 'Hawkins! To me ... at the double!'

Crouching low, Hawkins came scuttling down the coach, which was littered now with ammo bandoliers and empty brass cartridge cases. On either side of the carriage, the assault troopers were firing back through the shattered windows, hitting the floor every time the heavy American machine-gun ripped along the train.

'Sir?' Hawkins dropped down by a grim-faced Corrigan, with a sideways glance at the vomiting Captain Smythe.

'Casualties?'

'Slim Sanders got nicked. Otherwise all right, sir,' Hawkins reported, raising his voice as another rocket hurtled through the air, trailing fiery-red sparks behind it and slamming into the ground a dozen yards away.

'Fine.' Corrigan breathed a sigh of relief. 'Thank God for that. Now, those ruddy Yanks have almost got us up the creek without a ruddy paddle. They've got us bottled up at both ends. It's no use trying to hold on to this train' – Corrigan lowered his voice so that none of the others could hear – 'and you can bet your last penny that if we surrendered, they'd take no prisoners.'

Hawkins nodded his old head grimly. 'Dead men tell no tales, they say.'

'Exactly. So we've got to get off this thing – and we haven't got much time left. D'you think those vehicles back there would start up first go? I mean, it's bloody cold out there.'

'I had the lads give 'em a shot of juice after they were loaded, sir. The carbs are full of petrol, and there are blankets under each bonnet. With a bit of luck, they should. Why, sir?' Hawkins and Corrigan ducked as a sudden burst of machine-gun bullets tore into the coach, filling it with choking, acrid fumes and sending wood splinters flying everywhere.

Corrigan gave no answer. Instead he turned to Smythe, whose shoulders were still heaving. 'Captain Smythe!' he cried above the sporadic din of small arms fire. 'Pull yourself together, man! No time for games now! D'you hear?'

Miserably, Smythe looked up, his face ashen, vomit dripping from his scummed lips. 'Yes, Corrigan?'

'I've got a job for you. You're in charge of the drivers. I want you to work your way with them to the vehicles. No heroics. I want no casualties. Do you understand?'

Smythe nodded and wiped the back of his hand across his mouth. As he did so, Corrigan noted that he was still trembling violently. The poor bastard was scared, very scared – but Corrigan couldn't help feeling a certain grim satisfaction: Smythe would soon find out that war was totally unlike anything he had been led to expect back at the Depot in Catterick.

'All right, now this is the drill. Sergeant Hawkins and I and two parties of troopers are going to try to reach the end of the train, working our way along the tracks. We'll uncouple the guard's van, which is wrecked and blocking the end of the train. As soon as I do, Smythe, I want you and your driver to start up the first half-track and roll it off the train.'

'Yes, I understand, Corrigan. Then what?'

'Simple. You beat hell out of the Yanks with the half-inch machine-gun! But watch out for that bazooka of theirs. It's a killer. While you're doing that, we'll uncouple each flat car in turn and roll off the rest of the vehicles. The Yanks can keep the bloody train, if they want. We'll have to go it alone from now on. Clear, the two of you?'

'Clear, sir,' Hawkins snapped.

'Clear, Corrigan,' said Smythe – but his voice still sounded uncertain and tense.

'Right then, here we go. Hawkins, you to port. Me to starboard.'

'But, sir! Starboard's where–'

Corrigan cut short his protest with a brisk. 'Don't be a bloody old woman, Hawkins. I know how to look after myself. All right, the two of you... *Let's go!*'

Corrigan hit the snow hard. To his left, the Yanks crouched in the bushes were still blazing away furiously at the train, unaware of the plan Corrigan had set in motion. He felt a sense of eerie calm. His mind was working with remarkable speed and clarity. Any moment now they would be spotted, but he knew exactly what he was going to do; he felt absolutely, completely in control of himself.

'All right, lads, off you go,' he whispered.

81

Immediately Corrigan's group started to double forward silently through the whirling snow, while Corrigan himself waited, rifle at the ready, tensed expectantly for what had to come.

Suddenly there was an angry shout. A slug howled viciously off the steel wheel next to him. A dark figure loomed out of the snow, running directly towards him. Corrigan didn't hesitate. The rifle thumped at his side. The Yank screamed and flung up his arms, his stomach ripped apart by the slugs at such short range. Next moment he hit the snow, and an excited, angry cry went up on all sides: *'The Limeys are out of the train! The Limeys are out!'* – and Corrigan was pelting wildly through the snow after his men, a hail of slugs chasing his flying heels.

On the other side of the train, Hawkins heard the cries and shots and knew that Corrigan had been spotted, exactly as he had wanted to be – that was why the CO had chosen the side where the most Yanks were.

'All right, off yer go, lads!' he hissed. 'And keep yer bloody big heads down. You, Sanders, and you, Wolfers – come with me.'

'Why?' Slim snarled.

'Because I bloody say so,' Hawkins snapped, 'that's why. We're gonna nobble that bloody bazooka before it knocks a bloody great hole in Captain bleedin' Smythe's half-track. *Come on!'*

Corrigan yelled a warning. There was a great roar. Flame flashed scarlet. Something slapped him hard and hot in the face. A rocket slammed into the already ruined guard's van and exploded in burst of evil purple flame. Shrapnel flew everywhere.

Someone screamed piteously, 'I can't see... Somebody help me for God's sake! *I'm blind!*'

Groggily, Corrigan stumbled towards the trooper, who was swaying like a drunk, hands pressed tightly to his face. 'It's all right, son... All right now.' He grabbed him and forced his blood-wet hands from his eyes.

Corrigan gasped with horror. By the lurid, flickering light of the burning van he could see that where the boy's eyes had been, there were now two deep, suppurating pits. The bazooka had ripped out his eyeballs. He felt a sudden rush of bile flood his throat. The next moment he retched helplessly, as the boy stumbled away into the darkness.

In spite of the deadly bazooka fire, the leading troopers were now crowded around the coupling between the van and the first flat car, kicking at the frozen connection with their boots, hammering at it angrily with their rifle butts.

Corrigan pulled himself together and fought his way through them. 'For God's sake, don't crowd so much,' he ordered. 'If that bloody bazooka man–'

'*Look out!*' someone screamed in panic.

Behind them, that terrible, searing flame ripped the darkness apart once more.

They hit the snow as one. Corrigan felt the air torn from his lungs as the great rocket hurtled by like an express train at full stretch. He gasped for breath, head twisted to one side like a man being strangled. Above him, the bazooka rocket smashed into one of the Bren-carriers. The impact was so tremendous that the little armoured vehicle was ripped from its moorings on the flat car and flung like a toy high into the air. Next moment it slapped to the ground and immediately burst into flames.

'Oh, my God,' someone moaned, 'they're slaughtering us! Can't anybody do anything about that sodding bazooka? Knock it out?'

Fifty yards away, Hawkins prepared to do exactly that. Moving forward with Slim and Wolfers slightly to his rear, the little sergeant prepared to rush the bazooka position, tensing himself for the final scramble that could well mean death.

'All right,' he commanded, 'you two stop here.'

'But Sarge–' Wolfers began to protest.

'Shut yer trap!' Hawkins interrupted. 'Only one bloke can do this, young Wolfers – me.' He eyed the two-man bazooka team

84

crouched behind the protection of a heap of snow-covered sleepers, the Number Two man already inserting another deadly rocket into the long tube balanced on the first man's shoulder. 'If I don't make it, sling yer grenades at them – and don't forget to duck.'

'Christ, Sarge,' Slim moaned, 'you are a bloody old woman, aren't yer? D'yer think we don't know how to throw a bleedin' grenade?'

Hawkins didn't answer. His whole being was concentrated on the next terrible sixty seconds and what he had to do. He drew a deep breath, willing himself to be calm and praying that his Sten-gun wouldn't jam – as the cheap little sub-machine-guns often did. Then he was up and running, the Sten chattering frantically at his hip as he went.

With a startled scream, the Number Two went down, hands clutching his throat, the rocket dropping from nerveless fingers. But the Number One reacted with surprising speed. Dropping the launcher, he jerked a Colt from his belt and fired. Hawkins flung himself to the snow, feeling the heat as the slug howled off the track just behind him. Next moment he was up and rushing forward again. He pressed the trigger of his Sten.

Nothing happened! *The bugger had jammed again!*

The American with the Colt laughed. With his target clearly outlined in the flames of the burning carrier, he took careful aim, almost as if he was back on some peacetime shooting range. Hawkins flung the useless Sten at him. Luck was on the little sergeant's side. The Yank howled with pain as the Sten smashed into his face, and he went reeling back, pistol unfired.

Hawkins gave him no second chance. He dived forward. In a mad scramble, the two of them went down in the snow, Hawkins on top. For what seemed an age, the two of them heaved and tugged, each searching for an advantage. Then Hawkins had it: his two outstretched fingers shot inside the American's flaring nostrils. Without a moment's hesitation, he crooked his fingers and ripped upwards and out. The American screamed hysterically, his whole body tautening like a strung bow. Hawkins hung on desperately, the blood spurting hot and wet all over his hand. 'Come on! *Come on!*' he yelled frantically. 'Give me a hand – I've got the bugger!'

The Yank gave a great heave. There was a ripping sound. He screamed shrilly, but he was free. Not for long. Just as he rolled over flinging Hawkins to the ground, his hands groping for the little Englishman's skinny throat, Slim Sanders' cruel brass-shod rifle butt came slamming down onto the back of his head. Bone splintered, and he died there and then, slumped over Hawkins' prostrate body.

A moment later as Hawkins still lay there, gasping for breath like a man who had just run the four-minute mile, there was a great cheer and the throaty roar of a half-track bursting into life. Suddenly the air was filled with the stink of petrol, as Captain Smythe's half-track hit the ground and went rattling into action, the machine-gun mounted in the cab firing furiously.

With one hand Wolfers reached down and heaved the dead American off Sergeant Hawkins, yelling, *'Christ, Sarge – we've done it!'*

SEVEN

It had been easy. As soon as the last Tommy vehicle had disappeared into the night, pursued by angry tracer fire, the surviving Amis had come out of their hiding places like the rats they were, scuttling among the wreckage, ignoring their own dead and wounded and looting whatever they could lay their hands on.

Unnoticed, Hartung's men had swept down from the hill – and had managed to get to within twenty metres of the Amis, bent over their looted cigarettes and cans of corned beef, before being spotted. But by then it was too late. A quick burst, a couple of screams as the Amis slammed to the snow, and it was all over. Within seconds, the panic-stricken survivors were throwing away their weapons, shooting their arms up in surrender and crying, *'Don't shoot! Don't shoot! Kamerad!'*

For a little while, Hartung and Martini covered the trembling Amis lined up by the side of the flat cars, while the hungry young paras stuffed themselves greedily with whatever food they could find: chunks of cold corned beef, bars of bitter Tommy ration chocolate, handfuls of boiled sweets. At each new discovery the greenbeaks chortled aloud, like the schoolkids they really were.

But as the snowstorm abated and a pale, spectral moon sidled into the sky to the north, Hartung knew it was time they were on the move again.

Martini seemed to read the tough captain's thoughts. Gazing with distaste at the trembling bunch of miserable Amis, some of whom were actually sobbing with fear, he asked, 'What now, sir?'

Hartung sucked his teeth and flashed a look at the engine. It was still smoking away steadily, although the Dutch driver lay dead over his controls and the fireman hung out of the cab, his head smashed to blood pulp. 'Ever fancied in your long and varied criminal career pinching a train, Martini?'

'It beats walking any day, sir. Why d'you think I volunteered for the paras? I couldn't stick all that shitting marching.'

'Exactly. The question is, can we work the thing?'

Martini gave a gasp. 'You mean, pinch *this one?*'

'*Jawohl, ja!*'

'But sir, won't they be looking for it?' Martini objected.

'Perhaps. But my guess is that the whole Allied rear area is in a state of total confusion. Who'll bother chasing after one missing Tommy troop train? Besides, it's a long hike to the Meuse and our own people, Martini, and the boys are in poor shape. That train could save us a lot of blisters – and perhaps even worse.'

'Corporal Heinze in my Number Three Section used to be a fireman with the Reichsbahn before the war. He's always showing off the muscles he got from heaving coal. Perhaps he could drive the thing – I don't know.'

'I'll watch these rats. Get him, Martini, and see what he says. If he says yes, get the boys to uncouple all the wagons except the first coach. That should do us. All right – off you go.'

Ten minutes later the former fireman with the German railways was installed in the cab. 'I think I can manage it, sir. It's a German model. A thirty-seven Kloeckner locomotive. I once worked on it myself.'

'*Grossartig!*' Hartung called back, and beckoned to Martini, who was already supervising the paras uncoupling the flat cars.

'Sir?'

Hartung lowered his voice. 'The Amis, Martini. You realise we can't take them with us, don't you? They'd only be a hindrance.'

'We could always let them go, sir...' Martini said slowly, his gaze fixed curiously, even apprehensively, on Hartung, as if he

90

were already half-aware of what was to come.

Hartung shook his head. 'No, I don't trust them, Martini.'

'Then what ... what do you suggest, sir?' Martini asked carefully.

Hartung crooked his right finger, as if he were pressing the trigger of a gun.

Martini caught his breath involuntarily. He knew that prisoners were often shot on the battlefield, but mostly it was while the blood was hot and the adrenalin still racing fast and furious. This killing would be different: it would be carried out in cold blood.

'Sir,' he said softly, 'you know what they'll do with us if they catch us – I mean, if we *did*...' He left the rest of the sentence unsaid.

Hartung nodded slowly. 'I know, I know... But, we must ensure that they *don't* catch us, eh?' He sighed a little wearily. 'Martini, let's not fool ourselves. Germany has lost the war and we'll be lucky if we survive it, but for a couple of hairy-arse stubble-hoppers, we haven't had a bad run for our money. Think of 'forty-one, after Crete: the girls in black stockings, the Champagne, the medals... Back from Africa in 'forty-three: remember those Roman whores and the Chianti? Even this Spring wasn't so bad either – all those little girls back in the Reich, thinking we were heroes, only too happy to fall into bed with us and open their pearly gates... No, Martini, we've had good times. But *those* kids–' he gave a nod in the direction of the paras over by the train – 'they haven't begun to live yet. Why, I'd bet my last pfennig that the whole lot of them are still virgins – not had as much as a sniff at a whore's petticoat. I don't care what it costs *us*, Martini, but we've got to save them. We've got to give them a chance. Do you understand?'

Slowly, reluctantly, Sergeant Martini nodded his head. 'I understand, sir... But I don't want them to do it.'

'Agreed. They'll have no blood on their young hands, if anything goes wrong later. We'll do it together.'

'I want them inside the coach,' Martini continued. 'I don't want them even to see it.'

'Agreed again.'

'I'll get the greenbeaks aboard, then, sir.'

Without another word, Martini turned, leaving Hartung to stare at the Americans who were soon to die, their unshaven, runtish faces hollowed out to silver death's heads by the moonlight. What thoughts were going through their minds? he wondered. Did they know that they had minutes left before they left this earth for good?

Suddenly, with total certainty, Hauptmann Helmut Hartung knew that this was how his own life would end, too – abruptly, violently, in some God-forsaken place whose name he didn't even know…

'*No – please, mister! No… No!*' they screamed.

Some of them were on their knees, wringing their hands in the classic pose of supplication; others hiding their faces like small children trying to blot out a nightmare; some simply stood there, tears streaming down their ashen faces, shoulders heaving with sobs, as if they were heartbroken.

There was a horrified silence as methodically, with practised fingers, Hartung and Martini set up the tripod of the MG 42. The only sound now was their own harsh breathing – that, and behind them, the impatient panting of the locomotive as the paras fired its boiler, ready to move off.

Martini thrust home the long belt of ammunition. Automatically Hartung knelt and thrust back the bolt. There was a renewed burst of wailing and weeping from the Ami deserters. Hartung concentrated on the machine-gun. The very air seemed charged with guilt. He thanked God that his wet-tails couldn't see what he was going to do. Martini slapped the gun to indicate it was ready to fire, and Hartung looked up.

The sight of the hysterically sobbing, pleading Americans struck him like a blow in the face. He gasped for breath. A wave of horror submerged him. It was as if he were waking from one terrifying nightmare, only to be thrust into another, even more horrific one. His finger, wet with sweat despite the freezing night air, curled round the trigger. At his side, Martini tensed.

Just as he pressed the trigger, he caught a fleeting glimpse of one of his victims: a youth, his eyes wide and staring as if they might pop right out of their sockets at any moment, his mouth open in a silent scream... Then he began to work the gun from left to right, while Martini fed the belt of ammunition into it.

At a rate of a thousand rounds a minute, the machine-gun blasted the prisoners apart. One after the other they fell, bones smashed to gleaming white fragments amid the welter of red, faces ripped apart by the hail of bullets, bodies withered away before the very eyes of the two killers. Relentlessly, mercilessly, they hosed the line with slugs, the sound of their murderous weapon drowning the cries, the screams, the yells of their victims...

And then it was all over, leaving behind it a reverberating silence that seemed to last for ever.

EIGHT

'*What did you say, Beetle?*' Angrily the supreme commander, General Dwight D Eisenhower, stubbed out yet another of the sixty Camels he chain-smoked each day and glared up at his chief of staff, General Bedell Smith. In the ante-room of the high-ceilinged eighteenth-century palace of Versailles which currently served as his headquarters, the typewriters clattered, telephones rang and civilian girl clerks clacked back and forth on high heels, for all the world as if this was some peacetime office back in New York, and not the place where the fate of some five million fighting soldiers was decided.

With an angry frown, the chief of staff repeated the urgent message he had just received from the inspector-general of Hodges' First US Army.

When he had finished, Eisenhower, the big grin which had endeared him to millions conspicuously absent now, glared up at him from his huge, paper-littered desk. 'But it's impossible,' he gasped. 'Simply impossible. It *can't* be…'

Bedell Smith looked down anxiously at

the pale, strained-looking face of his boss; saw the deep circles of worry under the blood-shot eyes. 'Ike, I hate to do this to you, but it's true. Of course, the message from First Army was garbled. Hell – ain't everything been garbled since this damned counter-offensive began!' he added angrily, with a trace of that notorious temper of his. 'But there's no denying the facts. A freight train or troop train of ours has been bushwhacked, way back in the COMZ.'

'But couldn't it be the Krauts?' Eisenhower almost pleaded.

'No, sir, I'm afraid not. The first of our Joes on the scene after the bushwhacking was reported early this morning, about seven hundred hours, found a burned out British carrier next to a lot of abandoned flat cars. It bore the number forty-three and a black-and-red triangular divisional sign. I've just asked Ken Strong of Intelligence what they signify.' Bedell Smith paused, gave it to the commanding general. 'Apparently, forty-three is the outfit number of the Limey Reconnaissance Corps – a recon outfit, in other words – and the black-and-red triangle is the divisional insignia of their Iron Division. So, whatever *did* happen up there, the Limeys' divisional recon had something to do with it.'

Ike said nothing. Instead he lit yet another cigarette, his sallow, moon-like face creased with worry. This week *everything* seemed to be going wrong. Ever since the 16th, the whole world had been falling apart: the Krauts had caught him with skivvies down about his ankles; the guys at the front were running away; it looked as if it would only be a matter of hours before his armies in the Ardennes were split right down the goddam middle. And now *this!*

'Eighteen of our men,' Bedell Smith went on, taking advantage of Ike's silence. 'Eighteen men – mown down in cold blood, four of them obviously shot in the back of the head because they hadn't been killed in the first burst. It's a massacre all right – there's no denying it. And it's a massacre carried out by the Limeys.'

'But why, Beetle? *Why?*'

His subordinate shrugged helplessly.

'What were the Limeys doing in our area of operations in the first place?' moaned Ike, running his hand through his thinning hair. 'What the Sam Hill's going on? Christ, Beetle, I'm totally confused this morning!' Hurriedly Eisenhower made an effort to pull himself together. 'But this is for sure: we might be fighting for our lives in the Ardennes at this moment, but I'm damned if I'm going to let fine young American boys be massacred like that without doing something about it. If those Limeys did it, they're probably deserters on the run. There

97

are too many of that kind around as it is.'

Bedell Smith nodded his agreement. 'Ike, there's one way we can clear this thing up straight away.'

'And that is?'

'Get on to Monty. Have him check if one of his units was officially in the area. If he says no, then we'll know those goddam killers are deserters and we can put out a call to all COMZ units to be on the look-out for them.'

'*Look-out?*' Ike echoed. 'I'll tell them to shoot on sight – *and shoot to kill!*'

Slowly, very slowly, Field-Marshal Montgomery placed the khaki-coloured field telephone back on its cradle and pursing his thin lips, stared thoughtfully at the portrait of Field-Marshal von Rundstedt on the wall of the caravan opposite. It was nearly twelve o'clock, and outside, the headquarters clerks and the like were already lining up outside the cookhouse tent, jingling their mess tins and mugs and making the usual small talk of men to whom a hot meal meant a welcome change from the boring routine of office work.

They said that von Rundstedt drank these days; that he finished a half-bottle of his favourite French cognac before lunch. He never visited the front, either. Obviously he had resigned himself to being a figurehead –

an illustrious name to placate the army, while Hitler ran the war. Montgomery peered at the soldier's narrow face above the wrinkled hen-neck, and felt a certain amount of pity for his German opposite number. Ever since the failure of his bold plan to capture Arnhem and thrust forward into the heart of the Reich, he, too, had felt he was taking a back seat in the conduct of the war. Now it was Roosevelt and Churchill, encouraged by Eisenhower's confident, publicity-seeking manner, who were running things – and making a complete mess of it too.

But now at last, fortune was beginning to smile upon him once more. He knew that it was only a matter of days before a chastened Eisenhower came crawling to him on his knees, *begging* him to take over and save him and the US Army from the mess they had got themselves into in the Ardennes – all because of their own over-wheening optimism and lack of strategic foresight. Yet this latest business – what had Eisenhower called it? The 'Meuse Massacre'? – threatened to put paid to all that.

Montgomery took his gaze off von Rundstedt. '*Meuse Massacre!*' he muttered contemptuously to himself. How the Yanks loved melodrama! Always they had one eye on the newspaper johnnies and the headlines. Surely there had never been a war like this, fought in the newspapers and on the cinema screen!

Eisenhower's call had caught him on the hop. Dammit, the Yank had even been able to identify Corrigan's unit! So what explanation could he have given to his irate supreme commander? What else could he have done but deny all knowledge of the presence of a British unit in the American theatre of operations? Any other course of action would have destroyed his whole plan.

Now, of course, the question was: could Corrigan avoid being apprehended by the American authorities before Eisenhower finally climbed down and issued a plea for help? Afterwards would be a different matter – *then* he was sure he would be able to sort everything out with Eisenhower. In his great need, Ike would probably forgive anything and everything – after all, his whole future depended on his being able to get out of the Ardennes mess with clean hands...

For a moment Montgomery thought of the hard-faced young captain with the wounded cheek who had sat in his caravan only two days before, and wondered where he could be now and what he was doing. Then he pressed the button on the desk in front of him.

Immediately, his bespectacled sergeant-clerk appeared at the door of the caravan, as if he had been waiting outside all the time, ready to move in as soon as the buzzer sounded.

'Sir?'

'Jenkins, when did we last hear from Captain Corrigan's column?'

'Twenty-four hours ago, sir,' replied Jenkins promptly, with a glance at the clipboard which he always carried underneath his arm. Jenkins was never seen without it – in fact Montgomery sometimes wondered if he took it to the thunderbox with him. 'To be exact, sir, at fourteen hundred hours on the twentieth of December.'

'Since then nothing?'

'Nothing, sir,' Jenkins replied woodenly, his pale, pudgy face revealing nothing – though he already knew of Eisenhower's call and was smart enough to put two and two together.

Montgomery thought for a few moments. For some reason Corrigan was no longer communicating with him – which was just as well. But whatever had really happened down there in Belgium, he knew instinctively that Corrigan had survived it. The fact that he was no longer in radio contact with his HQ signified nothing – indeed, it was all to the good. It meant that for the time being, there was less danger of the Yankee radio snoopers being able to link Corrigan – he of the celebrated 'Meuse Massacre' – with *him*.

Montgomery paused momentarily. Could

Jenkins really be trusted all the way? He decided he could be. 'All right, Jenkins, now this is what I want you to do. I want you – on my express authority – to remove from the files the written copies of all signals so far passed between this headquarters and Captain Corrigan. And I want no records kept of any future communications either.'

Sergeant Jenkins looked shocked. 'But King's Regulations, Sir–'

'Let that be my problem, Sergeant,' said Montgomery softly, knowing as he spoke that he was making Jenkins an accomplice to a military crime. 'For the time being, Jenkins–' and a cynical little voice at the back of his mind told him it could be for a great deal longer – 'we have no official knowledge of Captain Corrigan and his assault troop. They no longer exist. Understood?'

BOOK TWO

THE GULAG RATS

'He who eats with the Devil, has need of a long spoon'.

Old Russian Proverb

ONE

From across the frozen snow of Red Square came the muted stamp of thousands of feet and the sound of lusty young voices singing '*Katinka*'. Another division was marching to Moscow Station for shipment to the front.

Marshal Zhukov, nervous as always in the presence of Old Leather Face, allowed himself a faint smile. This time Stalin was certainly building up his strength. It would be the last offensive, taking the war right into the heart of the Fritzes' wretched empire, thank God!

Sitting at the far end of the huge, dimly-lit hall on his raised throne-like chair, Old Leather Face appeared unmoved by the sound of his young soldiers marching off to be slaughtered in their thousands at the front. Instead, he sat slumped in his chair almost as if asleep, making no movement, save to suck occasionally at his curved pipe, surveying his marshals through veiled Asiatic eyes. As usual, his wrinkled, leathery face revealing nothing of his inner feelings.

His marshals, squat, bemedalled, seemingly weighed down by their huge golden epaulettes, waited. They had been kept waiting like this for twenty minutes now, as if they were a bunch of common recruits. Nobody would have guessed by the way Stalin treated them that here were some of the most powerful men in the Soviet Union, with power of life and death over millions of soldiers.

Although he was long used to Old Leather Face's tricks, Zhukov couldn't help frowning angrily. He was making them wait deliberately – deliberately humiliating them, reminding them in spite of their victories, of *his* overwhelming power. With a snap of my nicotine-stained fingers, he was saying to them, I could have each and every one of you executed – just like that. And not a voice in the whole of Soviet Russia would be raised in protest.

Suddenly Stalin clapped his hands. Rossokovsky, the youngest of the marshals, started as if he were the rawest of recruits. On the throne-like chair, the dictator allowed himself a faint smile.

Instantly, Stalin's runt of a hunchbacked secretary appeared from behind the silken curtains, as if he had been waiting there all the time, ready to spring into action immediately. 'Comrade Stalin?' he whined.

'Vodka,' commanded the Soviet dictator, removing the pipe from his mouth and stroking back his old-fashioned curved moustache. Within seconds the secretary had disappeared and reappeared carrying a tray with a bottle of vodka and a bowl of salt on it, as if by magic.

The shaven-headed marshals waited until Stalin completed the vodka ceremony, forming a 'V' of skin between his thumb and forefinger, pouring salt on it, licking off the salt and then tossing down a clouded glass of the ice-cold vodka with an audible gasp. Now, Zhukov told himself, the cunning old bastard is going to make his announcement at last.

Stalin began. 'In exactly three weeks' time,' he said slowly, his Georgian accent very noticeable now, his dark, cruel eyes circling the assembled company, 'on the morning of the tenth of January, nineteen forty-five–'

'We attack?' Zhukov couldn't contain himself.

'Yes, Comrade Marshal – with all three fronts. We shall drive full out from Poland, heading for East Prussia in the north and Czechoslovakia in the south, with our central front aiming for the heart of the Fritzes' lair.'

The marshals smiled, the tension broken at last. Now they knew what was expected of them. It would be a great victory. Only Zhuvok didn't seem to share the excitement of his comrades. His broad, flat, peasant face with the dimpled chin of an aggressive, pugnacious man remained obstinately dour.

'You do not welcome this news, Comrade Marshal?' Stalin said softly. There was a cryptic smile on his wrinkled face, but his dark eyes remained cold as ever.

'*Da, da, Tavarisch Stalin,*' Zhukov said hurriedly. '*Boshe moi,* it is the order we soldiers have been waiting for since nineteen forty-one, when the treacherous Fritzes first attacked our Soviet Fatherland! But I must point out with all due respect,' continued Zhukov, hating the wheedling note in his own voice, but aware all the time that he was facing an Asiatic despot as bad as any Mongol Khan, 'that the Fritzes still have a sizeable army not only facing us, but also held in reserve in the west, on the Anglo-American front. The latter could be withdrawn in an emergency and thrown into the battle against ourselves...'

His voice trailed away as he saw a self-satisfied, cunning smile begin to cross Stalin's face. The bastard had something up his sleeve...

'But my dear Marshal,' said Stalin – the old bourgeois form of address was always a warning signal. Behind Zhukov, a junior marshal hurriedly took out a handkerchief, dampened it with Eau de Cologne and smoothed it across his sweating brow. Fear and tension had suddenly descended upon the big, gloomy hall. 'That reserve has already been committed. Since Saturday, the sixteenth of December, all three armies of the Fritz Field-Marshal Model have been engaged in battle with the armies of the western plutocrafts.'

There were gasps of surprise from the marshals. No wonder the handful of western liaison officers hadn't been allowed to approach them for the last few days. Stalin, devious as always, hadn't wanted them to learn of the German attack in the west.

Zhukov persisted. 'But Comrade Secretary,' he said, low-voiced and humble, 'knowing that madman Hitler and his terror of the Red Army as we do, would he not break off his attack in the west and release Model's troops to bolster up his eastern front? After all, the Fritzes and the Anglo-Americans do subscribe to the same decadent capitalist creed.'

Stalin nodded his head in agreement. 'Of course, you are entirely right. He would if he could. But I have already taken steps to ensure that Hitler will continue his attack in the West *whatever* the threat from our invincible Red Army on his eastern front.'

'May I be so bold as to ask *how*, Comrade Secretary?' asked Zhukov, ignoring a little warning voice which was urging him to remain silent. At his side, Rossokovsky whispered out of the corner of his mouth, *'For God's sake, Zhukov, don't go too far!'* Five years ago, the handsome young marshal with his string of mistresses had been inside the Gulag. Only the war and the need for his military talents had saved him from that hell-hole. But even after all the tremendous victories Rossokovsky had won for Stalin since 1943, he still lived in fear and trembling at the thought of being sent back.

But for once, Stalin wasn't angry at being questioned. Indeed, he smiled again – a big smile now, that made his eyes almost disappear into a sea of wrinkles. *'How?* I shall tell you, Comrade Marshal. I intend to give Hitler a victory.'

'A *victory?'* There were startled cries from all sides.

'Yes. I intend to help the Fritzes beat the Western Allies – for a while, at least. This will ensure that the Germans become so involved in their attack in the west that they will be unable to withdraw their forces to meet our glorious Red Army until it is too late. By the time Hitler realises his mistake we shall be standing at the gates of Berlin itself. Then, my comrades, we shall deal with the western capitalists, sweeping them before us into the sea. It will be another Dunkirk – but this time the Red Army will kick them out of Europe *for good!'*

For a moment the assembled marshals were too stunned at the boldness, the sheer magnitude of Old Leather Face's scheme to be able to speak. Even Zhukov was lost for words.

Again Stalin clapped his hands, and the hunchback appeared from behind the silken drapes, rubbing his bony hands. 'Comrade Stalin?'

'Comrade Beria – show him in now.'

Bemused, bewildered, the marshals looked at each other, open-mouthed like gawping, barefoot peasant boys seeing their first automobile.

One minute later, Beria, the head of the Secret Police, the most feared and hated man in Russia after Stalin himself, was ushered in. As he advanced towards Old Leather Face, he completely ignored the marshals, his attention concentrated solely on his fellow Georgian.

The two monsters slapped and kissed each other, jabbering away in their own unintelligible tongue. Watching, Zhukov felt physically ill, his stomach churning at the sight of the fawning pervert who commanded the greatest secret police *apparat* the world had ever seen. Whatever had Mother Russia done, Zhukov asked himself helplessly, as he had done a thousand times before, to have deserved such leaders?

Finally Stalin released himself from the secret police chief's grip and said, 'Comrade Beria – report!'

Beria immediately began to hold forth in

his wheedling woman's voice, toying with his gold-rimmed pince-nez as he spoke. 'In accordance with instructions given to me by Comrade Stalin, I have instituted a series of measures to ensure that the Americans do not receive any support from their capitalist allies, the English. In his great wisdom, Comrade Stalin' – here he bowed and rubbed his pale woman's hands unctuously, beaming at the man on the throne – 'has ordered that the Fritzes must cross the River Meuse. It is vitally important to the success of their attack. Now, the only ones who can stop their crossing are the British. Sooner or later, therefore, the hard-pressed Americans in that area are bound to swallow their pride and look to their decadent capitalist allies, the British, for assistance.' Beria paused for a moment, smiling smugly at the assembled marshals. 'Gentlemen, I intend to see that that assistance will *not* be forthcoming!'

A stunned silence greeted the secret police chief's announcement. At last Zhukov, the senior marshal, found his voice again, but this time, as he spoke, he made no attempt to conceal his dislike of the oily, bespectacled secret policeman.

'Just one moment, comrade,' he said, in his gruff, no-nonsense soldier's voice, ignoring the warning look on Stalin's face, 'I am sure your agents are well placed and many, even though the area in which they operate is so many thousands of kilometres away from Russia. But pray,' he gave Beria a contemptuous smile, 'how can even *your* famed service prevent the British Army from operating some thousand kilometres away from the nearest Red Army divisional command?'

Beria smoothed his pale white hand across his bald pate, pursing his painted lips like a cheap whore. Behind Zhukov, the junior marshal was dousing himself with cheap cologne once more, and at his side Zhukov could sense Rossokovsky's growing tension. What a pack of cowards we Russians are, thought Zhukov; even *his* heart was thumping away like a trip-hammer at his own temerity.

'How?' Beria said at last. He looked pointedly at a pale-faced Rossokovsky. 'I am sure, comrades, that some of you have heard of the so-called Gulag Archipelago, where we attempt to rehabilitate those traitors, reactionaries, pimps, whoremasters, black marketeers, perverts and worse who attempt to subvert our glorious Soviet Fatherland? In the days of the Czars, such types would have vanished for good in Siberia. But due to the great generosity of Comrade Stalin, we now prefer to make some attempt to return even the worst of these scum as law-abiding Soviet citizens.'

Rossokovsky let his gaze fall and stared

113

miserably at the marble tiles. Seething with rage, Zhukov clenched his big fists. How dare that perverted swine Beria humiliate a brave soldier like Rossokovsky who had suffered so much for Mother Russia? But he controlled himself.

'Now,' Beria continued, completely unaware of the wave of hate and disgust that swept his way, 'in nineteen forty-two, a whole camp of those Gulag rats, some twenty thousand strong, was overrun by the Fritzes in the Ukraine. Naturally, forgetting everything the Soviet system had done for them, the scum immediately went over to the fascists – to a man. As a reward, the fascists took them westwards with them as soon as they began to retreat, in late 'forty-three. In that year these treacherous rats were settled in farms and factories in the border areas of Belgium and Luxembourg, taking the place of men lost in battle.'

Beria paused for breath. Outside, there was a heavy, threatening rumbling sound and the metallic clatter of tracks, as tanks rolled by. But even the noise of the armour didn't disturb the marshals' concentration. For now Beria had them interested. What kind of plan had he dreamed up for those poor wretches from the Gulag, now so far away from their homeland on the other side of the world?

Beria had the answer. 'In September, when

the Americans overran the area, I asked their authorities to round up all Russian civilian workers in the Low Countries for processing and send them back to the Soviet Union.' He gave the marshals a wintry smile. 'Fools that the Americans are, they agreed. They collected the rats in four main camps south of a Belgian town of Marche, not far from–'

'From the eastern bank of the River Meuse.' Zhukov beat him to it – the burly marshal had travelled in the west during his days of military school in Germany and knew the area well.

'Exactly, Comrade Marshal.' Beria seemed in no way offended that the marshal had attempted to steal his thunder; he knew that no one, not even Zhukov, had any idea what he was going to say next. 'The Americans also agreed that we should be allowed to send a panel from Moscow to screen our fellow citizens to ascertain whether their behaviour had been treacherous in any way during their captivity.'

'Which it *had* been,' interjected Stalin from his throne, seeming to awake from his doze. 'Any Russian who falls into the hands of the enemy – unless he is seriously wounded – is *by definition* a traitor.'

'Naturally, Comrade Stalin,' simpered Beria, rubbing his hands. 'So thanks to that idiot of a general, Eisenhower, we sent a screening committee – which of course was made up of my agents. In due course, the committee was allowed by the Americans to ship in supplies to the internees.' He smiled again. 'And those supplies were weapons. So, comrades, at this moment in Belgium, right in the middle of the no-man's-land between the Germans and the English, lightly guarded by a handful of second-rate American troops, we have the equivalent of two rifle divisions.' He beamed at them, seeing from the marshals' faces just how impressed they were with his cunning.

'And now,' growled Stalin, 'the time has come for those rats from the Gulag to fight and die for their Soviet Fatherland.'

Once more Stalin clapped his hands, and the hunchback appeared from behind the drapes, followed by white-clad waiters, bearing glasses and bottles of vodka. Hurriedly they started to pass out glasses and fill them with pepper vodka, while Stalin tapped the floor impatiently, with his old-fashioned knee boot, as if he couldn't wait now to dismiss them to their commands.

Finally all glasses were filled, and the marshals prepared to drink to Stalin's toast, whatever it might be.

Hastily, Stalin raised his glass. 'Comrade Marshals, I give you the rising of the Gulag rats,' he smirked evilly, '*and the death of the English! Nastrovya!*'

Even Marshal Zhukov, thick-skinned as he

was, and a soldier not given to fantasies, felt a cold finger of fear trace its way down his spine as he imagined the strange conflict soon to take place on the Meuse between Russian and Englishman, both doomed from the very start. Then, dutifully, he raised his glass with the rest. '*To the rising of the Gulag rats... And to the death of the English!*' he bellowed in his deep bass, the sound echoing and re-echoing in the gloomy rafters of the Kremlin. '*Nastrovya!*' Next instant, he hurled his empty glass at the wall with all his strength, as if he hated the whole damned place and would have dearly loved to bring it crashing down to its foundations, complete with its despotic master.

But on this throne, Old Leather Face grinned at the red-faced marshal slyly, even triumphantly; he could read Zhukov's mind, and knew just how powerless he was to put his seditious thoughts into action...

TWO

'Attention, attention, you Gulag rats!' barked the agitprop flanked by his bodyguards, Hook and Tin-Teeth, both of whom were professional killers and now openly carried the round-barrelled Soviet Tommy-guns recently smuggled into the resettlement camp.

In the hut, the men grouped round the roaring, pot-bellied stove, their bearded faces hollowed out like skulls in the ruddy glare, stopped their chatter. Others sitting on their bunks, the legs of which rested in bowls of water to keep off the bugs, ceased running burning strips of paper down the seams of their shirts to kill the lice, and looked up.

All of them were afraid of the cunning little bespectacled agitprop with his twisted, bitter mouth; he had the power of life or death over them now. One word from him, and they would be on the Bitch's death-list. Once back in Russia, there would be no going back to the Gulag for them: it would be the NKVD firing squad against the nearest wall.

Silence fell over the darkened room; the

only sound was the crackle of logs in the stove, and from outside, the steady tread of the American sentry on the crisp snow beyond the wire.

The agitprop took his time, savouring the power he possessed over these men, some of whom were themselves hardened professional killers and all of whom were veterans of the Gulag and years in Russian and German captivity. Finally he spoke, while Hook, the one-armed killer, and Tin-Teeth, with his gleaming set of stainless steel teeth, kept their eyes warily fixed on the Gulag prisoners. 'At last you rats are going to be allowed to prove yourselves. Moscow has made its decision, and you will carry it out.' He raised his voice and called to the next room: 'Comrade Veruskaya, the rats are ready for you now.'

The door was flung open. For a moment the hut was flooded with ice-cold air. A huge, heavy-bosomed woman stood there, dark hair cropped as short as a man's. The prisoners gasped, the older ones pressing themselves back against the wall in terror. It was the Bitch!

The head of the Resettlement Committee strode imperiously into the centre of the room, followed by her simpering, pretty little blonde secretary, and struck up a pose, booted feet planted squarely apart, long Russian cigarette jutting out of the corner of her mouth. Hastily the 'secretary' – whom everyone knew to be her lover – tugged the cloak from the Bitch's broad shoulders, revealing the full bulk of that heavy-bosomed body.

Slowly the Bitch mustered their faces in the ruddy light, then clicked her fingers. Hurriedly the 'secretary' took a flask from her pocket and handed it to her. Deliberately, knowing that every eye in the place was following her moves greedily – for most of them hadn't tasted vodka in years – she placed the flask to her lips and took a long, satisfying pull at it, before handing it back to her little mouse of a mistress.

'*Horoscho*,' she announced, wiping her ham-like paw across her mouth. 'The time for action has come. Now you Gulag rats will have the chance to redeem yourselves – though I hardly think you deserve it, scum that you are.' Her dark, bold eyes blazed with contempt. 'Still, at least you have your worthless lives to sacrifice for your Fatherland. *They* should suffice.'

She halted for breath, looking round at these men who now knew that the Soviet system had them in its grip again, and taking pleasure in the looks of fear in their skinny faces.

'It will be your task to link up with the Belgian communists and with them, create as much havoc and confusion as possible behind American lines. The Fritzes are attacking to the east. Our information is that they should be in this area within forty-eight hours. A panzer column is on the way, trying to reach the Meuse. You must be gone before it arrives.' Her broad Slavic face contorted in a sneer. 'Though no doubt some of you rats would be only too happy to be back with your Fritz friends once again, eh?' She stared challengingly at the men nearest her, but they lowered their gaze as if embarrassed.

Now she hurried on, anxious to waste no more time. If she was to enjoy Katya's smooth young body before it all started, she must be quick.

'Naturally, the decadent Americans who guard us will not allow us to escape without a struggle. Therefore they must be liquidated!' For the Bitch, the word seemed to have no special importance; since she was a veteran of ten years in the NKVD, this was hardly surprising. For the Gulag rats, however, hardened as they were, it signified brutal, cold-blooded murder. Here and there, there were shocked gasps.

The agitprop snarled threateningly. '*Davai... Davai...* Enough of that, you pigs!'

The Bitch went on, 'Comrade Kutuzov' – she indicated the agitprop, who bowed fawningly– 'and his trusted comrades will be armed and will lead the attack on the

121

Americans. The rest of you will follow, un-armed, and carry out their orders. If you die in the attempt,' she shrugged contemptu-ously, 'so be it. Russia will be rid of another piece of scum. If you live, then I shall do my best to see that the authorities are informed of your change of heart. That is all. Agitprop, we attack the Americans at dawn!'

A moment later, the huge lesbian, her simpering mistress and the agitprop and his professional killers had all departed. Among the Gulag rats there was a heavy, foreboding silence broken only by the crackle of the pine in the fat stove. Each man stood motionless in that blood-red gloom, wrapped in a thick cocoon of his own thoughts...

It was Piotr the Stump who first voiced out loud what many of them were thinking. Tapping his peg-leg, he gave a growl of anger. Before falling foul of the NKVD in '41 and being thrown into the Gulag Archipelago, the old soldier had spent a quarter of a century fighting for the Czar and his Soviet successors in half a dozen bitter campaigns on two continents. 'It ain't right, mates – it ain't right at all.'

There were murmurs of agreement from his cronies, most of them 'politicals' or soldiers like himself who had been blamed for Stalin's own incompetence and thrown into prison in the bad years before Stalingrad. But none of them spoke. There were traitors everywhere, even in this hut, who would betray their comrades in suffering in return for release from the Gulag Archipelago. If Piotr wanted to burn his mouth first, let him; *then* they would say their piece.

'The Americans have been good to us,' Piotr said doggedly, staring at his brawny forearms, gnarled with the sabre-cuts of battles long ago. 'They are a politically naive people, but they are good. Food, cigarettes they have given us. Once one of them gave me a drink of that whisky of theirs, which the English with skirts make. By the Holy Virgin of Kazan, was that some drink!' He shuddered at the memory. 'I had my hundred that day, comrades, that I swear. *Nyet,* the Americans are our friends. We *cannot* kill them in their beds as that great perverted cow commands.'

'But what are we to do, Little Brother?' asked VD, a huge man, once a notorious womaniser who now kept his riddled penis wrapped up in a little cotton bag packed with iodine. 'Should we not *warn* them?'

Piotr shook his grizzled head. 'I wish on my mother's memory that we could, comrade. But look.' He leaned across his bunk and gently removed the edge of the black-out curtain.

VD gasped. Outside, clearly outlined in the hard Winter moonlight, stood the agitprop's bodyguard, the one-handed Hook, Tommy-gun cradled under his arm, guarding the door.

'You see?' said Piotr sadly, letting the sacking curtain fall again. 'The Bitch doesn't trust us. No, we cannot save our American friends on guard tonight. But when the Bitch gives the order to attack, we *can* try to get away and warn those off-duty outside the camp.'

There was a murmur of approval from his cronies. VD asked, 'And then? To the Fritzes? Shall be make our way to their lines?'

'No,' Piotr said firmly, falling once again into the old habit of making decisions and giving commands and suddenly feeling like a soldier again after his years in the Gulag and German exile. 'We will go west – to the Americans, our friends. Russia is the past.' Tears began streaming down his old soldier's face as he realised what he was saying. 'America is the future. Now comrades, pack your bundles and prepare to move out. We march to the future, come what may...'

Now it was nearly dawn. A heavy silence lay over the camp. The world seemed dead. In their watch-towers the Americans shivered or slept. Even the night wind was silent, and the skeletal trees were motionless.

Yet an attentive ear might well have caught the faint scrape of leather across frozen snow, the soft clink of a rifle sling, the gasp of hurriedly controlled breath, as the killers of the Gulag crept out of their lairs for the slaughter, like wolves sniffing the night air.

In her quarters, the Bitch struggled into her uniform, that of a colonel in the NKVD, the tunic heavy with medals. On the rumpled bed the 'secretary' slept face downwards, her skinny naked back red with the puffed weals of the knout, still wearing the garter-belt and black silk stockings the Bitch liked her to don for these occasions.

In his hut, the agitprop sat sipping the good bean coffee which the Americans dispensed so liberally and which brought a fortune on the Belgian black market. In between sips he gave his orders to his assembled henchmen. 'Slaughter the Americans ruthlessly,' he commanded, 'then disperse the rats once the killing is over. Let them stream across the land aimlessly, anywhere they want to go, as long as they hinder the progress of the Anglo-Americans eastwards to meet the Fritzes. *Ponemayu?*'

His killers nodded their assent, relieved that they wouldn't be the ones who would have to brave the freezing cold and tackle the Western Allies, armed only with their bare hands and homemade knives.

In his hut along with his companions, Piotr prayed as he had never prayed in all his life – despite the godless heathen masters to whom

125

he had been subjected for so long. By the light of the solitary candle, which flickered in the draught and flung gigantic, wavering shadows on the dripping, bug-ridden walls, he intoned his chant in the deep bass of the Russian Orthodox Church, followed by his fellow-inmates, careless of what those pimps, whoremongers and perverts outside might think as they crept forward to carry out their murderous business.

Then he turned to them, prayer forgotten, as the first shot echoed outside with a sound like the snap of a dry twig underfoot on a hot Summer's day. 'Comrades,' he declared, his eyes blazing, 'we must survive. Perhaps some of us will never live to see that glorious day when there is peace in the world again and the Fritzes have finally been ousted.' He gazed at the haggard, worn faces of his friends – men who, like him, had seen so much horror in these last ten years. 'But those of us who *do* live on must swear that they will save our Holy Mother Russia – will deal with that swine in the Kremlin, Stalin, where the time is ripe.'

Piotr raised his hand to give a benediction, and as he did so, the first distant scream of horror ripped through the pre-dawn silence. Ignoring it, Piotr made the sign of the cross above the bent shaven heads of his friends in the Russian fashion, murmuring, '*God go with you, rats of the Gulag...*' And then they were streaming outside, with Piotr hobbling behind them as best he could towards the horror of the massacre...

The cruel slaughter of the guards was almost over now. Here and there a lone American tried to fight it out, barricading himself inside one of the huts and firing until the last of his cartridges were spent. But the rats were unstoppable now. They had looted the Americans' liquor stores and were fighting drunk. They fell upon the survivors, screaming the old battle cry, 'Urrah', laughing hysterically as they were hit and dropped to the snow, still drinking in the moment of death. All around, Americans were being ripped to pieces, their bodies slashed and sliced until they were nothing more than unrecognisable bloody gore. Here and there one of the survivors tried to surrender, pleading for mercy, kneeling bareheaded in the snow, hands clasped and upraised in the classic pose of supplication. But there was no mercy shown this morning. The supplicants were beaten to death where they knelt, and the rats, carried away by blood-lust and drink, continued to beat the lifeless corpses until they could go on no more.
Watching the slaughter, her brawny arms placed protectively around Katya's frail body while the agitprop and his bodyguards kept them covered, the Bitch smiled grimly,

eyes gleaming with barely suppressed excitement, the lower half of her body suddenly weak with sexual longing.

'It is exactly as Comrade Beria wanted it,' the agitprop exclaimed, as a bunch of the rats, completely drunk now, began a crazy Cossack dance on the body of a slaughtered American, throwing empty bottles into the air as they danced.

The Bitch nodded. 'Turn the rats loose now, agitprop. Let them flee westwards towards the English. By the time those decadents have dealt with them, the Fritzes will be over the Meuse, and Comrade Stalin' – even the Bitch lowered her voice at the name in reverence – 'will be a happy man. *Davai... Davai...* Hurry – there is no time to lose, comrade.'

Agitprop turned to Hook, his bodyguard, who had speared a looted ham with his gleaming hook and was gnawing it greedily. 'All right, you dog, stop stuffing your guts. Fire a burst. The rats have had their fun. Now let's get them moving.'

Hurriedly, Hook dropped the ham into the dirty snow and thrust up his Tommy-gun, snapping the trigger back with his hook. Lead stitched the air. Without waiting to see if the shrieking, struggling, drunken men would react or not, he lowered the weapon and fired a burst straight into the nearest mob. Men reeled back screaming or slumped to the ground dead.

'*West!*' Hook bellowed above the uproar. '*Run west, you scum!*'

Suddenly the slaughter and the looting were forgotten. The rats broke at once, clutching and clawing at each other in their haste to escape the hail of lethal bullets. Like the Golden Horde of another age, they swept across the snow in their hundreds, heading west.

Standing on the heights above the camp, Piotr moaned as he saw the hideous deeds carried out by his own fellow countrymen. For a moment he hung his head in shame, while VD and the rest waited around him, impatient to be off before they were submerged by the horde now streaming their way. How few, how pitifully few of the Americans, had they been able to warn in time! How few had escaped the slaughter!

'Comrades,' said Piotr in a broken voice, 'it's no use. I cannot go with you.'

'*Why?*' VD exploded. 'Because of your wooden pin? Don't worry, little brother, I shall carry you on my back if necessary.'

'No, it's not just that – many thanks all the same, VD.' Piotr's old soldier's face hardened. 'There has to be justice done. That sow down there must not be allowed to escape her rightful punishment.'

VD looked at the other man in astonishment, noticing how much younger Piotr looked all of a sudden, in spite of his almost white hair. Authority and decision had swept away the years. 'You mean you are staying, Piotr?'

'Yes. I may die, comrades – I probably will,' he said, his voice harsh, almost cruel-sounding. 'But if I do, I shall take the Bitch with me... Now, comrades, go – before that scum overtakes you.'

'Piotr,' began VD, but Piotr waved imperiously for him to be silent. VD gave in. '*Dostvedanya*,' he whispered, knowing that he would never see the old soldier again.

'*Dostvedanya!*' Piotr replied. And then they were gone, streaming down the other side of the hill, leaving him up there, as motionless as a statue, staring down at the camp with murder in his unblinking grey eyes...

THREE

All day they had been crawling steadily southwards through the rugged, snowbound Ardennes hills towards the Meuse. The weather had been terrible. In their freezing, open armoured vehicles they had fought every inch of the way along the steep, winding mountain roads, battling against the blizzard. The look-outs' faces were stung purple by the flying snow, their eyebrows white with the bitter, glittering crystals. Time and time again the vehicles had skidded on the icy roads, the drivers cursing furiously as they wrestled to prevent them from veering into the ditch on the left of the road, or worse, plunging over the edge and down into the valley far, far below.

They could almost have been the last men left alive in this white, whirling, merciless Winter world. Only once did they hear the faint sound of motors coming from far away, and an hour or so later, in a gap in the snow storm, they glimpsed a long, miserable trail of refugees on the road below, their pitiful possessions heaped on their wagons and carts, wending their way slowly westwards.

The fact that they seemed to be alone in

the middle of the biggest battle of the campaign in the west didn't worry Corrigan; on the contrary, it pleased him. It meant he could crowd his vehicles together, safe against air attack or observation, and communicate with them by hand signal. There was therefore no need to use his radio and run the risk of being picked up by the German radio detector units – who, as he knew of old, were the best there were, always up front with the fighting troops and attempting to locate and identify enemy outfits.

Now the assault troop were crawling forward at a miserable ten miles an hour; the pace was slow, but at least this way they were secure against anything but direct observation on the ground. All the same, Corrigan knew his hard-pressed, frozen troopers couldn't stand it much longer. In an hour it would be completely dark, and by then he would have to get them under some sort of cover so that they could thaw out and brew up some char. There would be an issue of rum, too – although strictly speaking that was reserved for when they were in direct contact with the enemy.

Corrigan, sitting in the leading half-track with Hawkins and Smythe, rubbed the snowflakes from his face with a hand that had no feeling, and stared to right and left. They were crawling up yet another steep

Ardennes ascent now, and the tracks of the vehicles were spinning alarmingly. Next to him, Slim Sanders, crouched intently behind the wheel of the half-track, was cursing fluently to himself as he fought the vehicle up the slope. Corrigan sucked his teeth thoughtfully. It was an ideal place for an ambush: steep drop on one side, heavily-wooded slope on the other. A man and two boys could hold up a whole regiment in a position like this.

'*Sir!*' Suddenly Hawkins' homely Yorkshire voice cut into his thoughts alarmingly. '*Look!* At twelve o'clock!'

Corrigan turned to his front and narrowed his eyes against the driving snowflakes. He gasped. A flare was hissing into the white gloom like a bird of prey. He stared up at it, following its flight into the heavens. Then, with a suddenness that startled him, it exploded with a soft *plop* and slowly, very slowly, began to descend to earth, staining the snow below and the row of anxious upturned faces an unnatural, sickly green colour. Finally it hit the ground and died a slow, hissing death. Then all was silent again, save for the whine of the labouring engines and the breathing of the watching troopers.

De Vere Smythe gulped. 'What... What does it mean, Corrigan?' he asked anxiously, pressing himself against the armoured side of the half-track, as if he expected a shower of bullets to come winging his way at any moment.

Corrigan's gaze remained fixed ahead, but his fingers were already feeling for the safety-catch of his infantryman's rifle. 'Don't quite know, Smythe. A flare, that's all. I can't believe the enemy is this side of the Meuse.'

'More Yank looters, sir?' Hawkins suggested, already signalling to the vehicles behind them to prepare for trouble.

'Don't think so, Hawkins. Why would they want to give the game away in advance? Besides, I think we gave them a bloody nose back there on the railway. They won't be back for more just yet… Sanders, get ready for trouble. Remember: swing towards the ditch if anything happens.'

'I'm not bleedin' stupid, sir!' Slim cried through gritted teeth. 'Get a nice bleedin' headache if we go over the other side!' He continued to fight the treacherous road.

Behind them, the other assault troopers leaned over the sides of their vehicles, eyes narrowed to slits, trying to penetrate the flying snow, while Corrigan tensed, every nerve strained as he waited for the first angry busts which would indicate trouble.

Nothing happened. Five minutes later they had cleared the pass and the road ahead of them was clear: a stretch of virgin snow, un-marked by human footprints, with not even a fallen branch to bar their progress.

Almost reluctantly Corrigan lowered his rifle, his gaze still flashing suspiciously from one side of the road to the other. But if there was anyone lurking there in the trees, he wasn't showing himself. It was a perfect Christmas card scene, straight from Woolworth's gift-counter: snow-heavy firs and banks of windswept white snow.

Hawkins breathed out hard and lowered his Sten. 'Now what d'you make of that, sir?'

'Yes,' said Smythe in a shaky voice, 'why the flare? Who fired it, Corrigan?'

Corrigan shrugged a little angrily. 'Good grief, Smythe, I'm not a bloody mind-reader. How am I supposed to know? All I know is that somebody out there fired a flare, that's all.' He relapsed into a sullen silence.

On and on they went. Now the sky to the east was beginning to darken rapidly, and as the light faded, the cold intensified, seeming to creep into their very bones. Even the old sweat Hawkins, who never appeared to notice any extreme of temperature, hot or cold, started to shake, his teeth chattering audibly. Corrigan knew it was time that they found cover for the night. But where?

It was ten minutes later when Smythe, his lips purple with cold, suddenly broke the silence. 'I say, Corrigan. I can see smoke over there at ten o'clock... Can you see?'

Corrigan swung up his glasses, brushing

away the snowflakes that had collected around his eyes. Smythe was right. Rising slowly above the firs to their left was a thin trail of blue smoke. He sniffed, smelled the homely warm odour of burning wood – and shuddered involuntarily. What a boon it would be to sit down right now in front of a warm stove, with the logs crackling away merrily and the tiles hot to the touch! He was almost giddy with longing for warmth.

'All right, Slim, steer in that general direction.' He turned to the line of vehicles crowding the road behind his half-track, and cried above the whining engines, 'Stand fast, the rest of you. We're going to check it out...'

Hawkins nodded to the frozen troopers behind him, and cold as they were, they responded immediately: safety-catches were clicked off, bolts were jerked back, grenades held at the ready.

At five miles an hour, the leading half-track turned of the road and started ploughing through the gleaming new snow, sending up a great wake of white behind it. In the back, the young soldiers tensed, weapons at the ready.

'Looks like a farm track, sir.' Hawkins pointed to an abandoned farm cart, almost buried in snow to their right. 'Could be some civvies up there.'

'Could be,' Corrigan said non-commit-tally. 'Let's wait and see.' Out of the corner of his eye, he noted that Smythe had drawn his .38 and was holding it in his gloved hand – which was already trembling uncontrollably.

Sending up a flurry of snow, they swung round a bend in the trail, and Slim slowed down immediately. Some two hundred yards to their front lay one of the typical walled farmhouses of the area, looking more like a fort than a farm. On three sides were the farm buildings, with the main house in the centre and a great gate to the front. A steady stream of smoke was coming from the high slate chimneys.

Slim shot a glance at Corrigan, who nodded. In first gear they ground forward, each man in the half-track staring moodily ahead, wrapped up in his own thoughts and fears, his body tensed apprehensively, heart thudding excitedly, as they drew nearer to the strangely silent group of buildings. Oddly, there wasn't even the sound of a single animal to greet them – and yet still the smoke came streaming from the tall chimneys...

The half-track rolled through the gate with a loud, echoing clatter. Next moment Slim hit the brakes – hard.

'My *God!*' Corrigan gasped, almost being pitched out of the vehicle. 'What the–'

The dead bodies of men and women lay

strewn around the courtyard, the women's legs spread and their black skirts thrown up to reveal fat white thighs. From a pulley on the barn to the right, a man was hanging, his head twisted to one side, his face a dark purple, his tongue hanging out like a strip of leather. In the middle of the square, another lay speared to a trough by a hayfork; and worst of all, nailed to the door of the main house, a priest had been crucified upside down, his penis sliced off and thrust in his mouth.

Hawkins and Wolfers were first to move. Without a word of command from Corrigan, they dropped lightly over the side of the half-track and silently crossed to the farmhouse. For several moments the only sound was the steady throb of the half-track's motor, while those in the vehicle stared hypnotically around at the slaughtered farm labourers and their women.

Then, from inside the farmhouse, Hawkins' voice broke the heavy, brooding silence at last.

'Nobody, sir,' he called, his voice sounding strange and unnatural, 'at least, nobody alive.'

Wordlessly, Corrigan signalled to Slim to drive in. As he did so, Corrigan's gaze fell on a plump, youngish woman lying on her back in the snow. Her legs, already stiff with *rigor mortis,* had been supported by the handles of

138

a barrow, so they stuck straight in the air, revealing the secret flesh below the fallen skirt and the trickle of black, frozen blood that came from her savaged body.

'In heaven's name!' Smythe breathed, and retched.

They drew up outside the big oaken door to the farmhouse, yellowing tobacco leaves drying above it; the usual manure heap lay underneath the kitchen window. Corrigan dismounted and stared about him. The place looked no different from a hundred continental farmhouses that he had been billeted in since the start of the Invasion. Only the smell was different. The usual odour of animal and human manure, stale cabbage and swedes was completely overpowered by the sickly, coppery smell of blood. Much blood.

At last Corrigan broke the heavy silence. 'Hawkins?'

'Sir?'

'Get the chaps to clear the corpses away. Put them in the barn over there. We'll take the house for tonight... And see that sentries are posted as soon as the rest come up.'

'Sir!' Hawkins sped away.

Corrigan looked at the darkening sky. It wouldn't be long before it was pitch-black, and he wanted the assault troop under cover and those ghastly bodies out of the way before then. With a shudder, he turned and headed for the house.

Outside, the wind howled a banshee dirge. Snowflakes lashed against the little windows and shutters rattled as the storm raged on. Out in the barn, where the dead had been lain, a door banged restlessly back and forth – but no one was going out there to close it. No fear!

Inside the farmhouse the petrol lanterns hissed and the yellow flames of the candles flickered wildly, throwing grotesquely distorted, wavering shadows on the dirty white-washed walls. But in spite of their exhaustion and the long, freezing day behind them, the troopers couldn't sleep. As they lay huddled in their blankets on the straw-covered floor, balaclavas pulled over their heads for extra warmth, each one of them felt a sense of uneasy foreboding – a foreboding compounded by the knowledge that only fifty yards away in the barn, lay the dead bodies of innocent men and women, brutally and mysteriously done to death as they went about their humble duties. No – even the most unimaginative of the veteran troopers couldn't quite shake off that creepy sensation of impending doom.

Instead of sleeping, they crouched in their blankets, smoking fitfully and in silence, listening to the howl of the wind and the muted conversation of Sergeant Hawkins, Sanders and Wolfers – but knowing as they did so that the three of them were talking only in order to keep their spirits up; their hearts weren't in it.

'Sowin' yer wild oats!' Slim was saying scornfully, glancing contemptuously around at the faces huddled together in the semi-darkness. 'Some of you young bleeders ain't sown as much as a bleedin' cornflake! And as for that new officer we've got, I've shat better before breakfast!'

Hawkins forced a grin, though his old, faded eyes remained grim and tense. Wolfers said, 'You ain't half a moaner, Slim. Right old ray o' sunshine, mate.'

'Got something to moan about, ain't I? Christ, it ain't half friggin cold in here!' he shivered dramatically.

'Want ter borrow me electric blanket, Slim?' Hawkins asked, and winked at the other. For once he was grateful to the little Australian; at least his patter took the lads' minds off this awful, brooding place and its dread mystery.

'It ain't a friggin electric blanket I want, even if yer had one, Sarge. It's a nice, big, juicy Sheilah with plenty of pepper in her pants!'

'Knock it of, Slim!' Wolfers moaned melodramatically, grabbing at his blankets. 'Yer'll have me wankin' meself stupid if you go on like that.'

'Yer go blind doing that!' warned one of the listeners.

'Who wants to be a bleedin' pilot anyhow?' someone else chimed in, groaning in mock-ecstasy. 'Oh, it's lovely! I think I'm falling in love with myself!'

'Soddin' schoolboys,' Slim sneered. 'Probably wouldn't even know how to toss themselves off proper.' He pulled the blanket over his head with a snort and closed his eyes.

Next door in the little room he shared with Smythe, Corrigan heard the muffled talk and exclamations and felt a certain relief. At least his men weren't letting the mystery of the slaughtered civilians get them down; they seemed in pretty good heart in spite of everything. Even Smythe had forgotten his fears and was snoring softly underneath his blankets in the far end of the room, below a cheap and gaudy watercolour of the 'Last Supper' which, together with a black crucifix, were the room's sole decorations. Obviously the murdered farmer and his workers had been highly religious people.

Once again he cast his mind back to the hideous scene in the courtyard and to the question of who might have been responsible; but once more he could find no solution to the mystery. In the end he dismissed it from his mind and began planning the morrow.

Time was running out now. He couldn't afford to waste any more. At first light he would make a direct drive for the western bank of the Meuse. If the Jerries hadn't crossed it already, it wouldn't be long before they did – and to judge by what he had seen since they left Holland, they would meet precious little opposition – unless Horrocks' Thirty Corps arrived here pretty damn soon. Yes, tomorrow he would hit the Meuse and report back to Montgomery. Thereafter he would see about finding a bridge, if any were still left standing and make the crossing.

Corrigan yawned and huddled deeper in his blankets, hands under his head, staring at the gloom above his head and listening to the howl of the wind outside. Slowly, his eyes closed and he began to drift off into an uneasy sleep. But his dreams were haunted by visions of frightened, bullet-riddled peasants, blood oozing out of the great gaping holes in their shattered bodies, and strange, wavering creatures with chattering Sten-guns, who left arrow-like marks like sparrows in the snow as they pursued their ghost-like victims.

Smythe snored on softly.

Wolfers held up his black market wristwatch to catch the faint silver light of the spectral moon shining above the woods beyond the farm wall. Twelve-thirty still! How bloody slowly time seemed to pass when a bloke was on stag – especially at this time of night. No wonder the Yanks called it the graveyard shift. He wound the watch up as tight as it would go then counted slowly to sixty, breathing out after each second. He held the watch up again, hoping. It was *still* twelve-thirty! Had the sodding thing stopped? He held it up to his ear, but no: the watch was ticking away loud and clear.

Wolfers stamped his frozen feet in the snow, shifting his position so as to be sheltered a little from the icy wind by the ancient, moss-covered grey walls. He hated this stag. First stag was okay, the safest time. The last stag just before dawn stand-to was all right, too. But the midnight-to-one stint was a bugger. If anyone was going to attack, they would do it now...

Wolfers gave a faint shudder, then laughed softly at his own fears. Silly twit! There probably wasn't a soul within a radius of twenty miles of here!

At least, not *alive*...

Once more Wolfers felt the small hairs at the back of his head stand erect with fear. It was only with an effort of will that he managed to stop himself swinging round to check if there was someone behind him, ready to pounce...

Time stood still. The wind continued to howl, every now and then whipping up fierce squalls of icy white snowflakes. Miserably, Wolfers pressed himself closer against the wall, sometimes seeming to disappear for minutes on end behind the curtain of whirling snow. And still it stubbornly refused to be one o'clock, when Slim Sanders was due to relieve him. Angrily, the big Yorkshire trooper cursed to himself, peering again and again at the green-glowing dial of his wristwatch.

He leaned against the wall to take the weight off his frozen feet and closed his eyes. For a few moments he thought of the ATS girl he had had at the back of an air-raid shelter just before D-Day: a real old 'knee-trembler' that had been. His mind wandered. He remembered the dinner his mother had served up on the last Sunday of his embarkation leave. His old man's heavy worker's ration card had gone on that: Yorkshire pud, made with a real egg and none of yer bloody powdered muck; half a crown's worth of roast, all for him; roast taties done with the pud; and as many brussels sprouts with real HP sauce as he–

Suddenly Wolfers' eyes flickered open.

Something or somebody was moving out there!

Again he felt fear trace an icy finger down his spine. He raised his rifle instantly and peered cautiously into the silver gloom, his heart thudding in his ears. Who was it? *What* was it?

He had a sudden vision of something long dead and smelling of the grave crawling towards him, its claw-like skeletal fingers reaching out to grab for his neck... He swung round, nerves jangling.

Nothing. Just the barn, as quiet as the grave... He groaned. Why did he have to come up with phrases like *that?* He would be pissing down his leg if this went on much longer. Great balls of fire, why couldn't Slim come out of the house and relieve him? *Surely* he must have completed his stag by now?

The young Yorkshire giant with the spotty, ugly face and over-active imagination breathed out hard. He *must* try and stay calm; he would be getting the screaming heebie-jeebies next. There was nothing out there except the wind, and as for the stiffs in the barn, well, they were just stiffs – and he had seen plenty of *them* over the last six months without pissing himself, hadn't he? Anyway, in a few minutes' time he would be back inside in the fug and warmth of the farm, sipping hot cocoa from the troop dixie – providing the other greedy sods hadn't already nicked it. There might even be a buckshee cracker and corned beef going, if he was lucky. He licked his lips in greedy anticipation. It was all in the mind. It had been the same with all them tall tales back at Catterick about the 'phantom of the cookhouse'. The sanitary wallah had seen it first, an old sweat with three rows of ribbons and not a tooth in his head; it had popped out at him one night when he had gone over for a cup of 'sarnt-major's char'. Proper put the wind up him, he said. Then their troop sergeant, old 'Dollali Tap', who had had too much sun in India, had gone looking for it, armed with a bayonet. 'I'll fuckin' phantom 'im, if I can get this 'ere toothpick close enough to his goolies,' he had said. But he had come back as pale as a ghost himself, whispering something about a thing that had passed him noiselessly, 'like a bleeding shadder.' Course, in the end it had turned out—

Wolfers jumped. There was something there. *There was!*

Only a handful of feet away, a dark, oval, yellow face with slanting eyes like a Chink was staring right at him, the features impassive in the silver gloom, revealing nothing, saying nothing, doing nothing. They could have been the eyes of a dead man.

Wolfers gulped hard, blinked his eyes open and shut, heart going like a trip-hammer. But it was still there, staring, staring, staring.

'*Who... What...*' he began.

The words seemed to wake the creature out of its strange immobility. It darted forward. Wolfers bellowed like a stricken pig. It

147

was a man all right. He had grabbed the young trooper's balls and was squeezing ruthlessly. Through watering eyes, Wolfers caught a fleeting glimpse of more and more of the strange yellow figures beginning to slide out of the darkness and into the farmyard.

With a sudden effort, Wolfers smashed his fist into the other man's face. He heard him grunt with pain, felt hot blood flood his knuckles – realised in the same instant that his attacker was no zombie, but a real flesh-and-blood human being.

'*Stand to!*' he screamed. '*Stand to! We're being bloody well attacked!*'

Wolfers dropped his rifle, his face contorted with pain. *Still* the little yellow man refused to relax his grip on his genitals. Agony blazed through the lower half of his body like fire. His groin felt as if it might explode at any moment. He knew it would be purposeless to attempt to break the vice-like grip the attacker had on him – he would faint before then. Instead he grabbed the yellow man's head and with both hands, exerting all his strength, he started to pound it against the wall, back and forth, back and forth. His attacker started to moan. The pressure on his balls began to ease up. But Wolfers didn't stop. Carried away by a mad fury, a killer's blood-rage, he smashed his attacker's head to pieces, sending splinters of flesh and bone flying everywhere, until at last his attacker went limp and dead in his blood-filled hands. Only then did he relax his grip and allow him to sink to the snow, while all around, his comrades ran to meet the new challenge, firing from the hip wildly at they went...

FOUR

Again Slim brought up his looted shotgun and took aim. He had sawn the barrel down now, so that it wasn't much bigger than a service revolver. He pressed the first trigger. The Gulag rat rushing towards him, firing the Sten from his hip, caught the blast full in the face. It disappeared in a welter of red gore. His hands splayed and clawed at the empty air. Next moment he plunged into the snow, instantly staining it a bright crimson.

Another Russian charged him from the right, screaming wildly and in triumph, obviously thinking he had caught the lone soldier off guard. 'Laugh on the other side of yer bleeding yellow face, mate!' Slim yelled, carried away by the blood-lust of close combat, and pressed the second trigger. The blast caught the running man in the groin and slammed him backwards as if he had been struck in the guts by a gigantic fist. He screamed and dropped his weapon. Clutching his shattered belly, from which the guts were already beginning to protrude, he staggered backwards, while Slim feverishly inserted fresh cartridges, crying, *How's that one for size, mate?* As if in slow motion, the man went down on his knees, swaying back and forth and moaning, his life fluids leaking away. Deliberately Slim went over and kicked him in the face – hard.

Next moment, the mysterious attackers were coming in again, screaming out in their own language, with here and there a loud, guttural '*Urrah!*'

Again the assault troop's machine-guns sung their song of death. White tracer zipped through the air like golf balls. The first burst scythed through the line of running men. They went down everywhere, galvanised into one last, frenetic burst of action like puppets controlled by some mad puppet-master, then writhing in agony in the blood-stained snow, as their comrades sprang over them – only to die themselves moments later.

Standing at the door, snapping off controlled shots to left and right, Corrigan had no time to reflect on the reckless, almost suicidal bravery of their attackers. There was a new danger to contend with. Dark shapes were creeping through the skeletal, snow-heavy trees to the right of the house, where they had laagered their vehicles to shelter them from the freezing night air.

'They're out to nobble our vehicles!' he cried. 'Smythe, take over here! You, Hawkins and Wolfers – follow me! *At the double now!*'

They bolted from the door, zig-zagging wildly as slugs stitched a lethal pattern at their flying heels. A yellow man loomed up out of the silver gloom. He raised his Sten. Corrigan was quicker. Up came the cruel, brass-shod butt of his rifle. It connected right under the man's chin. There was an audible click. He reeled backwards, neck broken. Corrigan sprang over him and ran on.

Slim Sanders came running towards them from the right. 'Don't shoot, cobbers! It's me!' he cried, trying to insert new cartridges in his awesome weapon as he ran. 'They're everywhere in the trees, sir,' he gasped. 'Heaps of the yeller buggers!'

'*Look out!*' Hawkins screamed fervently.

Both Sanders and Corrigan ducked instinctively.

Hawkins fired from the hip. A little man running out of the trees went reeling back, his flat face looking as if someone had just thrown a handful of strawberry jam at it.

Corrigan leapt over a low wall. The next second a grenade sailed through the air and exploded in a blinding flash of white light just behind him. Corrigan yelped with pain. His right leg felt as if it had just been slashed by a hundred razor-blades. He went down on one knee, shaking his head like a boxer reeling from a tremendous punch.

Wolfers flung himself in front of the groggy officer. 'All right–'

The spade hissed down, missing his head by inches. Instinctively Wolfers' big hand shot out and grabbed it, just before the little man could raise the improvised weapon for another blow. For a moment or two the giant and his undersized opponent swayed back and forth, grunting and cursing, struggling for possession of the spade. Then Slim's shotgun butt slammed into the enemy's back. The man gasped and went down on his knees. Next moment, Slim blew the back of his head off with both barrels of his shotgun, crying above his victim's last, lingering high-pitched scream, 'Silly bugger, Wolfers! What were yer tryin' to do? *Waltz the little yeller shit to death?*'

They ran on, supporting a hobbling Corrigan, the night air all around them echoing to the vicious stab and blast of close combat. Finally they blundered into the cover of the trees, already aware of the first low, obstinate moans as their unknown enemy tried to start the frozen motors of the assault troop's vehicles.

Leaning weakly against a fir and trying to catch his breath, Corrigan halted and assessed the situation. In a sudden burst of flame as another grenade exploded nearby, he could make out about twenty figures swarming about the vehicles, trying to hand-crank them into action, while another ten-odd sat inside, attempting to do the same job with the electric starter-motor. So far, he guessed, he and his party hadn't been spotted; whoever the enemy were, they clearly assumed that their comrades sacrificing their lives outside the main house were keeping the assault troop busy.

Another grenade exploded in a burst of angry flame. By its light, Corrigan caught a fleeting glimpse of a big man, dressed in what looked like British Army uniform, his surly face contorted with rage as he bellowed orders in a language Corrigan couldn't understand to his toiling little subordinates. Unlike the others, he was obviously a white man, and Corrigan knew instinctively that he had to be their leader. He made his decision.

'Listen,' he hissed. '*Waltzing Mathilda*'s in the best position.' He indicated the vehicle closest to them, his own command half-track, named personally by Sanders in a fit of unwonted patriotism. 'Let's seize it and give 'em a taste of the half-inch machine-gun. That should scatter them. But I want that big chap alive. Slim, do you think you can nobble him?'

Slim Sanders spat on his free hand. 'Easy as fallin' off a bleedin' log, sir. But what do you want the bastard for? Shoot the bugger, I say. Gooks and wogs, they're all the same.'

If the situation hadn't been so serious, Corrigan would have laughed out loud. He had never met a man so consistent in his prejudices as the little deserter from the Australian Army. 'Information, Slim – that's why. Got me, cobber?'

'Got yer.'

'All right.' Corrigan forgot the pain in his leg and drew a deep breath. 'Here we go!'

They surged forward, weapons blazing. A yellow man fumbled wildly for a grenade at his belt. Corrigan shot him. The grenade exploded in his hands, which flew off like two gloves fringed with red. Another tried to bar Wolfers' way. Wolfers slammed his Sten into his attacker's face. The man's scream was stifled by hot vomit as the trooper's boot crashed into his crotch.

Hawkins came in from the right, weaving in and out of the trees, firing as he went. Listening to the *thonk* of enemy slugs slicing the wood all around him, he was carried away by the mad excitement of close combat. Gasping like a man in the throes of orgasm, he fired from the hip, hosing slugs to left and right, screaming obscenities at the top of his voice. A man threw a grenade at him. Without stopping, he scooped it up, hardly aware of the fuse spluttering wildly, and flung it back. The man who had thrown it disappeared in a ball of scorching flame, his scream echoing after. Hawkins ran on.

Sanders vaulted over a low wall and found himself suddenly up to his knees in a snowdrift. One of the Russians turned, shouting excitedly. It was the last thing he ever did. Slim pressed the trigger and his shotgun thundered. The blast caught the man right in the face, which suddenly seemed to trickle down onto his chin in a thick, red, bubbling mess.

Cursing frantically, Slim pulled himself out of the snow. Another Gulag rat rushed him. He fired again. A sudden line of red buttonholes appeared along the length of the running man's chest and he went down, clawing the air as if he were climbing the rungs of an invisible ladder. Slim dropped to one knee and with fingers that trembled almost uncontrollably, frantically fitted new cartridges into the smoking breech. To his right he could hear the familiar chatter of a half-inch machine-gun. The boys had reached old *Waltzing Mathilda* and were in business already.

With a glance straight ahead, Slim Sanders took in the scene: the big white man was cursing and kicking at his men as they attempted to run for cover, while the slugs from *Waltzing Mathilda* sliced the air sending up little spurts of snow all around them. Slim gave a grin of satisfaction. Those little yeller buggers wouldn't help the big bloke when the shit started flying. They would be too busy looking out for Number One...

He drew a deep breath and counted to three. Next instant he was up and running, his head tucked down between his skinny shoulders as if he were pelting through pouring rain, shotgun clutched tightly to his side. A dark figure popped out from behind one of the trees and ripped off a burst of fire. Slim fired back, straight from the hip. The man was catapulted into the air and landed in the boughs, already dead. Slim darted on.

From somewhere to his right, near the big man, who was still yelling at his men, there came a low moan as one of the Russians hand-cranked a White scout-car. Thick blue smoke poured from the exhaust. Excitedly the big man sprang on the mudguard, obviously expecting the car to start at any moment. Louder and louder grew the whining. Then, while slugs from *Waltzing Mathilda* continued to howl off the scout-car's armour, the sluggish, frozen engine gave in a series of throaty coughs.

Suddenly the engine erupted into wild, noisy life, with the driver gunning the accelerator for all he was worth. It was exactly the opportunity that Slim had been looking for. He burst out of the trees. A Russian turned, startled, reaching for his pistol. Slim beat him to it. The shotgun thundered at his side, and his victim flopped face forwards into the snow. Angrily the big man swung round, face contorted in fury.

Slim knew he had fired both chambers, but didn't hesitate for a moment. 'Freeze it right there!' he commanded. 'Get those hands up in the air! Come on, let's be havin'' you! *Pronto, vite, schnell!*'

Whether or not the big man understood English, he *did* understand the threatening jerk of Slim's shotgun. He raised his hands swiftly.

Slim gave him no opportunity to reconsider. He ran forward and thrust the muzzle of the empty shotgun into the big man's belly. 'In the White – quick!' he snarled.

Half-stumbling, the big man blundered into the open cab of the scout-car. The driver looked at the two of them in blank incomprehension, but again a snarl from that wolfish, bronzed Australian face and a threatening jerk from the shotgun sufficed. He moved back so that Slim could clamber in after his prisoner.

'All right,' cried the Australian above the din of small arms fire, 'take her away. Hit the gas... *Gildy!*'

Fiercely, Slim rammed the muzzle of his shotgun into the big man's ribs. With a wince of pain, the man cried something to the driver, who let out the clutch; with a great shudder, the wheels freed themselves from the frozen snow and the White shot forward, Russians scattered wildly on all sides, caught completely by surprise. A moment later they were bouncing and jerking across the rough surface of the frozen snow, followed by *Waltzing Mathilda,* heading straight for the house and safety.

FIVE

Now the brooding pre-dawn silence was broken only by the soft moans of the wounded and the occasional sharp crack of a rifle from outside the farmhouse, followed by a muffled *thump* as a rifle bullet flattened itself on the thick, ancient walls. The loss of their leader had obviously rattled the Russians so badly that they had lost all interest in stealing the assault troop's vehicles. Now they seemed to be content with keeping the men in the farmhouse bottled in.

Carefully Corrigan checked out each of his wounded troopers, followed by Sergeant Hawkins, who as usual was fussing over his men like a mother hen. Corrigan was aware that their prisoner was watching his every move, but was happy to let him stew in his own juice. He wanted information from the man and he was going to get it; but first he would let him wait and contemplate what was to come.

Finally Corrigan completed his rounds of the pale-faced, shocked young men, their limbs now swathed in thick yellow bandages, and turned to Sergeant Hawkins.

'All right, Hawkins, no need to worry yourself like an old cluck. Basically only flesh-wounds – nothing we can't handle ourselves until we reach a proper sawbones. Satisfied?'

'Satisfied, sir. Thank God there was nothing serious.'

Corrigan nodded and turned to face their prisoner.

The big man had the heavy-knuckled, hanging hands of an industrial worker – a miner or steelworker possibly, Corrigan reckoned. He wore the white British overall of the Belgian partisans – *L'armée blanche* – but instead of the black, red and gold armband of the Belgian national flag usually worn by the partisans, he wore a hammer and sickle badge and a red scarf of parachute silk wrapped round his neck. You didn't need a crystal ball to see that the big prisoner was a communist.

Corrigan remembered Monty's warning back at Twenty-first Army Group HQ and strode purposefully towards the big man, who stared back unbowed and unafraid at the men all around him.

Corrigan mustered his best French. '*Qui es-tu? Pourquoi est-ce-que tu attaques mes soldats? Allez vite! Parle!*'

The big man's face contorted with contempt. Deliberately he spat on the floor and jerked a thumb like a small sausage to his chest. '*Ik ben vlaams,*' he snarled, and seeing that the Englishman didn't understand, added in thick , guttural tones, 'I am Flemish ... not Walloon.'

Corrigan's face registered surprise; then he recalled that their prisoner had also spoken some unknown language to their yellow-faced attackers. Of course – languages were second nature to the Belgies. 'Ah, you speak English,' he said, a little stupidly.

'Yes. Seaman. Worked Ostend-Dover crossing for five years.' He held up his right hand, fingers outstretched. 'What do you want?'

'Why did you attack my column?' Corrigan snapped. 'We're supposed to be allies, you know. And who are those little yellow fellows? *They're* not Belgian.'

Again the big man spat contemptuously. He folded his muscular arms across his chest and remained silent.

Corrigan had half-expected the reaction. The prisoner was tough, he could see that. But the bigger they are, the harder they fall...

'I shall get it out of you, you know,' Corrigan said softly. 'I'll ask you one more time.' He repeated the question, but again the big man remained obstinately silent.

This time Corrigan didn't hesitate. 'Sergeant Hawkins,' he barked, not taking his gaze off the prisoner.

'Sir!'

'Go into the kitchen, Sergeant, please, and bring me the pail you'll find there and any long-handled broom you can find.'

161

'Sir!' Hawkins marched away. A minute later he was back with a white-enamelled kitchen pail and a twig-broom, home-made by the look of it – the kind Belgian farm-women used to sweep the farmyard clean on a Saturday evening before the day of rest.

'Thank you, Sergeant,' Corrigan said, taking the pail from Hawkins.

'Corrigan...' The voice was Captain Smythe. 'Whatever do you think you're going to do?'

'What I said. I'm going to make him talk.'

'But how?'

'Simple. Knock it out of the bugger!' said Corrigan. And he nodded to Wolfers and Slim Sanders to grab the big man's arms and pull them behind his back.

Smythe looked shocked. 'But we're ... we're *British*,' he stuttered. 'We don't *do* things like that ... do we?' His mouth dropped open as Wolfers whipped off his belt and wrapped it neatly around the big man's wrists.

'Don't we?' Corrigan asked cynically. Taking hold of the bucket, he paused for a moment, facing the defiant Belgian, whose eyes blazed with hate. 'All right, one last chance. Are you going to talk?'

The big man pursed his lips and attempted to spit in his face. Corrigan dodged just in time. 'All right,' he said calmly, 'if that's the way you want it, let's see how long you last.'

With a sudden movement Corrigan thrust the pail over the big man's head.

He writhed and heaved, but Slim and Wolfers held him while Corrigan took the broom from Hawkins, holding it by the brush end.

Smythe turned pale. 'Oh, my God, Corrigan – what are you going to do?'

Corrigan ignored him and taking a deep breath, thrust the broom back like a cricket bat. Suddenly he lashed out with all his strength. The broom hissed through the air and struck the pail a loud, ringing whack. The big man staggered violently and would have fallen if Wolfers and Slim hadn't been holding him. From beneath the pail, something red and wet started to trickle down his chest.

Smythe held his hand to his suddenly chalk-white lips. 'It's torture!' he whispered in a broken voice. *'Torture!'* But no one was paying any attention to Captain Smythe now. All eyes were fixed on the trembling man with the pail on his head and a crimson-faced, angry Corrigan, still holding the broom. Slowly he started to raise it again, chest heaving as he summoned up all his strength.

Thwack! The broom handle came hissing through the air again. Smythe jumped. It hit the pail with a hollow boom. Wolfers and Slim needed all their strength to hold the big man upright. Suddenly blood jetted from beneath the pail and dropped in bright-red gobs on the cartridge-littered floor. Sergeant Hawkins gasped.

Corrigan hit the pail again – and again. Now Captain Smythe was sobbing openly, the tears streaming down his face, mumbling incomprehensibly to himself. But no one even noticed. It was as if everyone was hypnotised by the terrible scene being enacted before them.

Over and over again, Corrigan, his face streaming with sweat, eyes blazing savagely, slammed the pail with the broom handle. With each blow his chest heaved, his breath coming in sharp, hectic gasps until finally even he had had enough. Dropping the broom as if it were red-hot, he turned to Hawkins. 'Take the bucket off his head... He's ripe now, I'll be bound.' He ran his sleeve across his glazed brow to wipe away the beads of sweat which were dropping like glistening pearls into his thick eyebrows.

Hurriedly Sergeant Hawkins stepped forward to carry out his command, as if anxious not to give Corrigan a chance to change his mind. He removed the bucket, and gasped at what he saw.

The big man's face was almost unrecognisable. His features seemed to have swollen up to almost twice their original size, the cheeks split and green like overripe plums, the nose twisted to one side, a bright crimson, the eyes narrowed to mere slits, with thick, black blood pouring from nose and ears. As for the tortured man's mouth, the lips had split in half a dozen places and gaps in his teeth showed through the bright-red gore that filled his mouth.

Miserably, trying to avoid looking up at the big Belgian, Hawkins pulled out his own khaki handkerchief and attempted to wipe away the blood. But Corrigan pushed him away angrily. 'No bloody sympathy, Hawkins!' he cried gruffly. 'That bugger would have killed us all in our beds if he'd had the chance!' His hand shot out and grabbed the Belgian by the front of his blood-soaked overalls. 'All right, you swine, out with it now! Or by Christ, I'll kill you next time!'

But the big man's spirit was completely broken.

'No... *No*... Please,' he quavered, raising his heavy hands as if to protect his martyred face. '*Nyet... Nyet!*' The plea ended as a near-scream.

'*Then talk!*'

'So lads, that's the way of it,' Corrigan summed up, while their prisoner, completely broken now, sobbed in the corner, shoulders heaving like a child. 'The big fellow is the leader of a communist partisan organisation. The little yellow bastards are former prisoners in the Gulag Archipelago who fell into German hands. When the Americans liberated them, they were put in camps before being sent back to Russia. Apparently they broke out a couple of days ago and are making a last, desperate attempt to redeem themselves in the eyes of the Russian authorities.'

'How do you mean, *redeem* themselves, sir?' asked Hawkins.

Corrigan smiled, but there was no warmth in his eyes. 'In the Red Army you don't let yourself be taken prisoner. You fight to the last man and the last bullet. If you're taken prisoner, you're regarded as a traitor and treated accordingly if you ever return to Russia. No Red Cross parcels and nice old grannies knitting you pullovers in the Workers' Paradise. If you go into the bag, it's the firing squad for you.'

Hawkins whistled softly, as if impressed. 'Thank Christ we're in the good old British Army then!'

'But why try to nobble *us*, sir?' Wolfers protested, brow creased in a puzzled frown.

Corrigan shrugged. 'I've only got a vague idea. And he' – he indicated the sobbing Belgian – 'only knows what he's been told by his party bosses. But in essence, the Russians want us to get deeper into the shit here in the west so that they can grab as much territory as possible in the east. They want the Jerries to succeed with this new offensive of theirs because it'll take the pressure off the Red Army.'

'But they're our allies, sir!' Wolfers said, puzzled.

'Are they?' Corrigan asked, eyes full of boundless cynicism. 'I worked with the Red Army back in 'forty-two in Persia. I wouldn't regard them as allies – more as fellow conspirators, out for what they can get. I wouldn't trust them as far as I could throw them.'

There was a sudden silence as the men digested Corrigan's statement, broken only by the odd shot from outside. Here and there some of the young troopers frowned or shook their heads, as if in disbelief. During the middle years of the war they had been used to hearing the propaganda of the British Communist Party, and to seeing the slogan 'Second Front Now' painted on every wall and bridge; their image of the Red Army was of a loyal, democratic, war-winning ally. It came as a shock to them to learn that their Russian allies were now fighting against them. It took some digesting.

But not for Slim Sanders. He grinned suddenly and nudged Wolfers, who was unusually solemn and thoughtful. 'Didn't I always tell yer they're all the bleedin' same, the whole bleedin' shower of 'em? First we fight the bleedin' Jerries! Then the bleedin'

Yanks! Now it's the bleedin' Russians! I tell yer, young Wolfers, the *whole bleedin' world is against the assault troop!*'

The outburst raised a laugh and the spell was broken. It was time to consider what to do next.

'We'll leave at first light,' Corrigan began. 'I reckon we're about twenty miles from the Meuse now, but in this kind of weather we'll need all day to get there, so I want to make an early start. Now, what I'm afraid of is that they'll start sniping as soon as we try and make it to the other vehicles.'

'We could rush them with the half-track, sir,' someone suggested.

'Agreed. But before they fled from the other vehicles they may have tried to booby-trap the path, perhaps even the vehicles themselves. We might just go rushing into something rather unpleasant.' Corrigan frowned. 'We need time – we can't just go rushing out under fire.'

'What about the Belgie?' Smythe suggested. The captain still looked somewhat pale and drawn now, but at least he had recovered his powers of speech.

'How do you mean, Smythe?'

'Well, if he *is* their leader, make him order them to hold their fire and withdraw out of range.' He smiled faintly. 'You seem to have a way with him, Corrigan, after all, don't you?'

Corrigan shot his fellow-officer a hard

168

look. A change had come over Captain de Vere Smythe, that was for sure. He had grown up; he had learned the true facts of war. It had nothing to do with bands and parades, bullshit and blanco. The real shooting war was something vastly different – and at last Smythe seemed to have discovered that. 'It's an idea, Smythe,' mused Corrigan, turning it over in his mind.

Outside, one of the roosters locked in the barn with the bodies of the murdered civilians started to crow faintly. It would soon be dawn. Here and there a man yawned. It had been a long night and none of then had had much sleep.

Corrigan looked at the Belgian sobbing in the corner. The man's will was broken completely; he would do as he was told. Yet there was a lingering doubt at the back of Corrigan's mind. In his limited experience, these working-class communists were tough, very tough – unlike the pansified, middle-class parlour pinks he had met in society drawing rooms in London before the war. They had become communists because they'd been hungry, not because commun-ism was fashionable at university; they fought for their perverted creed to the end.

'But what if he double-crosses us, sir,' asked Slim Sanders, breaking the heavy silence and expressing Corrigan's own unspoken doubts. 'We can't understand the lingo he talks to his men. What if he tells us one thing and them something else, eh?' He looked almost accusingly at Corrigan, an angry scowl on his skinny little face. 'Out we come and find ourselves with our knickers down around our bleedin' ankles. What then, sir?'

Corrigan forced a laugh. 'What then, you little rogue?' he echoed, with more conviction than he felt. 'Why, we pull 'em up again smartish, so that the wind doesn't get up our arses!'

SIX

'The Meuse!' announced Captain Hartung, as the corporal next to him in the cab of the locomotive eased back the throttle and the little train began to slow down.

Next to Hartung, Sergeant Martini craned his neck and stared through the dirty grey of the early dawn at the dull silver snake of the river far below. But Hartung's gaze went automatically to the east, beyond the far bank, vainly combing the landscape for signs of the flickering pink colour which would indicate that German artillery was nearby.

'Our comrades haven't made it yet, then?' Martini asked, expressing aloud the big officer's unspoken thought.

'No, doesn't look like it, Martini. But there's one advantage in it for us.'

'What's that, sir?' Martini asked, as the locomotive chugged up a long incline between tight, snow-heavy banks of a cutting.

'The bridges will still be in the Amis' hands, which means they won't blow them until the very last moment. With a bit of luck we might find one intact that we could cross.' His bearded face suddenly glowed with excitement. '*Himmel, Arsch und Wolken-bruch!* Wouldn't it be something if we could take a bridge and hold it until our own people arrived, Martini? It would be the great days of nineteen forty all over again!'

Martini, however, didn't share the captain's enthusiasm. 'Those days are over, sir. The clock's in the pisspot. We'll be lucky if we get out of this with just a black eye,' he said in a sombre voice, watching the smoke stream backwards in a solid white block.

'Suppose you're right, Martini,' said Hartung, reluctantly coming down to earth again. 'The great days are over. But even so I'm damned if I'm swimming the Meuse – not in December. You know I've got a weak chest.' He winked.

'You – a weak chest, sir?' Martini echoed scornfully. 'I've seen you rolling naked in the snow in Finland with the temperature twenty degrees below zero!'

'I was younger and more stupid then. But seriously – if we can get across the river down there without getting our feet wet, I'd be a happy man.'

'Agreed, sir. We're going to have to abandon the train sooner or later. Eventually we'll either be rumbled by the Amis or we'll run out of fuel.' He jerked a thumb at the coal tender swaying behind them.

'Yes. So we've got to get across the Meuse before we run out of steam. Now, we can

172

expect the normal land bridges over the river to be under heavy guard, especially at a time like this. After all, they're the key targets of our panzer divisions.'

Martini nodded his agreement, as the locomotive laboured mightily up the steep cutting.

'But what kind of guards would they have on a railway bridge? I mean, they wouldn't expect our forward troops to come up by train, would they?' Hartung answered his own question. 'Of course not. So my guess is that they might only have a few clapped out Belgie soldiers guarding it, looking out for saboteurs, agents, that kind of thing. I doubt very much if they'd have the usual barricades, with guns covering them and regular infantry. You can't run a railway line like that. It'd be far too cumbersome.'

'So assuming we do find a suitable bridge, when would we cross, sir?'

'As soon as it's dark. Run in slow, and then, once we're on the thing, go flat-out so that they're confused and have no time to react. As soon as we're over and safely out of sight, we'll then abandon the train before they can take counter-measures.' He beamed at the big NCO, whose face, like his own, was flecked with coal dust; in fact, the two of them looked more like miners at the end of a shift underground than members of the Reich's élite parachute army. 'With a bit of cunning and a bit of luck, Martini,' Hartung chortled, 'you and me will be back with mother tonight, toasting our dice-beakers in front of a nice warm stove and supping bucketfuls of nigger sweat laced with firewater.'

Inspired by his CO's words, Sergeant Martini raised his right leg and let off a tremendous fart. *'Heil Churchill!'* he cried exuberantly. Already in his mind he was sitting there with his big boots on the glowing stove, knocking back big mugs of black *Ersatz* coffee laced with Schnapps, just as the captain had promised. 'By the Great Whore of Buxtehüde, sir, it seems a million years since I was last warm and had something–'

'Sir!' cried the corporal driving the train in alarm. *'Look!'*

Almost before the two of them had time to do so, the corporal hit the brakes and jerked the wire above his head to open the sandbox. The big steel wheels shrieked ear-splittingly, the sand dropping all around on the rails to give them a grip, as the desperate driver tried to bring the engine to a stop. There, blocking the track ahead was the trunk of a fallen tree.

Hartung swallowed hard, suddenly bathed in sweat, as the engine slid and shrieked ever closer to the huge obstacle, willing it to stop in time. If it didn't... He shuddered, hardly daring to think the thought through.

At last, with mere feet to spare, the locomotive's wheels gripped with an awful sound that made Hartung grimace as if in pain and grit his teeth, and a moment later it came to rest, its front submerged in branches, and Hartung's nostrils were suddenly assailed by the heavy scent of pine resin.

'*Phew!*' Martini breathed out hard. 'Nearly pissed in me boot that time!'

Hartung mopped his wet brow. 'Yes, it was damned close. All right, get the men. Let's have a look-see at the damage. Let's hope we can clear the shitting thing quickly.' He flashed a look at the silent firs marching up the sloping bank to his right like spike-helmeted Prussian guardsmen. Thank God this was Belgium and not Russia. There, the woods would have been swarming with Popov partisans by now.

Dropping to the ground, Hartung stamped knee-deep through the bright white snow to where the tree-trunk lay across the track, followed by the shivering young paras. For a few moments he mustered it, considering the best way of dealing with the damned thing with the minimum loss of time; then he started to rap out his orders, his breath fogging a thick grey on the freezing dawn air.

'Bayonets out... Start cutting the foliage away first ... knot your toggle-ropes together to form lines... Martini, get a loop round that end... Come on, you bunch of wet-tails! *Los! Los!* We haven't got all day!'

It happened with startling suddenness. The young paras were completely absorbed in their task, working in silence, each youngster well aware of the urgency of the situation, when there was the sharp, hard crack of a sniper's rifle.

A metre away from Sergeant Martini, a blond boy who had taken off his heavy helmet straightened up suddenly, face ashen and completely bewildered, as if he couldn't understand what was happening to him. Right in the middle of his high forehead, a neat, perfect, little purple hole had been drilled. Next moment he pitched face-down into the snow, the back of his head blown apart by the bullet.

For what seemed an eternity, the paras remained frozen into a horrified tableau like the cast at the end of some cheap melodrama, staring down at the dead youth in shocked disbelief. Then suddenly they woke up, as bullets started to cut the air all around them, howling off the steel tracks. All around them the woods were full of little running figures yelling that well-remembered cry of *'Urrah!'* that sent cold shivers down Captain Hartung's spine.

Martini reacted first. *'Down!'* he cried. As

the startled young paras flung themselves into the snow, too surprised as yet to make use of their weapons, Martini swung round to face his attackers, feet spread apart, firing his Schmeisser from the hip. Wildly he loosed off an entire magazine, the hail of bullets cutting the trees and bringing the twigs raining down in a green flood. Here and there the odd lucky slug felled one of the running figures, taking the steam out of their first attack. As soon as his magazine was empty, Martini dropped to the ground, rolling on his back to fit another and crying angrily to his men, 'Come on, you bunch of perverted banana-suckers, return their fire! *Feuer!*'

At last the young paras woke to their danger. Now they started to return the enemy fire, which though scattered and wild at first, was rapidly becoming more accurate and controlled as the ambushers began to drop to their knees and seek cover.

Captain Hartung dived to where Martini lay cursing, the slugs whipping up the snow in angry little flurries all around him. 'Listen, Martini, whoever those bastards are – guerrillas, partisans or asparagus Tarzans – they've got us by the short and curlies. We've got to shift this shitting tree!'

Martini slammed home his mag. 'Right,' he said grimly through gritted teeth, 'but they'll pick us off like flies if we try.'

Just then a group of dark figures burst

from the trees to his right and started pelting heavily across the tracks, perhaps in an attempt to cut them off. They never made it. Without seeming to aim, Martini ripped off a burst, and the men went down screaming, ripped apart by that terrible blast of fire, lying writhing and moaning in the snow, staining it scarlet with their own blood.

'We've got to feign an attack. Hold them off long enough to allow the rest to push the tree clear.'

'And I'm to volunteer to lead the attack?' There was a broad grin on Martini's dirty face.

'Exactly.' Hartung grinned back. Thank God he had an 'old head' like Martini backing him up in a tight corner – and this really *was* a tight corner: there had to be at least two hundred of the bastards up there in the trees.

'I suppose you're going to promise me the Iron Cross, Third Class for this, sir?' Martini quipped, as he checked the number of spare magazines he still had left. 'I've been longing to win one of them ever since nineteen thirty-nine.' He winked.

'No, you big rogue. I'm promising you the biggest blonde pavement-pounder in Berlin and a barrel of suds once we get home!'

'Well, why didn't you say so before, sir?' Martini bellowed. 'Now that's *really* something for a hairy-arsed old stubble-hopper to risk his life for!' He sprang to his feet enthusiastically, ignoring the slugs that immediately started winging his way. 'Right then, all you heroes of my section – on yer feet! *Come on, you dogs! You don't want to live for ever, do you?*'

About the same time Sergeant Martini made his bold statement, a worried-looking Captain Corrigan prepared to make his own break-out from the farmhouse through the communist partisans.

Outside, it had started to snow again. As Corrigan peered out of the window, soft, sad snowflakes were drifting down, already beginning to obscure the leaden morning sky, reducing visibility even more. Now, virtually no shapes could be distinguished, save the snow-covered mounds formed by the bodies of the dead and the assault troop's vehicles. But Corrigan knew the enemy was still out there, watching and waiting. It was no use fooling himself. The cold wouldn't deter them. They could stand up to arctic temperatures. He made his decision.

'Smythe, Hawkins – we're going out now. I'll take *Waltzing Mathilda*. The rest of you, follow on foot, nice and close behind and I'll give you fire cover while you start the vehicles.' Behind his back he crossed his fingers, praying that they would start first time. 'All right, Sanders and Wolfers, bring up the prisoner.'

'Come on, hero of the working class,' Slim

sneered, pushing the beaten Belgian to his feet. 'Come and talk to yer nice yellow friends.' And he gave the tightly bound prisoner a shove that sent him staggering helplessly towards the door.

Corrigan caught him just before he slapped into the wall. 'Good. So you know what you're supposed to do, don't you? Tell them to keep out of our way and there'll be no trouble. I give you my word of honour as a British officer' – behind him, Smythe gave a tight cynical laugh, but Corrigan ignored it – 'that you'll be set free unharmed once we're on our way. Do you understand?'

Numbly, his face bent in defeat, the prisoner nodded.

'But don't fool yourself,' Corrigan snapped harshly, placing the muzzle of his rifle underneath the man's chin and raising it so that the Belgian was forced to look at his hard, cold, threatening face. 'One false move – and I'll blow the bloody face off you. Got it?'

The Belgian gulped. 'Yes,' he said weakly. 'Got it.'

'All right, Wolfers, open the door. Here we go!'

Wolfers flung open the door, and using his rifle, Corrigan thrust the prisoner into the open, keeping the weapon tucked cruelly into the soft flesh beneath the jaw so that the Belgian had to keep his head tilted as if he had a wry neck.

180

Corrigan waited momentarily, staring around him. Then he turned to look at the half-track *Waltzing Mathilda*. Nothing! The whole area seemed empty. He stared down at the snow. There were no new footprints. 'Okay,' he snapped, 'shout up! Tell them in their own lingo that you're in bad trouble if they try to pull any tricks. Get on with it!' He pulled the rifle away a little so that the Belgian could speak, and suddenly felt very foolish as the big man followed his instructions. Hell, the little yellow fellows could be miles away by now, and his prisoner might be talking to thin air!

Finally the Belgian was finished. Still nothing happened; there was no sound save the soft hiss of the falling snow.

Corrigan began to feel not only foolish, but irritated too. He turned to his men. 'All right, mount! Sanders, start her up… The rest of you, follow.'

Five minutes later they were with the vehicles, cranking them up and attempting to start the engines, the steel plating icy to their touch, while Corrigan and his crew kept watch in *Waltzing Mathilda*. Every one of them was nervous and on edge, yet still there was no sign of their attackers of the previous night.

One of the reluctant engines started, filling the morning air with blue fumes and the stink of petrol, while crew members crawled underneath to check for mines or booby traps. But there were none. It seemed as if their attackers had vanished into thin air.

Corrigan, however, was taking no chances. 'Hawkins and Wolfers, you come with me,' he ordered, as the column prepared to move out. 'We'll walk it for the first hundred yards, just in case,' he added, with a hard look at them.

Hawkins knew what he meant. It was quite possible the Russians had laid mines in their path under cover of darkness.

Solemnly the little procession walked through the gate, the Belgian in the lead, followed by the vehicles, whining along in first gear. All eyes searched the snow to left and right for the tell-tale signs of anti-tank mines, but again there was nothing: just fresh snow, its surface perfect and smooth, completely undisturbed. Obviously their attackers had learned their lesson, or were scared for their leader. Either way, they weren't putting any obstacles in the way of the assault troop.

Corrigan decided the coast was clear. 'All right, Wolfers and Hawkins, we'll mount up again.'

'And his nibs?' Hawkins jerked a gloved hand at the Belgian who was trembling in the freezing dawn air.

Corrigan hesitated momentarily. 'Oh, let the bugger go. I think he's learned his lesson. He'd only be an extra burden for us.'

'Sir.' Hawkins raised his foot and gave the woebegone prisoner a token kick in the rump. 'All right, mate, bugger off. Give my regards to Uncle Joe when you see him.'

Ignoring Hawkins' dig at Stalin, the burly Belgian staggered forward a few paces, then turned to stare at them, his slits of eyes reflecting a mixture of doubt, fear and hate. For a moment he obviously thought he was going to be shot as soon as he turned his back on his captors. Then he decided he wasn't, after all, stumbled off, hands still behind his back, breaking into a shambling trot until he disappeared into the firs to their right. Hastily the three men swung themselves over the side of *Waltzing Mathilda*.

Sanders, at the wheel, didn't wait for the command to start. Straight away he slammed home first gear and let out the clutch. The half-track creaked forward almost immediately, gathering speed swiftly, while behind them the rest of the convoy did the same, throwing up a great white flurry of snow in their wake. Corrigan breathed a sigh of relief and relaxed for the first time since they had left the farmhouse. They had done it. They were on their way to the Meuse at last.

But Captain Corrigan's assault troop wouldn't get away with it as easily as that. The communist partisans weren't finished with them yet...

SEVEN

Hastily the corporal driving the locomotive took it back down the line, as ordered by Captain Hartung. Up in the trees, Sergeant Martini's party were still keeping the partisans at bay, and red and white tracer was zipping back and forth lethally among the firs. The angry cries and howls of agony of a close-range firefight filled the air.

Ignoring the slugs flying in all directions, Hartung stood up and raised his arm. The corporal eased on the brakes. The locomotive chattered to a stop. The driver waited. Now the paras who had been working for the last thirty minutes on the tree trunk scattered into the ditches on both sides of the track, leaving perhaps a metre of the trunk still barring the rails. The driver licked his lips. He was more afraid of Hartung than a whole regiment of guerrillas. If he made a mess of this operation and derailed the train, there would be all hell to pay; Captain Hartung had a rough old tongue.

Hartung blew three sharp blasts on his whistle – the signal for Sergeant Martini to withdraw from the woods. The next instant his hand came down sharply. The corporal reacted at once and threw open the throttle. The big steel driving wheels chattered violently and the whole locomotive shuddered like a greyhound straining at the leash. The driver let her go. At twenty kilometres an hour, the engine clattered forward. To his right, Sergeant Martini and his squad came running heavily through the snow, bullets throwing up little spurts of white at their heels. Behind them, the partisans were growing bold again, beginning to emerge from the cover of the trees and give chase, yelling excitedly as they did so.

The driver opened the throttle still more. Slugs were pattering the whole length of the train now. The driving wheels chattered. The boiler shook. Hungry flames leapt out of the fire-box as another shovelful of coal was slung in. Clouds of smoke belched from the stack. A grenade exploded below the tender, erupting in a burst of angry scarlet. Shrapnel howled through the air. The driver held on for all he was worth. It was now or never. They were going to crash!

At forty kilometres an hour, the locomotive struck the end of the tree. It shook crazily. The fireman dropped his shovel and screamed hysterically, '*We're going over!*' The corporal hung on grimly as the locomotive swayed back and forth, as if suddenly struck by a gale. Next moment the tree was flying to one side, with showers of wood splinters

185

and clouds of thick, black smoke obscuring his view.

They were through!

'*Mount up!*' Hartung shrieked, and fired a last burst at the running partisans, hardly caring whether he hit them or not. The paras needed no urging. Frantically, pushing and shoving in their haste, they sprang aboard.

Moments later, a panting Sergeant Martini and his section, now covered by fire from the paras already in the big single coach, flung himself gasping into the cab next to Captain Hartung.

'Great crap on the Christmas tree, sir, I reckon I deserve that blonde pavement-pounder ... and the barrel of suds ... right now!'

And with that they were off, thundering away down the track, leaving the shooting behind them, grinning like gleeful schoolboys let out of school...

Twenty miles away, Captain Corrigan also began to relax as the column started to swing down the road that would lead them to the Meuse. Evidently their attackers had taken fright. Like the treacherous rats they were, they had slunk back to their hideouts in the thick Ardennes forests, there to wait for further orders from their masters on the other side of the world in Moscow.

The men in *Waltzing Mathilda* began to

relax, too. Most of them had clicked on their safety-catches. Some smoked. Wolfers even sang – between bites at a piece of greasy 'Compo' bacon scooped out of a can – relating the exploits of that notorious spider with his enormous 'bazooka' and the innocent 'Miss Muffet on her tuffet' and launching merrily, if unmusically into the ribald chorus: '...*Big balls, small balls, balls as big as yer head; give 'em a twist around yer wrist, and sling 'em right over yer head... Get hold of this, bash-bash, get hold of that, bash-bash... I've got a luverly bunch o' coconuts. I've got a luverly bunch o' balls...*'

At the wheel, Slim Sanders grimaced. 'Have a heart, Caruso!' he moaned. 'Can't yer give it a rest for a while?'

Without even bothering to remove the grease proof paper, Wolfers took another enormous bite at the long roll of bacon, smearing his heavy chin with grease in the process. 'Thought I'd cheer you up a bit, mate,' he said, munching happily. 'Go on, smile! Give yer ears a visit.'

Muttering angrily to himself, Slim Sanders concentrated on his driving. The snow was thickening and the narrow country road was treacherous.

'...*Up came a spider, sat down beside her, whipped his old bazooka out and this is what he said...*' Wolfers continued happily, as they rattled on.

Time passed. The countryside seemed completely deserted. If the renegade Russians *were* out there, Corrigan reflected, they were keeping themselves mighty well hidden. He made an effort to dismiss them from his thoughts. As soon as they reached the Meuse, he would radio Monty's HQ and inform him of the situation along the river. If the 'Master' was in agreement, he would then cross the river and start the job he came here to do: a recce of the terrain to locate the spearhead of the German advance. That was something the commander of Thirty Corps, General Horrocks, would want to know in a hurry, once the great move to the back-up position started – and somehow Corrigan had the feeling that the Americans wouldn't be able to supply that information. As Monty had rightly said, this was outlaw country and everything here was uncertain and confused.

'Corrigan?'

The clipped tones of Captain Smythe roused him from his thoughts. He shook his head a little, as if waking up from a heavy sleep. 'What is it?'

Smythe pointed a finger to the left. 'Isn't that a dog over there? If it is, I suppose we must be getting close to civilisation.'

Corrigan pulled out his binoculars, rubbed away the film of icy mist and focused them on a small creature bounding energetically across the snow towards them. Its long tongue was hanging out of its muzzle, and on its back was a mysterious object that he couldn't quite make out, though he could see a kind of aerial protruding from it, flashing like a silver whip. 'Yes, it does seem to be a dog. Though God knows what–'

'There's another one, sir!' Hawkins' voice broke in excitedly. 'Just coming out of the trees at three o'clock!'

Corrigan swung his glasses round in the direction indicated. Hawkins was right. Another dog, now clearly recognisable as an Alsatian, was racing towards them; like the first, it carried a heavy pack on its back with an aerial flashing in the grey light. Behind it was another just emerging from the wood, head bent as it sniffed the snow, ears pressed back tightly against its wolf-like skull. Evidently the animal had spotted something it didn't particularly like. Suddenly it, too, seemed to pick up the scent and came pelting over the glistening white snowfield towards the assault troop's vehicles.

'Deucedly funny,' Smythe said, putting into words Corrigan's own thoughts. 'Three dogs like that... Do you think they might be wild or something? Let loose by some farmer before he took off on a refugee train heading west?'

Corrigan didn't answer; he was too busy focusing his glasses again. Another two dogs had just emerged from the trees, both carrying packs identical to the others and were now hurrying in their direction.

'I once saw this *filum*,' said Wolfers, his latest bawdy song forgotten now. 'Think it was based on a book by Jack London. Anyway, there was this pack of wolves in the Arctic–'

'Shut up, Trooper Wolfers!' Corrigan silenced him crudely, biting his bottom lip in angry, puzzled irritation.

Wolfers duly relapsed into a sulky silence.

Now the dogs had spread out, as if obeying some unknown command, and, like a living fan, were converging on the slow-moving line of vehicles from left and right, encouraged by raucous cries from the bored troopers, who were calling 'Come on, Fido!... Hurry up, boy, and get yer dinner!' and the like.

The dogs seemed to respond to the cries. They increased their efforts, bounding across the snow, feet going like clockwork, tongues hanging out, panting visibly, two jets of grey coming from their dilated nostrils.

'Two to one, the big one!' cried jubilant voices from the carrier behind *Waltzing Mathilda*, as a grey Alsatian, flecked with patches of black, started to draw ahead of the rest, heading straight for them. 'Come on, laddie... That's the style – you're winning!' One trooper held up a can of Spam and yelled, 'Here's yer bone, laddie... A tin of armoured pig! Bash on, that's the style!'

Now happy cries went up from all the vehicles as the dogs raced ever nearer, ears flat to their skulls, racing all out, as if this was a dog-track back in Blighty and they were greyhounds, desperately chasing the dummy hare.

'*The winner!*' cried the comic in the carrier as the dog drew level with it and started running alongside the little tracked vehicle, perhaps hoping that if it performed well enough it might be adopted or at least get a free feed.

But as Corrigan watched its performance, he couldn't help feeling a sense of inexplicable apprehension. This dog was unlike any that he could recall. There was no tail-wagging, no joyful barking, no lively springing into the air. The grey and black Alsatian had a look of attentive curiosity that was almost human about it; it seemed almost to be looking for a *weakness* in the carrier...

Suddenly Corrigan saw it change course, falling a little behind the carrier, heading straight into the white wake churned up by its tracks in the snow.

'What the hell?' Corrigan began. 'Look out–'

But it was already too late. The dog was beneath the carrier and in between the churning tracks. Suddenly the carrier erupted in volcanic fury. Scarlet flame interspersed with brilliant white flashes shot into the grey sky. Next moment the carrier followed, whirling round and round like a child's toy.

The explosion hit Corrigan in the face like a blow from a flabby fist. Instinctively he opened his mouth to prevent his eardrums from bursting and closed his eyes for an instant. When he opened them again, the carrier lay on its front, its tracks still racing like the legs of an upturned beetle, and dark shapes lay sprawled all around it in the extravagant postures of men violently done to death.

Corrigan had it in a flash. The Russian partisans had tricked them after all.

'*The packs!*' he cried fervently. 'The packs they're carrying are filled with explosive! They've been trained to go under vehicles... That aerial thing is a detonator! Don't let them get near you, driver! *Fire! Fire ... for Chrissake!*'

For a long moment they were all too stunned to react. Then, as one of the dogs started to lope towards *Waltzing Mathilda,* wild firing broke out on all sides.

But the big black brute seemed to bear a charmed life. Tracer cut the air all around it. Slugs whipped up flurries of snow at its feet. But always it dodged in the nick of time. And it was getting closer and closer. They could almost sense it looking for the chance it had been trained to exploit – a chance to slip under the flying tracks, to its death and their destruction...

Now it was only yards away, its aerial whipping back and forth, the pack of high explosive bobbing up and down on its lean back, saliva dripping from its long yellow fangs as it threw its long, wolf-like head back and forth. Suddenly it dived forward. Corrigan caught his breath. This was it! But just then a dark object sailed through the air, and Smythe yelled, *'Duck... Duck everybody!'*

The grenade exploded the next instant, inches in front of the racing dog. But it did the trick. The pack of high explosive disintegrated the following moment in a thick, angry red sheet of flame. *Waltzing Mathilda* rocked from side to side like a ship caught in a tempest. The blast-wave whipped their clothes tight about their bodies, forcing them to close their eyes and gasp for breath. But when they opened them again, the dog was gone, strewn over the snowfield in bits and pieces of red gore and smoking rags of pelt.

Next moment the troopers were hurling grenades on all sides, knowing that this was the only way to rid themselves of the killer dogs. The morning air was filled with the rattle of tracks, the roar of engines, the *crump* of grenades and the pitiful, frenzied howls of dying, horribly mutilated dogs, left to writhe in agony in the blackened snow.

'Talk about the fuckin' Hound of the Baskervilles!' snarled Slim Sanders, his face dripping with sweat, as he braked at Corrigan's command so that the officer could go back and take stock of casualties. 'Christ – who the hell could think of a bleedin' rotten trick like that, mates? I ask yer, cobbers, *who could?*'

But no one had an answer for the little Australian. Instead, they just stood there numbly, watching Corrigan, outlined stark black against the brilliant white of the snowfield, slowly move from body to body, cutting off the identity disc from each man and closing his eyes, if he still had eyes to close. And as they watched, each one of them knew that one day, soon, it could be them...

EIGHT

'Huy,' Captain Corrigan said sombrely, as the leading half-track negotiated the steep bend, and to their right, the little town with its road and railway bridge over the Meuse came into view far below. 'We bed down here for the night.'

At his side, Sergeant Hawkins breathed a sigh of relief at the news. It had been a long day. Soon it would be dark and the temperature would fall dramatically again. It would be good to get the boys under cover and get hot food inside them before they set off again across the river and into the front-line area the next day. It would improve their morale. The business with the dogs and the deaths of their comrades had depressed them. Many of them hadn't said more than half a dozen words all that long, freezing day.

'Champion!' Wolfers said, wiping a piece of snot from his red, dripping nose. 'The Yanks like their grub. I bet they'll lay on a real slap-up meal for us!'

'You and your ruddy belly,' Hawkins said. 'Is that all you ever bloody well think about?'

Wolfers, happy at the prospect of food, grinned back at him. 'Not allus, Sarge.

195

When me guts are full, I think of cunt.'

Now they were negotiating the last bend of the steep descent to the Meuse, and the convoy began to close up, slowing down to walking-pace as they neared the road bridge. As usual, the approaches were covered with a rash of military signposts, with white tapes running the length of both sides to indicate that they were mined.

As a veteran, Corrigan was immediately aware of an uneasy atmosphere about the place. Wrecked vehicles lay everywhere: on one side an abandoned weapons-carrier, its sides pockmarked with bullet-holes, on the other a crashed ambulance, its windows shattered like cracked ice. Corrigan frowned. A good unit would have got rid of them; they were bad for morale.

Now they started to roll through the first of the American defences. Black GIs manned the snow-covered weapon pits – probably service troops, since blacks didn't serve in combat units in the segregated US Army. Yellow-eyed and looking scared under their helmets, they kept their heads down as the convoy rumbled by.

'Them darkies don't look too happy to me, sir,' said Hawkins softly.

'No, they don't,' Corrigan agreed. 'In fact they look plain terrified.' He nodded a greeting to a group of infantrymen in tight, long black slickers, their faces unshaven, their eyes furtive and anxious; but again he received no response.

Corrigan bit his bottom lip. The rattled GIs weren't a pretty sight; he could almost smell their fear. They were getting closer to the front now, and you didn't have to be Sherlock Holmes to deduce that things were bad up there.

They rattled on between high, dull-looking nineteenth-century houses, their windows tightly shuttered. The flags which had probably decorated their facades only a week before had gone now, all signs of welcome for the Allied liberators painstakingly removed. It was almost as if the occupants had fled, but somehow, Corrigan doubted it. He had the impression of scared, white-faced civilians crouching behind their locked doors, ears pressed to the wood, listening apprehensively to the clatter of their tracks, wondering what they signified.

'Barricade ahead, sir!' called Sanders from the driver's seat.

Corrigan forgot the unseen civilians and turning, saw that large concrete rolls had been staggered across the bridge ahead of them, guarded by tangles of concertina wire with armed sentries on both sides. In the middle of the road stood a big man in a helmet and white gabardine trenchcoat, grease-gun in his arms, obviously waiting for them to stop. A little further on, pointing

197

straight at them was a manned 57mm anti-tank gun.

'Slow down then, Sanders,' Corrigan ordered, and waited till the driver had drawn level with the man in the trenchcoat, who he could now see was wearing two silver bars on his shoulders. 'Can we get through, Captain, and find billets for the night?'

The American stared up at him coldly. He had one of those dry yellow faces animated by pitch-black, sinister eyes that Corrigan had often remarked on in Americans. The man looked to him as if he had been left out in the sun for a week in Death Valley.

'Identify yourself,' said the GI in a husky, menacing voice.

'Captain Corrigan, Assault Troop, British Iron Division,' said Corrigan, a little annoyed. It had been a hard-fought day and he was in no mood to play games with Yank rear-échélon wallahs.

'Flim-flam,' said the American, obviously unimpressed. 'Got any ID?'

'Listen,' Corrigan growled, trying to control his temper. 'I am a captain in the British Army. We're supposed to be allies. What right have you got to stop me?'

Slowly the American patted his grease-gun and with a jerk of his head, indicated the 57mm anti-tank gun, the barrel of which was swinging round to sight on *Waltzing Mathilda*. '*That*,' he said laconically.

'Oh, come off it,' Corrigan snapped, face angry now. 'I've had a bloody day, lost six of my chaps. I want the rest of the troop under cover before it gets dark. Now will you please get out of the way and let us through.'

The American sniffed, deaf to the other man's outburst. 'You look like a Limey, buddy,' he said deliberately, 'you sound like a Limey; you probably *are* a Limey...' Fuming, Corrigan recalled having heard all this somewhere before. 'But brother, this is a key objective, and I've got to be sure, or the commanding general'll have my ass.'

'I am *not* your brother!' Corrigan barked, doubling his fists and fighting to restrain himself.

The American seemed not to hear. He jerked a lazy thumb at a wrecked jeep to the far end of the bridge, its front axle shot away, with two stiff objects covered by a tarpaulin lying next to it. 'Krauts, dressed as GIs... Tried to bull their way through this morning. They passed away – sudden like...' As he drawled on, the GI's dark, snake-like eyes stayed fixed on Corrigan's face, as if he were trying to find something there known only to himself. It made Corrigan suddenly feel distinctly uneasy. 'So ya see, we've got to be a might careful with any guy trying to cross this bridge. Who knows?' his dark eyes narrowed to slits. 'You could be Kraut.'

'Well, we're not,' Corrigan snapped firmly,

only controlling his temper for the sake of his tired, hungry men, 'take it from me.'

The Yank smiled patiently. 'But I can't do that, friend. I–'

'*Sir*... Sir! Captain Rizzi!' called an excited voice from the other end of the bridge.

Rizzi swung round. 'What is it, Weiniger?' he asked, addressing a bespectacled NCO in a peaked stocking-cap who was still calling to him and waving his arms with excitement. 'Can't it wait?'

'No, sir,' the sergeant called back. 'Just came through from HQ. Vitally important.' He lowered his voice in hushed respect. 'From General Hodges himself, sir.'

'Jesus H,' Rizzi moaned. 'What the Sam Hill have I done wrong now? All right, buddy, just hold it there for a moment. I'll be back.' He broke into a sudden, unathletic trot, leaving Corrigan, by now beside himself with rage, to stare at his retreating back.

'Fuckin' Yanks! Worse than gooks and wogs,' Sanders sneered contemptuously. 'Couldn't fight their way out of a bleedin' paper bag.'

'Watch your lip, Sanders,' Hawkins hissed warningly. 'It might have escaped your eagle Aussie eye that them Yanks has got a bleedin' great pop-gun pointing right at us.'

Only Wolfers seemed unaffected by the delay. He sucked his big, ugly front teeth contemplatively and said to no one in particular, 'Wonder what kind of grub them Yankee cooks is going to dish up for supper? Hope it's one of them tinned chicken dinners of theirs – with ice-cream... Lashings of chocolate ice-cream!'

But as it happened, Trooper Wolfers wasn't destined to eat tinned American chicken or lashings of chocolate ice-cream that particular night. That night, Wolfers' capacious stomach would remain achingly empty.

For what seemed an age the officer and the sergeant conferred, shooting suspicious looks at the troopers waiting there, who stared back at them in impatient bewilderment.

Then it happened. Rizzi straightened up and gave three shrill blasts on a whistle which had appeared as if by magic in his hand. Suddenly men came pouring from the houses on both sides of the opposite end of the bridge, struggling into their overcoats, slapping on their helmets, unslinging their weapons, while red-faced NCOs bellowed orders at them.

'What's going on?' asked Wolfers, as the soldiers streamed towards them, Garands at their hips, while others converged on the convoy from their own side of the bridge, weapons at the ready. 'Did we say something wrong?'

'Yes – what the devil *are* they playing at?' rapped Smythe, tugging at his cap angrily. 'They're treating us like third-class citizens!

I'm a British officer – I'm not used to this kind of treatment...'

'Shut up!' commanded Rizzi, grease-gun levelled at the two surprised officers standing upright in the leading half-track, who could only stare at the angry, hate-filled faces of the GIs surrounding them on all sides. *I'm* doing the talking here. Now, you, Captain' – with a jerk of his little machine-pistol he indicated Corrigan – 'order your men to come down from those vehicles, hands in the air, as slick as cat-shit on lino. *Move!*'

'But what–'

'Do as I say, Captain,' Rizzi hissed, clicking back the bolt of his grease-gun menacingly. *'Now!'*

Helplessly, feeling an absolute fool and with his mind racing wildly, Corrigan raised his hands. One by one, his men reluctantly did the same.

'I'm damned if I'm going to go along with this farce,' Smythe said determinedly. 'I'm a British officer–'

Rizzi raised his pistol into the air and pressed the trigger. An ear-splitting burst of fire broke the heavy silence.

Hastily Smythe raised his hands.

Now, under the direction of the Americans, their faces heavy and threatening, the troopers started to go over the side of their vehicles one by one. Their personal weapons were immediately ripped roughly from them, and with a great deal of slapping and cuffing they were forced to the side of the bridge, hands still raised in surrender. Finally they were all disarmed, standing in a long, forlorn line like enemy prisoners-of-war, shivering a little as the dark shadows of night started to race along the Meuse valley.

Corrigan made an effort to keep his voice steady and unemotional. 'Now, Captain er ... Rizzi, you've had your way and we've caused you no trouble. Perhaps you could be so kind as to explain the meaning of this farce? Why have we been arrested like this?'

Rizzi stalked over, his skinny body visibly quivering with suppressed rage. 'I'll tell you, you Limey bastard!' he cried, his head twisted to one side and his sallow face suddenly flushed an angry red as he choked with fury. 'Because... Because you and your murdering swine killed eight of our boys – in *cold blood!*'

Suddenly it seemed that Rizzi could contain himself no longer. He raised the steel butt of the little machine-pistol, and before Corrigan could dodge, slammed it hard into the Englishman's surprised face. Corrigan went reeling backwards with a yelp of pain. Hawkins tried to catch him – too late. His head socked into the stone balustrade with a sickening thud. Next moment a black, wavering cloud swamped him and he fell unconscious...

NINE

All was silent now: no sound save the rustle of the night wind in the snow-capped first and the soft crackle of the logs in the fire-box as the locomotive got up steam.

Outside on the track, the paras, their faces tinged a soft red from the light from the fire-box, stared silently at the dark, stark silhouette of the railway bridge below. Some smoked moodily. Each man appeared to be deep in thought, for even the youngest and foolhardiest of them knew that soon their fate would be decided. After what they had done to their Ami prisoners, they knew what would happen to them if they fell into American hands...

Next to Sergeant Martini, Captain Hartung smoked pensively. Veterans that they were, they knew that a man who had washed himself and emptied his bowels stood a better chance of surviving if hit than someone who was dirty and whose guts were still full. Accordingly, they had bathed and shaved in the snow, then carried out their natural functions, to the amazement and wonder of the shivering young paras. For once, however, Sergeant Martini hadn't

204

bawled his greenhorns out; this was too serious a business for crude jokes.

Hartung blew out a stream of blue smoke and said softly, 'So, this is the drill, Martini. We go on very slowly. According to Corporal Heinze, who should know, a locomotive always slows down when approaching a bridge. It's regulations.'

Martini nodded and continued to puff at his cigarette.

'That should suffice to keep whatever guards the Amis have up there at ease. We'll keep to the slow speed until we're halfway across. Then, assuming the sentries have been posted on the eastern bank, facing the direction our own forces will come from, we'll speed up – go at them hell for leather. If there's any obstacle across the tracks, we'll blast through it like–'

'Shit through a goose?'

Hartung chuckled. 'Exactly – like shit through a goose. Naturally, once we're past the sentries, all hell will break out further up the line. According to Heinze, we could get a run of three or four kilometres if we're lucky – then they could switch us onto some branch line and stop us. So, the plan is to go all out for two kilometres or so, which I hope will clear us of the outskirts of Huy, then ditch the train. From there on, we hoof it – but somehow, old friend, I don't think we'll have far to march. Look!'

He jerked his thumb to the east, where the night sky was flecked by sudden, regular, wavering flashes of faint pink, split here and there by a brighter, whitish light, like the silent electrical storm one sometimes sees on a hot Summer night.

'Heavies,' said Martini, recognising the flashes immediately. 'The permanent barrage.'

Hartung nodded almost solemnly. 'Yes. It looks like it to me, Martini. That means the front can't be far away.'

Martini remained silent, absorbing the information for a few moments, staring at the flickering lights. As he puffed fitfully at his cigarette, he automatically shielded the glowing stub with his cupped hand so that it couldn't be seen from the bridge. 'Well, sir,' he said finally, 'I don't mind telling you, I'll be glad to get home.' He stretched and gave a little groan. 'I'm getting too old for these little games. *Himmel, herrje,* I seem to have spent half my life sitting in the dark, hungry and cold, waiting to go into action.'

Hartung nodded. 'I know, I know, Martini. Did I tell you I'll be thirty on Christmas Day? What a day to have a birthday! And I feel more like sixty. Remember Belgium back in 'forty? Storming the fortress at Eben Emael? How fit and eager we were then! We couldn't wait to get into action and have our first taste of the shit flying.' He sighed. 'It

206

seems like another world.'

'It was, sir,' Martini said sombrely. He took one last puff of his cigarette and dropping it to the snow, stubbed it out with a muttered curse. 'When do we move out, sir?'

Hartung flashed a look at the green-glowing dial of his watch. 'In exactly thirty minutes. The time now is eighteen hundred hours and twenty seconds.'

'Shall we circumcise our watches, then, sir?'

Hartung laughed out loud, suddenly feeling youthful and happy once more, like in the great days. 'Circumcising ... *now!*'

'Listen, Smythe,' said Corrigan grimly, as they squatted in the dirty straw of the freezing prison, with the troopers huddled all around, teeth chattering with cold. 'Look at it like this. In this year of Our Lord, nineteen forty-four, England is full of do-gooders and parlour pinks – people who live like right-wingers and talk like left-wingers. Those fellows are now preparing to give away our empire. They'll flog off India so that some poor old crone in Liverpool can have a pair of cheap specs. Later on they'll throw in Africa so that the poor can have free teeth. The Middle East and all its oil will go in exchange for buckshee hearing-aids. Ever since that damned Beveridge Report started all this Welfare State nonsense, those feather-bedded so-called intellectuals back in

London have been ruddy well knocking themselves over to give away the empire – *and it's the same bloody empire we're supposed to be fighting to save!* And the Yanks know it – oh, don't they just!' He rubbed his bearded chin and frowned dourly. 'The Yanks talk a lot of claptrap about democracy and all that sort of crap. But they're here for the grabs too. When our empire vanishes, thanks to *Major* Attlee and his ilk, *they'll* establish a new one. We're on the way out and they're on the way in. And they treat us accordingly. That's why we're in here right now, freezing our balls off and hungry – because the bloody Yanks have got no respect for us, with our parlour pinks, Beveridge Report, Welfare State and all the rest of the ruddy pie in the sky.' He paused, his diatribe over, and took a deep breath.

By now Captain de Vere Smythe had grown accustomed to Corrigan's bitter outbursts against the system and the world in which he found himself, and knew how to deal with them. He smiled tolerantly. 'Well, in that case, let's hope that they *do* get a bloody nose in the Ardennes. Then Monty can show them just what the British Army's made of. But first, Corrigan, we've got to get out of *this* place.'

'I know, I know!' Corrigan agreed miserably. 'But there's no point even attempting to reason with that fellow Rizzi. He simply won't listen. Somehow or other, those deserters who attacked us on the train were later shot in the back – God knows who did it. Rizzi's superiors obviously think we're the culprits – and in the US Army, you don't question your superiors, you just obey. So much for the New World and Democracy.' He laughed bitterly. 'Now the Meuse is wide open, and we're stuck in this hell-hole, while all the time Monty's waiting to hear from us. My God,' he cried, 'it makes you bloody well sick to think of it!'

'Sir...'

It was Hawkins. Turning, Corrigan saw that he had a tin mug pressed to his ear and jammed up against the thick, ancient prison wall so that he could listen to what was going on outside. While the other troopers had relapsed into frozen apathy as soon as the cell door had slammed shut and the guards had departed, he and Slim, veterans that they were, had set about trying to discover as much as they could about their new surroundings.

'What is it?' Corrigan asked, raising himself with a stiff groan.

'I think it's gunfire, sir.' Hawkins replied. 'Come and have a listen.'

Hastily Corrigan picked his way through the shivering bodies of his men, packed in tightly in the lousy damp straw – for the grey stone walls, covered with the graffiti of two hundred years of pain and suffering, simply dripped with moisture – to where Hawkins crouched, tin mug in his skinny little hand.

Corrigan took it and pressed it against the wall. Yes, there was no mistaking that soft rumble from far away; it was the permanent background music to war – the barrage.

Grimly he handed the mug back to an expectant Hawkins. 'You're right. It's the guns.'

'Does that mean the Jerries are on their way, sir?' asked Wolfers. The big, gangling Yorkshire lad was wearing his spare pair of long johns wrapped round his head like a scarf for extra warmth, and a long, glistening drop of dew hung from the end of his red nose.

Miserably Corrigan nodded.

'That means we could go into the bag?' Wolfers persisted.

Corrigan was too miserable to answer, but Slim Sanders snarled, 'Fuck that fer a tale! Them Yankees can go and shit in their hats and wear them back to front for all I care, but I'm not goin' into any fuckin' Jerry bag! It'd ruin my bleedin' sex life, it would!'

But no one laughed at the little Australian's outburst; the men were too down.

Hawkins sucked his teeth thoughtfully. 'I think Sanders is right, sir,' he said after a moment. 'If we don't do something soon, we might well end up in a Jerry POW camp.'

'But what do you suggest?' Corrigan asked. 'The Yanks won't let us out. If the Jerries come, Rizzi and his merry men will make a run for it and leave us to the mercy of the Jerries – that is, if they don't shoot us out of hand first.' He looked helplessly around at the thick, dripping, grey walls and the thick oak door. 'And I can't see any way of getting out of this place in a hurry. We haven't even got a bloody knife!' he cried in exasperation.

'But we have, sir,' Hawkins said mildly.

'What do you mean?'

Hawkins pointed to the big, battered enamel bucket at the end of the big cell, which was supposed to serve all their sanitary needs for the night. 'The piss-bucket, sir.'

'The piss-bucket!' Corrigan echoed. 'Don't talk rot, man.'

Hawkins chuckled, his eyes almost disappearing into his wrinkled, leathery face. 'Don't believe me, sir? Then let me tell you how me and another couple of naughty boys got out of the glasshouse back in 1934. It was at Aldershot, sir, and I was a real bad lad in them days. Crime sheet as long as Sanders' there, sir, and *that's* saying summat...'

In spite of his inner rage and frustration, Corrigan leaned forward to listen, intrigued by what that soft Yorkshire voice had to say...

TEN

'Los!' Hartung commanded.

Corporal Heinze eased open the throttle. Next to him, Sergeant Martini tensed, Schmeisser at the ready. There was a hiss of escaping steam, a metallic chatter of wheels. For a moment nothing happened. The driving wheels weren't gripping; it was already beginning to freeze hard again. Martini gulped hard and said a quick prayer. Heinze opened the sandbox and eased the throttle forward. The wheels gripped. The train gave a deep groan, as if reluctant to be disturbed from its immobility. The linking mechanism clattered. Next moment they began to move forward. Gently, Heinze gave the engine more power, and the green needle of the speedometer started to swing to the right. Martini flung Hartung a grin of triumph, and the big captain smiled back, teeth a brilliant white against the black of the coal dust which already caked his face yet again.

Now they were rattling down the long descent to the bridge, outlined a stark, skeletal black against the dull silver of the river below.

'Easy does it,' warned Hartung.

The driver nodded, too busy with his controls to answer. By his side, Martini felt his hands grow wet with sweat as they gripped the machine-pistol. At his temple, a vein began to tick with apprehension and excitement; it was as if he was going into action for the very first time.

'Here we go,' Hartung announced. *'We're on the bridge!'*

On they rumbled. From far down below in the gorge of the Meuse, came a deep, drumming echo. The sleepers vibrated gently under their weight.

Hartung leaned out of the fireman's side of the cab, narrowing his eyes against the flag of white smoke which streamed backwards, trying to penetrate the gloom, ready for the first sign of trouble, nerves tingling electrically. On the other side, Martini did the same, his face hollowed out to a red death's head by the flames from the open fire-box. Now they were almost halfway across, and still there was no sign of the Amis or their Belgian allies.

Suddenly Martini saw it: a bright, winking red light ahead of them, perhaps a hundred metres away. It stuck out in the white gloom like a dire warning of the hell that was about to be unleashed.

'Red light, straight ahead!' he sang out urgently.

'But we're supposed to stop, sir!' cried

Corporal Heinze stupidly.

'Hit the tube, you silly shit!' Hartung bellowed over the rattle of the train. 'This is it. *Go!*'

For a moment it seemed that the young driver might refuse the order. Obviously his years with the Reichsbahn had taught him that it was a heinous sin not to stop at red. Then he remembered where he was and jerked open the throttle. The locomotive shot forward. Hartung held his breath and crooked his forefinger around his trigger. Any moment now the old, old song of death would commence...

Suddenly there were little glowing yellow lights on all sides: old-fashioned lanterns. Faces flashed by them – angry, surprised, dumbfounded. A big man in a helmet raised a pistol. *'Ami!'* yelled Martini, and pressed his trigger without even thinking. The automatic shuddered at his side. The cab filled with acrid smoke. The man in the helmet reeled back shrieking, to slip under the flying wheels. Blood shot up and splashed against the side of the cab.

Next to the cursing, sweating driver, Captain Hartung pumped off single shots to left and right in the confused darkness, hearing slugs patter off the locomotive's sides like tropical rain, knowing that every metre gained took them closer to victory.

Now they were nearing the far end of the

bridge. Vicious stabs of scarlet flame split the darkness everywhere. Tracer zipped through the air like swarms of angry red hornets. By the intensity of the fire, Hartung guessed that there had to be scores of the shitting Amis out there. He fired into the darkness wildly, knowing that their luck was running out – and fast.

A slug howled off the cab. He ducked. Now all was anger and chaos. Would they ever get through? Something slapped against Hartung's helmet, rapping against it like the beak of some monstrous bird. He recoiled groggily, putting out a hand to prevent himself from falling. In the same moment the driver slumped over his controls, his heavy jaw shattered, his last, dying cry smothered in a mess of blood, gore and broken bone.

Hartung moaned aloud – but his moan was drowned almost immediately as a white-glowing armour-piercing shell rammed into the side of the train. Metal struck metal with a loud, ringing boom. The boiler exploded at once with a furious, whirling red glare. Steam escaped in a mad hiss. Everywhere there were screams, cries, yells, with paras jumping crazily to the track, right into a mad flurry of zipping white tracer that ripped the air apart in lethal fury.

Hartung fell, landing on his knees on a sleeper and yelling aloud in pain. The locomotive was burning furiously now. Behind it, the coach had begun to whine and groan like a tortured being, as slowly but surely it started to pitch over the side. Girders splintered like matchwood beneath it. Then the night was filled with a great, awesome roar that drowned even the sounds of battle as the coach went over, the bodies of the dead tumbling from it like so many broken dolls. Next instant it sailed into the void. Blazing fiercely now, it turned over in mid-air almost lazily, while Hartung, crouching there on his knees, watched openmouthed like a village idiot.

Now, inexorably, the locomotive was following it, teetering on the edge, burning furiously, steam still jetting from its wrecked boiler. It swayed violently, as if possessed of a life of its own. Then abruptly, startlingly, with a great rending of metal and splintering of sleepers, the great black monster plunged over the edge. A second later it hit the icy waters of the Meuse with a deafening impact and exploded in a great, echoing roar that seemed to go on for ever...

Now they were hammering relentlessly on the walls and door of the cell with their mugs. *'Let us out! Let us out!'* they cried in chorus, while Hawkins and Sanders waited behind the door as planned, tensed and apprehensive.

Outside, cries of alarm and panic were ringing out on all sides. Jeeps could be heard starting up in the icy night air. Whistles shrilled. NCOs bellowed angry orders and from further away came the bitter crackle of small arms fire. And all the while, frightened voices cried out the same dread warning: *'The Krauts have hit us! The Krauts are coming! We're bugging out – now!'*

'They're not going to fall for it, Corrigan!' Smythe cried above the racket, as an acrid smell of burning began to seep in underneath the cell-door. 'They've just abandoned us to the Jerries!'

'Keep trying,' Corrigan urged, desperately seizing the only available piece of furniture, a three-legged stool, and hammering against the door with it. 'A Jerry POW camp? Somehow I don't think that Captain Rizzi's going to let us off *that* lightly–' He broke off suddenly. Booted feet could be heard running down the stone-flagged passage outside. 'Here they come!' he warned.

The men renewed their hammering, and behind the door, Hawkins and Sanders steeled themselves for action. In their bleeding hands they held long slivers of enamel which they had chipped from inside the piss-bucket, and as Hawkins had claimed, their improvised weapons were razor-sharp and deadly. Hearts beating like trip-hammers, the two men waited, knowing everything depended upon them now.

There was a clatter of chains, then a rusty squeak as a key was turned in an ancient lock.

Corrigan flashed the two men a look. Hawkins nodded and gulped. Sanders leered.

The door was flung open. The passage was crowded with armed men, all pointing their weapons at the cell-door, illuminated by the incandescent white light of a flaring Coleman lantern. In their midst stood Rizzi, a .45 in his hand, a streak of blood trickling down his sallow face, and murder in his black eyes.

'Don't think I'm going to leave you guys here so that the Krauts can put you in a POW camp,' he sneered. 'No, *sir*. Before I go, you're going to pay for what you did to our–'

Hawkins sprang forward – and tripped over the stool that Corrigan had used to hammer on the door, sprawling full-length in the doorway.

Rizzi cursed. Smythe sprang forward. '*No!*' yelled Corrigan desperately. Too late. The Yank's big pistol thundered at pointblank range, the slug tearing Smythe's face off. He rose inches off the ground and slammed back against the opposite wall, dead even before he hit it, sending blood splattering to left and right like scarlet rain. Sanders bellowed with rage. His arm shot out. The razor-sharp piece of enamel sank deep into Rizzi's skinny belly. He gave a great gasp, seeming to crumple up like a deflated balloon. Gasping for breath as if he was running for his life, Sanders stabbed him again. Still Rizzi didn't go down, though his knees began to buckle under him like those of a new-born foal. 'Christ,' Sanders gasped, his face greased with sweat, 'why don't you bleedin' well *die!*' With an awful sucking noise, he withdrew his weapon, his hand now dripping scarlet to the knuckles, and thrust it home one more time. Rizzi gave a terrible gasp, the left side of his face wrinkling up as if with a sudden attack of goose pimples. He shuddered violently. A tiny trickle of dark-red blood seeped out of the corner of his mouth, then grew instantly to a torrent, flooding his mouth, dripping through his teeth. With infinite slowness, Rizzi at last began to go down, watched by American and British with mesmerised, awed fascination. Then suddenly, he collapsed in a heap on the floor, the only sound the faint gurgling of death in the back of his throat.

The spell was broken. Hawkins kicked the Coleman lantern to one side. Wolfers sprang forward, grabbing Rizzi's pistol. Suddenly all was confusion, cries and chaos. Next moment, Corrigan, trying not to look down at the crumpled shape at his feet, was tucking the grease-gun to his hip in the corridor, and commanding, in a voice so calm and collected that he barely recognised it as his own: *'No more bloodshed! We're allies... Please drop your weapons and raise your hands...'*

ELEVEN

Scarlet flame stabbed the chaotic darkness. Heavy machine-guns rattled. Tracer, white, red, and green, zipped lethally everywhere. On all sides angry, panicked cries rang out in German, English and French. Somewhere a voice was crying out in the plaintive, flat tones of the Mid-West, *'Say, buddy won't ya give me a hand?... I can't see... Say, won't anybody help me?'* Up above the town, on the left bank of the Meuse, the tracks were burning fiercely, and in their gaudy red light could be seen twisted rails hanging into the river and the mangled wreckage of what had once been a carriage. Below, the water itself still hissed, and at periodic intervals great bubbles of trapped air erupted on the surface with an obscene belch. Somewhere down in the old town the church bells tolled urgently, their din mingling with the wail of air-raid sirens. It was a scene of total confusion. Huy had never experienced a night like this since the French had sacked it three centuries before.

Corrigan pressed the trigger of the grease-gun he had taken off the American in the prison, and it erupted against his hip. Two men huddled together further up the cobbled street – German, American, Belgian partisan, he neither knew nor cared – screamed pitifully as the burst of slugs ripped into them. One whirled round in crazy animation, smashed through the thin ice of the horse-trough and sank slowly into the waters to drown. The other sat down abruptly against the wall, face turned upwards in the crazy red light as if begging God in heaven to save him. As Corrigan raced past his dead body, followed by his unarmed troopers, he saw that he'd just killed two Americans.

'Christ, what a bleedin' balls up!' gasped Slim, as he ran on.

Now confused gunfire was pouring down from the windows of the tall eighteenth-century buildings that lined the street, as the Belgian partisans of the White Army dug out their hidden weapons and began to fight the unknown enemy. Praying that they would make it through the gauntlet of bullets to where the vehicles had been parked, Corrigan rushed on, firing from the hip to left and right, with the rest of the troop at his heels.

A rickety wooden bridge across a side-arm of the Meuse loomed up. A dead body lay at its entrance. Corrigan sprang over it. Ahead of him, a grenade exploded. Angry violet light split the darkness, revealing a dark

222

figure feverishly sawing at the ropes suspending the bridge with his bayonet.

'Hold it there!' Corrigan gasped.

'*Leck mich am Arsch!*' the angry curse came back in German.

Without pausing to wonder what in God's name a German was doing here so far from the front, Corrign fired – and missed. Behind him, Hawkins raised his US Colt and fired. The bullet hissed past Corrigan's right ear and momentarily he felt its searing heat on the side of his face. The German howled and reeled back on the side of his face. The German howled and reeled back, his face dissolving into a mass of blood and gore in his hands. Lifeless, he slammed to the cobbles.

'*Grand Place*,' Wolfers yelled, as a flare suddenly lit up the night sky, illuminating the blue-and-white enamel street sign above his head. 'They took us down here, sir. The vehicles must be over–' The rest of his words were drowned by the obscene howl of a mortar bomb.

'Strewth!' yelled Slim. 'Now they're fuckin' mortarin' us! Won't be long before they start throwin' the bleedin' kitchen sink at us!'

As if on cue, a complete old-fashioned kitchen range came bursting through the wall of the house opposite as a mortar bomb exploded inside, sending a great shower of red-hot embers and bricks flying out with it.

'Holy Cow!' Slim cried, 'did you see that?'

'That'll teach yer to keep yer big Australian cake-hole shut!' Hawkins yelled, snapping off a quick shot to the right at a sniper in civilian clothes. With a howl the man fell face forwards from his perch and landed on the cobbles like a bag of wet cement.

Now Corrigan could see their vehicles packing the cobbled square to his front, the squat silhouettes of the White half-tracks outlined by the flames of a fire burning merrily in one of the adjoining buildings. Thank God for that, he thought, ignoring the screaming Belgian women rushing back and forth with buckets of water, trying to put out the flames; at least the warmth would help the engines to start in the freezing cold. He halted, chest heaving violently with the effort of the running through the winding streets. 'Sergeant! Sergeant Hawkins… Set up a defensive perimeter.'

'Sir!'

'Shoot anyone, friend or foe, who tries to break through.'

'*Sir,*' Hawkins repeated woodenly. He hadn't the strength to say more. It felt as if his poor old lungs would burst at any moment. Not for the first time, he wondered if he was getting a bit long in the tooth for this kind of lark.

'Drivers, to your vehicles!' snapped Corrigan, and together with Slim and the other drivers, he pushed his way through the crowd to where *Waltzing Mathilda* stood waiting.

Slim, eyes open as always to the main chance, caught one of the women bending to pick up a bucket, and slipping his hand underneath her skirt, gave her ample buttocks a delightful pinch. 'Sorry,' he said, 'can't see a thing in this light, can yer, missus?'

'*Merci,*' she simpered, suddenly coy, as he turned to run on. 'Any time, *M'sieu... Vive L'Amérique!*'

Just then he caught a fleeting glimpse of her face. 'Christ Almighty,' cried, aghast, 'it's Whistler's bleedin' Mother!' Then he jumped in behind the wheel of the big armoured half-track, while Corrigan cranked the starting handle for all he was worth.

Five minutes later, they were on their way again, slugs pattering off the steel sides of the vehicles like heavy Summer rain on a tin roof. At one corner, a screaming civilian suddenly ran out of the shadows straight into their path and disappeared underneath the churning tracks of *Waltzing Mathilda*. A bazooka opened fire a little further on, but the rocket missed the lead vehicle by yards. Next moment, a burst of machine-gun fire ripped the bazooka man to shreds, leaving him hanging over a windowsill, with blood jetting from half a dozen wounds as if from a punctured pipe. Five minutes after that, they were clattering out of the town and up the long incline that led eastwards. Corrigan's assault troop had done it again. They were free once more!

'Any luck yet, Wolfers?' Corrigan asked, as the little convoy ground its way onwards, Slim at the wheel peering anxiously through the thick dawn mist.

Wolfers lifted up one earphone and shook his head. ''Fraid not, sir. The Jerries are marching bloody brass bands all over the wavelengths. They're jamming everywhere. Ruddy well deafens yer, it does.'

Corrigan grinned sympathetically. 'Keep trying, Wolfers.'

'And watch yer language when you're speaking to an officer, Trooper Wolfers,' Hawkins added severely, as Wolfers returned to the task of trying to raise Montgomery's HQ.

'Don't be too hard on him, Hawkins,' said Corrigan, wiping the dampness of the fog from his drawn unshaven face. 'He and all the rest of the men have been through a hard time these last twenty-four hours.' Then he turned his thoughts to the day ahead. 'Now this is what I plan to do. At present we're stooging around the eastern bank of the

Meuse on a north-south course. Once we're out of these hills, I'm going to head due east until–'

'Until we hit the Jerries.' Hawkins completed the sentence for him, jerking his head to the east, whence came a distant rumble of gunfire, muted now by the fog.

'Exactly. I don't like it any more than you do, but that's what we're here for – to carry out reconnaissance.'

Gloomily, Hawkins nodded his understanding. 'Not that yer could do much in the way of a recce on a morning like this. By gum, yon Jerries could be out there in front by the battalion and we wouldn't be able to see them until we was right on top of 'em.'

'You're right, Hawkins. And I don't have to tell you what would happen if we bumped into an advance Jerry patrol armed with bazookas.'

'Fer Chrissake, sir!' Slim groaned from the driver's seat. 'There's no need ter paint a ruddy picture! Who do you think'll go for a Burton first? Yours truly – Mrs Sanders' handsome son.' He bent even closer to the driving slit in the armour plate and peered into the grey clouds, as if he fully expected to see German infantry looming out of them at any moment.

It was nearly nine in the morning, with the fog as thick as ever, when the first alarm came. For nearly a quarter of an hour they had been toiling up a country road strewn on both sides with abandoned equipment, gas-masks, steel helmets, entrenching tools, greatcoats, even rifles and hand grenades – all in the olive drab of the US Army. As Hawkins commented drily, sucking at his unlit pipe, 'Don't need a crystal ball to see what's going on here, do yer, sir?'

Corrigan nodded grimly. 'Looks like the US First Army's been taking quite a hammering.'

Suddenly the troopers in *Waltzing Mathilda* stiffened, hands damp with sweat as they clutched their weapons. Up ahead could be seen the shadowy outlines of a dozen or more figures in the fog – waiting, or so it seemed, for them!

'Stand fast!' snapped Corrigan urgently, ripping his infantry rifle off his broad shoulder and clicking off the safety-catch. 'Wolfers, signal to the other vehicles to halt!'

At a snail's pace, the lead half-track crept forward. Crouched next to Corrigan, Hawkins could feel his heart beating furiously. At the side of his wrinkled brown face a nerve began to tick alarmingly. 'Who the fuck *are* they?' he demanded angrily.

Corrigan didn't answer. He was too busy trying to penetrate the gloom to where the mysterious figures waited. 'Ready for quick evasive action, Slim,' he hissed out of the side of his mouth.

'You're not kidding, sir,' replied Slim through gritted teeth.

Suddenly a piteous voice called, 'For God's sake, are any of you fellers American?' The voice was that of a broken man – a man who had sunk into an utter, bottomless despair.

'*Phew!*' gasped Slim. 'Soddin' Yanks.'

Relieved, Corrigan lowered his rifle and called, 'No, we're English… What's up?'

'Thank God… Thank God,' sobbed the unknown speaker. 'Ya hear that, fellers – they're Limeys!'

A moment later Slim was braking, and he, Corrigan and Hawkins were staring down from the half-track at the spectacle below.

A skinny pony pulling a cart laden with what were obviously wounded men stood panting before them, twin jets of grey breath spurting from its distended nostrils. Every bone in the poor creature's body stood revealed in the morning light, its sides glistening white with hoar frost. Next moment, the animal crumpled to its knees, head hanging pathetically to one side. Within seconds it had died in front of their astonished eyes.

'God Almighty!' breathed Hawkins. 'The poor dumb creature.'

'What about them poor dumb soldiers?' hissed Slim, and stared at the dozen or so Americans huddled around the cart, some of them without helmets, many without weapons, and all very obviously at the very end of their tether.

Corrigan sprang over the side of the half-track, trying to ignore the stench of the wounded and the trail of blood-stained, watery faeces the woebegone little group had left behind them on the snow. They had dysentery, that was obvious. 'Who's in charge here?' he asked, staring around at the Americans' haunted, unshaven faces, their eyes wild, wide and bulging out of their sockets.

'Me, Captain,' replied the hoarse, broken voice which had first called to them.

Corrigan swung round to see a bedraggled-looking soldier, whose hair was already turning grey. On the sleeve of his ragged greatcoat, the skirts frozen hard with ice, were the three stripes of a sergeant. His right hand was wrapped in a thick, blood-stained bandage.

'What happened?' asked Corrigan. 'The Germans – did they do this?' He nodded to the wounded men, moaning softly in the blood-stained straw at the back of the cart.

Almost sadly, the sergeant shook his greying head. 'No, sir. It wouldn't have been so bad if it *had* been the Krauts. That would have made sense. But it was our allies, our very own *allies* who did it.' Again, he shook his head, as if the world were too much for him.

'You mean ... *Russians?*' Corrigan turned round and exchanged worried glances with Hawkins and Sanders.

The American sergeant nodded. 'That's right, sir. Jesus, I never seen nothing like it. The way–'

Corrigan cut him short. 'When, Sergeant? When did it happen?' he asked, in a tone that revealed his own alarm all too clearly.

The wounded sergeant swallowed hard, obviously making an effort to gather his wits. 'Late yesterday evening, sir. We were bugging out with the rest of the guys when we got caught in a Kraut mortar attack. Things got kinda confused after that – I guess it was every man for himself. We'd been on the run for an hour or two and it was getting dark, so I started to look for a place for my men to spend the night. And that's when it happened...'

'Go on,' urged Corrigan impatiently.

'These goddam Russkis jumped us – there must have been a coupla hundred of the yellow bastards. Jesus, half my boys weren't even armed – they'd lost everything they had in the big bug-out. We didn't stand a chance...' With a moan of despair, the American sergeant covered his face with his hands and gave vent to a series of heart-rending sobs.

Looking grim-faced, Corrigan placed a hand on the man's shoulder and offered him his flask of government-issue rum. Inwardly, his thoughts were racing. Could these be the same Russian partisans who had surrounded them back at the farmhouse? If so – and it sounded likely from the sergeant's account – they had certainly covered some ground since then. But what if they were still in the area and poised to strike again? He paused, reflecting. His orders from Monty were to cross the Meuse, advance into US First Army territory and locate the German spearhead. *That* was a hazardous enough mission. But now there was the extra danger of another brush with two hundred blood-crazed Gulag rats to contend with.

The American sergeant with the wounded hand took a gulp of Corrigan's rum and returned it to him, his red-rimmed eyes clearly revealing the horror he had experienced. '*Why* did they do it?' he pleaded helplessly. 'Jesus – we're supposed to be allies! *Why?*'

Corrigan shook his head. The reasons were too complicated, and now wasn't the time to explain; he had other things on his mind. 'Politics, Sergeant,' he replied. 'Just call it politics and leave it at that. Now, these Russians – do you think they're still after you? Do you think they might be still in the area?' He gestured around at the gloomy, fog-bound scene, as if the killers might be out there already, lurking in the trees; but there was nothing to be seen, but sad, grey, billowing clouds of mist curling noiselessly in and out of the undergrowth, deadening all sound.

'Oh, they were right behind us all right, sir,' answered the sergeant, suddenly afraid once more. 'We heard them a couple of times calling to each other in their own lingo. They'd have spotted us for sure if it hadn't been for the fog.' He gripped Corrigan's arm in fear. 'You've got to get us out of here quick, sir. The murdering sonsuvbitches could jump us any minute!'

Corrigan freed his arm. 'I'm afraid that's not on, Sergeant. Don't worry – we'll give you what we can in the way of weapons. Even with the wounded, you'll be able to reach the Meuse by this afternoon.'

'You mean you're going on, sir? Right into them?' the sergeant asked incredulously.

'Yes.' Corrigan nodded to Hawkins to get the men back onto the vehicles.

'But you're crazy!' said the sergeant, gripping his arm again. 'The forests up ahead could be swarming with them!'

'It's a risk I'm afraid we've got to take,' Corrigan said softly. He was beginning to wish the man and his comrades would go. The looks of unreasoning fear on their ashen faces were enough to unnerve the strongest of men; they looked as if they had seen the devil himself. 'Now, my sergeant will give you what handguns we can spare and some tins of bully beef. We'll cover you for ten minutes, then we'll move out. Clear?'

'Brother, you're not shitting. Clear it is.' The sergeant raised his voice and cried urgently to his men. 'Come on, fellers, let's go! Let's get the Sam Hill outa here. The Limeys are staying... *Move it!*'

'But the rations, and the rifles–' called Sergeant Hawkins. In vain. Even the American wounded were desperate to be on their way again. Raising themselves from the cart, they hobbled after their companions, who had already stumbled into an awkward run, crying, 'Wait for us, buddies... Hey, don't leave us! Wait...'

Within seconds the fog had swallowed them up as if they had never been, their forlorn cries dying away in the distance as the grey mist descended upon them once more.

Slim gave a sardonic grunt. 'Christ, those Yanks really are creamin' their shivvies. Never seen nobody do a bunk as quick as that!'

Corrigan appeared to be about to say something and then changed his mind, but Hawkins read his thoughts. 'These things are sent to try us, sir.'

'Yes,' Corrigan agreed, clambering over the side of the half-track again. 'As if the Jerries weren't bad enough, it looks as if we've still got a couple of hundred rampaging Russian partisans to worry about.'

'Dear Mother, it's a bugger,' said Wolfers in a sinking voice. 'Dear Son, so are you.'

But nobody laughed.

Time passed agonisingly slowly as they crawled on through the fog. Their nerves were stretched to breaking point, every trooper straining his eyes to penetrate the gloom, the drivers cursing constantly as the mist swirled and thickened before them, obscuring visibility still further.

They seemed completely alone in the world, with nothing but dripping firs and the harsh cawing of unseen rooks for company. Twice, a flock of birds suddenly flew up from the trees, dragging their harsh cries behind them in mournful despair, and both times the troopers started, fingers instinctively taking first pressure on their triggers. But the Russians the American sergeant had warned them about were nowhere to be seen.

At noon, a weary Corrigan, his eyes red with strain, ordered a stop, instructing Hawkins to form the vehicles up in a defensive laager, reminiscent of the way American settlers arranged their wagons for the night for protection against Redskin attacks. Happily, the weary drivers formed the square and turned off their engines, while the stiff troopers dropped from the half-tracks and began the ritual of brewing up, ripping open the wooden crates of 'compo' rations with their bayonets and pumping up the little petrol-burning Tommy-cookers.

Sergeant Hawkins watched for a moment, making sure that one man of each vehicle crew stood sentry while the remainder cooked; then he turned to Corrigan. 'Mind if I pop off for a moment or two, sir?'

'What are you going to do,' quipped Corrigan. 'Take a little stroll in the country and savour the air?'

Hawkins' old face wrinkled into a craggy smile. 'Not exactly, sir. I've got a dose of the trots – I think it's that bloody tinned meat and veg stew. I bet they make it from bits of old nag. I've got to take a shovel for a walk.'

Corrigan grinned sympathetically. 'I know the feeling. But don't go too far, will you?'

'No fear, sir. Not with them blood-thirsty heathen Russians out there. Now, if you'll excuse me, sir.' And with that, he swung Corrigan a hasty salute, grabbed the nearest shovel from the side of a half-track and doubled away to the cover of the trees.

'Don't forget your Army Form Blank, Hawkins,' Corrigan shouted after him.

'Got bags of it, sir,' Hawkins cried as he ran, holding up a sheaf of brown issue lavatory paper. Then he vanished into the dripping trees, unbuckling his braces as he went.

Corrigan smiled after him for a moment; then he strolled over to where Wolfers was pumping away at his cooker, his broad Yorkshire face already aglow with hungry anticipation. 'And what little culinary delight are you going to prepare for yourself today, young Wolfers?' he asked.

'I was thinking of doing a tin of fried bully beef, and then seasoning it with some of them pilchards in tomato sauce, sir. I reckon the two of them together'd go down a treat. Anyhow,' he added a little defiantly, seeing the look of disgust on Corrigan's face, 'it'd make a change.'

'Yer,' Slim butted in, 'it'd give you bleedin' ptomaine poisoning an' all!' He shuddered. 'Strewth, Wolfers, yer must have guts of cast-iron to eat that kind of grub!'

'Go on,' Wolfers snorted. 'At least I don't eat soddin' kangaroos, like you lot in Aussie. I'm civilised.'

'*Kangaroos!*' Slim exclaimed, his thin cheeks flushed. 'Who told you that? That's the kind o' swag Abos eat – not yer white man!'

Corrigan decided to leave them to it, moving to another group before the argument really became heated. In spite of what they said to each other, the two of them remained firm friends; indeed, Wolfers seemed to be the only friend the smart little Australian had. Why, Corrigan didn't know.

Hawkins had finished taking his shovel for a walk and was just beginning to fasten his braces, when he heard the sound. He froze instantly. Somewhere ahead of him in the fog-shrouded firs there was something moving! Cautiously he sniffed the air.

The odour indicated human beings. But this wasn't the smell of the German. He knew *that* of old: a compound of iron-hard Ersatz soap and smoked bacon, the German soldier's basic ration. This smell was quite different: it was heavy with the stink of human sweat, garlic and coarse black tobacco. Could it be the Russians the terrified US sergeant had told them about? Sergeant Hawkins crouched low, gripping the entrenching tool by the handle to use as a weapon if need be, cursing himself for having left the laager without his gun.

Time seemed to pass horribly slowly. As the minutes ticked by, Hawkins began to feel the freezing cold steal up his feet, legs and into his guts. Still he dared not make a move.

Then he saw them: shadowy figures stealing through the wet fog to his front, as if following some sort of trail through the dripping firs. As silent as ghosts and as eerily frightening in their silence, they advanced stealthily through the trees. Sergeant Hawkins, though not an imaginative man, felt the short hairs at the back of his neck standing erect. It was the Russkis all right – he would recognise those slant eyes and yellow faces anywhere.

Now he could see that the American sergeant hadn't exaggerated: there were at least a couple of hundred of them, many of them mounted on horses presumably stolen from local farms. Some of the men were armed with handguns, but most simply carried clubs and sticks. In terms of weaponry they wouldn't be difficult for his lads to tackle – after all, each half-track mounted a half-inch machine-gun. But there were a hell of a lot of them – and they looked hungry for blood. Supposing they simply swamped the handful of troopers by sheer force of numbers? Hawkins felt his hands go wet with sweat, in spite of the creeping cold which had turned his nether limbs to ice. Please God, don't let them see me, he prayed fervently. *Please!*

It was Slim who first sensed trouble. Hearing a shout from the trees, he looked up to see Hawkins running towards him hell for leather, and what appeared to be a group of men on horseback giving chase from some distance away. As they drew closer, Slim recognised the mounted figures and immediately yelled across to Corrigan, *'Look! It's them bloody Russians again!'*

Panting for breath, Hawkins reached the safety of the ring of vehicles and flung a glance behind him. The mist was thinning now and the faint, yellow rays of a weak December sun had begun to filter through the firs, revealing a wild, disordered mass of galloping riders bearing down on the assault troop. Leading the attack were about half a hundred Russians mounted on a motley assortment of horses, ranging from great, lumbering Flemish farmhorses to riding ponies that might have belonged to Belgian ladies. Each rider was armed to the teeth and obviously intent on trouble, and in the very front was a wild-haired fellow, holding a bottle in his free hand, thundering along on a big bay.

In an instant Corrigan had seen enough to know that Slim was right. These were the same Russians that they had bumped into before. 'Stand fast,' he cried, as the men all round him fumbled with their weapons and the rest of the column began to bunch behind.

Suddenly the man on the bay could be seen to toss away his bottle and stand high in the stirrups. A white fog emerged from his mouth as he shouted something to his comrades. A great cry of '*Urrah!*' went up from the other riders.

'Here they come!' yelled Corrigan.

Suddenly the bay was racing forward at

breathtaking speed, ears pressed flat against its head, neck quivering, long mane streaming out in the wind, with the other riders and horses surging on in a rough line behind him.

'It ain't possible!' Wolfers cried in amazement. 'It's like something out of the pitchers.'

'Them toothpicks they're carrying ain't out of the pitchers, yer silly young–' But the rest of Slim's words were drowned by another hoarse cheer, this time from their right, as another group of partisans burst from the trees, carried away by the crazed blood-lust of battle. '*Urrah! Urrah!*' they cried, as they came stumbling and blundering across the snow towards the tightly packed circle of vehicles.

'Fire at will!' Corrigan yelled above the racket, and taking aim, pressed his trigger. The rifle slammed back into the hollow of his shoulder. A rider came tumbling down from his horse, which ran on, panicked and riderless. Almost simultaneously the others to the front of the convoy opened fire on the riders, while the frantic machine-gunners in the cabs of the half-tracks swung their weapons round to tackle the Russians on foot, who were now only a matter of yards away.

Now horses and riders were going down everywhere in the savage slaughter, horses whinnying pitifully as they were hit, throwing their riders, stumbling to their hindlegs, flanks slashed with scarlet, heads tossing wildly from side to side as they writhed in their death agonies. But still the irregular cavalry pressed home their attack. In spite of the great gaps cut in their ranks by that terrible hail of gunfire, they came storming on, swirling round the vehicles, using every trick they knew: clutching the belly of their mounts, using their flanks as living protection – anything to get within killing distance.

The first rider made it. One ton of rider and mount came sailing out of the sky to land right on the deck of the half-track next to *Waltzing Mathilda*. In an instant the Russians on foot took advantage of the break in the fire and swarmed all over the vehicle, turning it into a savage bath of blood, wallowing in the slaughter like wild animals, slashing, gouging, hacking, chopping in a frenzy of killing.

But Corrigan had no time to lend assistance to the hapless troopers in the next half-track, for now the riders, what was left of them, were only a matter of yards from *Waltzing Mathilda*. Already a group of them had leaped over the sweating heads of their mounts and were charging the half-track.

Like a ship's crew attempting to repel boarders, Corrigan's men leaned over the side and fired. A giant of a man wielding a rusty old cavalry sabre went reeling, his right eye dissolving into a mass of red pulp. Hawkins ripped off a burst from his Sten. No less than five running figurers were bowled over, dropping on all sides, screaming, writhing, cursing as they died in the snow. *Still* the others came on.

Now they were attempting to clamber up the steel side of the half-track. Corrigan fired into a savage bearded face. At that range the impact was horrific. The Russian's face shattered into fragments, bits and pieces of gore splattering the side of *Waltzing Mathilda* with a red rain. Another Russian reached up and seized Wolfers' head in an armlock, the Yorkshire lad's face suddenly turning purple as the Russian exerted pressure. The trooper shook like an enraged animal, then flung back his enormous body. The Russian came with him. Next moment he was lying on the floor of the half-track, to be trampled to death by half a dozen pairs of cruelly-studded boots.

Corrigan caught a glimpse of a raised arm and a vulpine face under jet-black eyebrows. In the nick of time he darted to the left. An axe hissed through the air, slamming harmlessly against the metal plating. The Russian howled at the shock and dropped his weapon. He never got a second chance. Corrigan rammed the brass butt of his rifle into the Russian's face. The attacker reeled back, spitting out gleaming white teeth from the scarlet hole which had once been his mouth.

Then, just when a desperate Corrigan thought they were going to be overwhelmed, the Russians broke off their attack. Yelling wildly, fighting each other in their frenzied attempts to escape, they fell back into the forests from which they had come, leaving behind them a carpet of dead bodies and pitifully writhing horses.

It was a long, long time before Corrigan could fully comprehend that the attack was over. Then, as the sounds of the firefight finally died away in the circle of snow-covered hills, to be replaced by the whimpers of the stricken animals and the moans of his own wounded, he shook his head like a man trying to wake up from a deep sleep. 'See to the casualties, Hawkins,' he commanded mechanically, fumbling to pull out a pistol from a holster attached to the side of the half-track. 'I'll deal with the horses, poor brutes.'

'Yes, sir,' Hawkins said numbly, moving as if his limbs were made of lead, his eyes completely empty of emotion.

Corrigan dropped over the side of the vehicle, landing on the body of the Russian he had just killed, which made an eerie belching sound as the gas escaped from the stomach. Corrigan didn't seem to notice.

Revolver held tightly to his side, he advanced on the dying horses to put them out of their misery.

'Be careful, sir,' Hawkins cried in warning, 'they may come back...' Then the little NCO stared down miserably at the slaughter in the back of the second half-track, where his 'lads' lay sprawled in gory confusion.

Slim Sanders added his voice to Hawkins'. 'They'll be back all right, sir. You can bet yer bottom dollar on that.'

But for once the smart little Australian deserter was wrong.

TWELVE

The Bitch waited at the door, staring across the smoke-filled room thronged with drunken, sweating members of the Repatriation Committee. By dawn they all knew the Germans would be here. Now, in true Russian fashion, they were celebrating, stuffing themselves with fine American food and drink for one last time before they fled west. If Beria had his way, they would be flying to Moscow, via Paris and Cairo, within the week; and even the most devoted communist among them wanted to enjoy the fleshpots of the decadent west before Mother Russia embraced them in her icy arms again. For once, the Bitch didn't object. She had carried out her mission successfully. Beria would undoubtedly reward her with a post in Moscow, and she had found Katya, who would be coming with her. Indeed, there was cause for celebration.

'Look, dear comrade.' Katya's voice cut into her reverie.

The Bitch turned round – and gasped with pleasure. Katya was dressed in a shimmering silken sheath, its fringed hem well above her black-clad knees, its neck plunging to reveal a firm white bosom which needed no bra to support it.

'Well?' demanded Katya, and like a little girl displaying her first party frock, she pirouetted delightfully.

The Bitch clasped Katya's delicate white hands in her own ugly red paws. *'Beautiful!'* she whispered, entranced. 'You are absolutely beautiful!'

'The American captain – it was in his quarters. Perhaps it belonged to his mistress.'

The Bitch shrugged indifferently. 'No matter. He will be poking that particular Belgian hole no longer. Come, my dear,' she said, extending her arm like an old Czarist gallant, 'do me the honour of accompanying me.'

Katya laughed happily, showing her perfect teeth, and accepted the proffered arm. Together, the massive woman in the grey-green uniform with the green epaulettes of a NKVD officer and the pretty, slim young girl walked into the smoke-filled room, ignoring the sly nudges and knowing grins of the men. Let their bourgeois little minds think what they like, the Bitch told herself. She had the power to make or break the biggest male chauvinist present.

Hurriedly, the agitprop wound up the handle of the looted American gramophone. The Bitch stood poised with Katya in her arms, waiting for the music to begin.

'Now, comrade,' the agitprop announced, as the record started to play and the room was flooded with the lilting melody of a Strauss waltz.

Stiffly, her enormous corseted bottom protruding grotesquely, the Bitch led Katya into the waltz, as the room cleared hurriedly and the others began to clap in the Russian fashion.

Cautiously, Piotr crept forward, his peg-leg muffled with sacking to deaden any noise it might make on the frozen snow outside the one-time camp administration building, knife gripped between his teeth Cossack-fashion and American grease-gun slung across his broad back. Each time he passed a window, he ducked, seething with rage as he heard the music, the chink of glasses and the excited chatter from within. 'Sons of whores!' he fumed. 'They're worse than the Imperialists... Living off the backs of the poor!'

He turned into a passage which he knew led into the kitchen the Americans had used for their little officers' mess – and stopped dead. A man dressed in the uniform he had come to fear and hate was standing there, urinating into the corner and drinking out of a bottle at the same time, swaying dangerously on his feet.

'*You!*' gasped the man, in the same instant

that Piotr reached for his knife. 'Piotr the Stump! What are you–'

'*Green cross whoreson!*' Piotr grunted, and thrust home his knife.

The NKVD man gave a great shudder as the blade slid into his soft belly. The bottle tumbled from his suddenly nerveless fingers and shattered on the floor. For what seemed like an age he hung there, gasping for breath like a stranded fish. Savagely, Piotr ripped the knife upwards, tearing open the officer's guts, feeling his blood pour hot and wet over his clenched fist. Then, cursing again, he withdrew the knife with an awful sucking noise. The man fell to the kitchen floor, dead.

Piotr didn't even look down. Now he was animated solely by rage and hate, his memory alive and burning with the wrongs done to him and the other Gulag rats. Had they not killed his wife and shipped off his only son to one of their schools to be 're-educated' – brainwashed, in other words, until they swore loyalty to that monster in the Kremlin and his perverted creeds? Had they not destroyed his own career, degrading him in front of his regiment, stripping him of his rank and honours like a common criminal – and he an officer who had shed blood for his country at least half a dozen times on the field of battle?

Face contorted with rage, his breath

coming in short, hectic gasps, Piotr sought and found what he was looking for: the two fifty-gallon drums of fuel which the Americans used for cooking. Hurriedly he tugged down the first big olive-drab can, hardly noticing its weight. The other followed a moment later. 'Now something to burn,' he muttered to himself, knowing that any sound he made would be drowned by the noise and music coming from the next room, where the pigs were enjoying themselves. 'Yes – and for the very last time!' he hissed, a mad gleam in his eyes, his features twisted by rage and hatred into a wolfish sneer.

Looking around, his eyes lit upon a bundle of old *Stars and Stripes*, the US Army newspaper, and *Yank*, their magazine. With the bundle clutched under his arm, he pushed and trundled the big can as best he could outside into the snow, then returned for the second one.

A couple of minutes later, he was almost finished. Hobbling back and forth excitedly he kicked the long line of newspapers and magazines stretched across the snow into place, so that it formed a crude arrow running from east to west and pointing directly at the house. It was an old trick he remembered from his days with the Cossacks, when there had been none of the complex radio equipment which military units used to signal to each other these days.

He stumbled back to the head of the arrow, arranged the paper more compactly, and flashed a look at the sky. It was just as he had hoped it would be: the fog had almost cleared, to be replaced by low, rolling clouds. It was still too bad for aircraft to fly, but it was good enough for *his* purpose...

He turned and stared at the house, from which now came the sound of raucous singing, and gave a hard, cruel smile. Let them sing. It would be the last time they ever did.

Heaving up the drum and holding it balanced there, he fumbled with the cap to open it. Suddenly the air was heavy with the cloying stench of escaping petrol fumes. Good. The thing was full to the very top. But then, the Americans always had plenty of everything. Once he had actually seen them waste over fifty litres of petrol to cool a barrel of beer. In the Red Army, they would have shot you for less than that. They would have called it sabotage. Slowly he trundled the barrel along the line of newspapers, soaking them with petrol, carefully ensuring that his own clothes weren't splashed. He knew he might die soon and he was prepared to do so – but not before he had dealt with those bastards who had ground the faces of his poor, oppressed people into the dust for so long. '*Soon ... soon!*' he crooned, a little crazy with anticipation now, as he forced open the second drum of gas and repeated the process, moving towards the house once more. Now, in the distance, he could definitely hear the faint rumble of the Fritzes' artillery. The weather was clearing. Soon they would be looking for targets of opportunity – and he would give them one! *By God, wouldn't he give them one!...*

'*Sto?*'

The harsh challenge took him completely by surprise. He was so shocked that he almost lost hold of the heavy drum. It was the man they called Hook: a one-armed killer who *really* deserved to be in the Gulag. He was standing there at the head of the arrow, swaying slightly as if he were already well over his hundred, but looking supremely confident. For in his hand, he held a looted .45 Colt taken from a US captain. And the gun was pointing straight at Piotr's heart.

'So, it's our *hero*, is it?' Hook sneered. 'The man with the George Cross and Order of the Red Banner. And what's he doing, playing with newspapers in the snow like an idiot child?' He laughed at his own humour, still swaying. But the big pistol didn't waver.

Piotr's mind raced wildly. He wasn't going to be foiled now. But what could he do? If he rushed him, he would be shot down in his tracks and that would be that. The Bitch would escape. He licked suddenly parched lips. Right now he would gladly have given his other foot for a glass of ice-cold vodka.

'All right, *hero*,' Hook snarled. 'Come on, over here and tell the Comrade Secretary what you're playing at out there in the snow.' He jerked up the pistol. 'And make it nice and slow. It wouldn't worry me one little bit if I had to blow your stupid patriotic turnip off here and now.'

'I'm coming,' Piotr quavered, lowering his head in defeat – but his hands were busily fumbling behind his back. 'Have I your permission to lower the barrel?' He nodded at the drum which he was balancing against his leg.

'You have my permission to go and piss yourself if you want... Now move... *Davai, davai...*'

Those words were Hook's undoing. Hearing that old, old cry with which he and the other Gulag rats had been whipped forward day after day, year after year, Piotr was goaded into action. With startling suddenness, his leg smashed out, and the barrel started to trundle forward, straight towards the sneering killer. In the very same instant, Piotr struck the match behind his back.

Hook's pistol barked. Piotr howled as a red-hot poker of agony thrust itself deep into his belly. He gasped with the shock of it. His knees started to buckle beneath him. Hook laughed out loud in triumph. Too late he saw the drum of petrol rumbling towards him. Next moment he was bowled over and the pistol was flung from his hand, his clothes instantly drenched with the escaping petrol.

Somehow Piotr forced himself to stagger towards the arrow. How, he didn't know. All he knew was that he had to live until he had done what he had come here to do. Trailing blood behind him, gasping harshly with the sheer agony of his stomach wound, he hobbled on, cradling the burning match in his cupped hands. Then, with one last, superhuman effort, he threw the match at the arrow.

With a great whoosh, a searing flame ran the length of the arrow like a gigantic blow torch, racing towards the arrow-head where Hook was still floundering.

Hook was engulfed as he struggled to his feet, the flames leaping up about his body, turning him instantly into a writhing human torch. Within seconds, the murderer was transformed into a hideous, charred monster. Where his face had been, there was only a black, crusted mask, his eyes replaced by two livid scarlet pools. With agonising slowness the thing raised a hand, through which the bones gleamed as white as ivory, and blindly started to totter towards the kneeling Piotr.

Piotr gasped frantically for breath now as he fought off unconsciousness, grease-gun held in shaking hands. He fired. The slug struck the thing squarely in the chest. It staggered, as if it had blundered into an unseen wall. For a moment it swayed there. Then, with dramatic suddenness, it fell screaming in its death-throes to the ground.

The single shot seemed to act as a signal. Suddenly, as the flames rose higher and higher, screams, cries, angry shouts and orders came from all sides. Piotr, already succumbing to the red mists of death, grinned weakly as he heard the Repatriation Committee rattle in panic at the doors. To no avail. They were securely locked from the outside. There was the sound of splintering glass. With infinite weariness, Piotr fought off the mists and raised his head.

The one with the stainless steel teeth was there at the window, a chair in his hand, systematically breaking the panes. Piotr didn't even aim. He pressed the trigger with a finger that felt as thick and as clumsy as a sausage. The little gun chattered at his side. Splinters of glass and brick howled through the air in a shimmering rain. The man sank back slowly his steel teeth shining stupidly and bulging from his mouth amid a welter of bright red.

Piotr felt the world begin to swim and waver before his eyes like a desert mirage back in those far-off days of his youth. He shook his head, trying to dispel the mists which were thickening once more. His eyelids seemed as heavy as lead.

Slowly the gun started to slide from his fingers. He mustn't let go... *He mustn't!* He had to hang on until the Fritzes found... But it was no good. His struggles at an end, Piotr pitched face-forwards in the snow.

In the very same moment, a couple of miles away, German forward observers spotted the blazing arrow flaring angrily on the horizon, and their phones started to rattle. It was almost too good to be true. They had spotted the Amis in Werbomont; obviously they were burning secret papers or something outside their headquarters. It was a dream target for the artillery. With a great baleful roar, the whole weight of the lst SS Division's fire-power descended upon the trapped NKVD officials...

Later, much later, the SS men would find the gross woman in the green uniform lying spread-eagled on her back, yellow false teeth bulging from her mouth, with one hand concealed under the skirt of a headless girl in black, and wonder...

BOOK THREE

DEATH TO THE PANZERS

'We are but warriors for the working day
Our gayness and our gilt are all
    besmirched
With rainy marching in the painful field.'

Shakespeare, *Henry V.*

ONE

'Fallschirmjäger, eh?' chortled General-
leutnant von Norden, his massive belly
trembling and his jowls making a slapping
sound as if they were applauding his
statement. 'But you're a long way off course,
my dear Hauptmann, *was?*' He dipped the
end of his cigar in his glass of looted cognac
and sucked it appreciatively.

'Blame Fat Hermann's flyboys for that,
sir,' replied Hartung, staring around the
staff officers grouped beside the divisional
commander and noting as he did so that the
officers of the Spearhead Panzer Division
seemed to do themselves pretty well, even at
the front. 'They were supposed to drop us
just over the Belgian border.'

Von Norden smiled encouragingly, his
pig-like yet intelligent eyes disappearing
momentarily into a mass of fat. 'Ah, the
brilliantined gentlemen of the Luftwaffe,
eh? Probably in too much of a hurry to get
back to their high-class whores and Champagne, I'll be bound. Before the offensive, I
was promised a whole squadron of fighter-
bombers by – er – Fat Hermann.' He smiled
at his officers, knowing that they, too,

259

shared his contempt of the Luftwaffe and that he could safely use the derisive nickname. 'And what did I get? One very ancient spotter aircraft, which crashed in a snowstorm on the first day of the attack.' He chuckled again and his gross body, dressed in the elegant black uniform of the Panzer Corps, shook violently. Then he took another look at the big, bearded captain in the tattered uniform standing before him, blue with cold. Tutting at his own inconsiderateness, von Norden beckoned hastily to an aide. 'Nigger sweat, Otto, with a shot of firewater – *schnell!*'

Gratefully a frozen Hartung, who had just struggled back to German lines with his handful of survivors, accepted the steaming cup of coffee and warmed his hands on it, while outside, the heavy guns rumbled and from somewhere in the distance came the sound of tanks clattering forward towards the front.

General von Norden allowed Hartung to drink for a few moments. Then, very professional and eager now, he turned to him once more. 'Well, Hauptmann Hartung, what can you tell me? With this terrible weather and no air reconnaissance, I know very little of what's going on between here and the Meuse.'

Fighting off his terrible weariness as best he could, Hartung told the general his story, recounting what had happened to his company after the Luftwaffe had landed them so far behind Allied lines.

'*Kolossal!*' the general snorted on hearing how they had hijacked the English troop train, and slapped his thigh with delight. 'In three devils' name, Hartung, you really deserve a bit of tin for that!'

Hartung continued, explaining how they had been forced to abandon the train when it had been hit and their driver killed; and how eventually they had managed to escape – those who were still on their feet – out of the eastern suburbs of Huy, where they had tangled not only with Americans, but also British soldiers.

'Tommies, you say?' von Norden queried quickly. 'On the *eastern* bank of the Meuse?'

Hartung took a quick sip of black coffee laced with Schnapps, then nodded. 'Yes, sir.'

Von Norden threw a significant look at his assembled staff officers. 'Well, there we have the mustard, don't we? The clock's almost in the pisspot!'

His staff officers nodded their heads grimly.

'It means Montgomery is moving his troops in strength from Holland, not only to the western bank of that damned river, but *across* it too.' Von Norden's gross face grew sombre. Suddenly it was as if he was quite oblivious of the world around him. A heavy silence fell over the room, broken only by the sound of Sergeant Martini's voice wafting across from outside, as he formed the survivors up. '...*Come on, you pissy pansies. You've had yer holidays. You're back with the real army now, so suck in those guts and rip up those stupid turnips of yours...*'

On any other occasion, Hartung would have grinned, but not now. The moment was too solemn. He had the impression that great decisions were being taken here, decisions that might determine not only the course of the present battle, but the fate of Germany itself.

Von Norden cleared his throat, and his officers sprang to attention, knowing that his deliberations were over and that soon they would be flying to carry out his orders. '*Meine Herren,*' he barked crisply, every inch the old-school Prussian officer now, 'disengage all units wherever possible. We are the spearhead of Manteuffel's Fifth. Let us concentrate on that role. The main point of our attack will be the town of Marche. Then, on to the Meuse with all speed.' Slowly his hard, searching gaze travelled from each officer to the next. 'Gentlemen, it is now a race between us and the Tommies – a race in which the prize is not only the success of this operation, but the future of our beloved Fatherland. We will never be able to mount another offensive in the west.

This is our last chance. We must cross the Meuse before the Tommies arrive in strength...!'

The big general's voice broke, and he ended on what seemed to Hartung an almost pleading note. Then the assembled officers were saluting and running off to carry out their instructions, and von Norden was left alone, looking shrunken, deflated, beaten...

Now it was almost light. To the east, the sky was beginning to flush white and the faint rumble of guns could be heard in the distance. Slowly the assault troop convoy rumbled on through the brooding forest, their tracks throwing up a wake of bright white snow.

It all seemed very peaceful – a Christmas card scene, almost; yet there was something ominous about the new morning. Standing upright in the half-track in spite of the keen dawn wind, Sergeant Hawkins flashed darting looks at the silent rows of firs, as if he half-expected the enemy to come bursting out with guns blazing at any moment. At his feet, Wolfers crouched over the B-set, ready to flash a warning to the next vehicle, some two hundred yards behind them on the forest trail. For once, he wasn't eating.

Even Corrigan felt a sense of apprehension. It was as if there was danger in the very air. But at least his fears had some rational basis. According to Montgomery's radio signal, the situation ahead of him was very confused, with pockets of Germans and Americans everywhere; but he *could* expect to meet the point of von Manteuffel's Fifth Panzer Army soon. Immediately he did, he was to signal Monty, since Horrocks' Thirty Corps was already on its way to the Meuse and the corps commander would need to know where to make his crossing in order to stop the German advance.

Corrigan put away his map, clicked off the little green light and stood up next to Hawkins, who was scanning the surface of the snow carefully in the thin white light. It was clean, devoid of any marks save for the dainty prints made by the teeming wildlife of the Ardennes forests.

'Deer, Hawkins,' said Corrigan soothingly, 'not Jerries. Might bump into one. Fancy a nice venison steak?'

Hawkins shook his head. 'No, sir. Give me a rasher o' bacon and real fried egg any day. Never did like fancy food.'

Corrigan smiled. Hawkins was a true Yorkshireman. Thank God there were still Englishmen like him!

At the wheel, Sanders started to guide the half-track up a steep snowy slope, driving with extreme caution. As always, the ascent was as slick as shit. One false move and they would be in the deep ditch on the other side. He had to take it carefully.

Time passed slowly. The only sound was the roar of the half-track's engine in first gear and the faint, distant rumble of the guns. At a snail's pace they toiled up the hill, Sanders cursing softly to himself.

Hawkins frowned. He knew he was a bloody old woman, but still he couldn't shake off his fear. He couldn't put his finger on the precise reason, but the fear was there all right, like an oppressive weight on his shoulders.

Suddenly it happened. Somewhere ahead of them the brooding silence was ripped apart by the throaty roar of a motor bursting into life. Hawkins' heart slammed against his ribs. At his side, Corrigan tensed and opened his mouth to call out an order – but there was no need. Sanders acted instinctively. He ripped the wheel to the right. The half-track skidded. Next moment it was sliding out of control, straight across the trail. 'Hold tight!' Slim yelled. They sailed over the embankment and slammed with a terrible bone-jarring jolt into the snow below.

'*Contact… Contact!*' Wolfers hissed urgently into his mike. '*Contact, Sunray Two… Contact!*'

The very next moment, a familiar black shape began to rumble over the top of the hill above them. *They had met von Man-teuffel's point!*

'They haven't spotted us yet,' Wolfers whispered into the set, as the eight-wheel German scout-car, its many aerials flashing back and forth like silver whips, came ever closer. 'The CO says let them come on. He wants to see what the opposition's like.'

'Roger,' replied the operator in the half-track behind. 'All under cover here. Norwich. Over and out.'

Wolfers couldn't help grinning in spite of the tension. '*Norwich*' – knickers off, ready and waiting! What a great old bunch of lads they were. Even now they weren't scared, despite the fact that they'd damn near had a head-on collision with the spearhead of the German advance! And it could well be that it was a handful of them against hundreds – thousands, for all he knew.

The white-painted armoured car with the stark black cross on its side, groaned ever closer to the spot where they had veered off the road. They tensed, crouching low inside the damaged half-track, fingers curled round the triggers of their weapons. Would the officer standing upright in the open vehicle spot their tracks?

Now Corrigan could see him quite clearly in spite of the poor light: a tall, proud, erect figure in a smart black uniform and bright silk scarf, binoculars slung around his neck. All of twenty and playing the hero, Corrigan told himself, half in contempt, half in pity. If things went well, the young fool would be dead within the next thirty minutes.

Now the scout-car was almost parallel with them. It slowed down suddenly. Wolfers tensed over his radio, ready to shout a warning. The others gripped their weapons in white-knuckled, sweating hands. Had they been spotted?

No – the tall officer bent and whispered something to his radio operator. The man nodded and spoke into his mike. The scout-car crawled on.

Relieved, Hawkins breathed out hard, but Sanders scowled as he lowered his sawn-off shotgun, angry at being cheated of his sport. 'I could have blown the bastard to Kingdom Come,' he snarled.

'Don't you worry your pretty little head,' Corrigan soothed him. 'You'll get your bellyful of combat before the day's out, take my word for it.'

Now the lead scout-car had almost turned the bend. Assuming the officer in command didn't spot the rest of Corrigan's vehicles hiding there, he would report the way ahead clear and the rest would follow. It was standard operating procedure for all recce outfits. Corrigan and his men followed its progress with bated breath, not even daring to speak. At the bottom of the hill, the scout-car halted. Someone gasped. Had they spotted something? A soldier in a white camouflaged cape, dropped out of the stationary vehicle and doubled heavily through the snow to the bend. He paused there, looked deliberately to left and right, shading his eyes with his hand like an Indian scout in a Hollywood western. Then, turning, he jerked his arm up and down three times rapidly – the infantry signal for 'advance'.

'They've bought it, Hawkins... *They've bought it!*' Corrigan cried gleefully.

'Here they come,' hissed Sanders. Like spectators at a tennis match, they all turned to look down the road for the first sign of the advancing column.

They didn't have long to wait. The first light tank breasted the rise in a flurry of snow and began to rumble down the hill, skidding and sliding as the driver fought for purchase on the slippery surface. A moment later another appeared – and another. Confident that the way ahead was clear, the drivers were devoting all their attention to holding a steady course on the track and were bunching badly, presenting an ideal target for the waiting troopers.

'Signal,' Corrigan hissed to a waiting Wolfers.

'Sir?'

'Snipers out. Knock out tank commanders

wherever possible. Piat men into the ditches. Fire on my signal.'

Immediately Sergeant Hawkins dropped noiselessly into the snow carrying the clumsy Piat anti-tank weapon, followed by Sanders, his shotgun slung over his skinny back so that he could carry the Piat bombs. Meanwhile, Wolfers relayed the message to the men hidden beyond the bend.

'Signal ... one red flare,' Corrigan added, and dropped over the side himself, clutching his infantry-man's rifle.

Now all was tense expectation. Unaware that their every move was being watched, the black-uniformed German tank commanders in their turrets helped the drivers below to fight the treacherous slope, each man concentrating on the difficult task of staying on the road.

As the last tank breasted the top of the hill, skidding wildly, its track throwing up a wild white wake of snow, Corrigan raised his rifle. The tank commander, a tall, skinny boy, slid into his sights. Fate had chosen him to be the first to die.

Corrigan tucked the butt firmly into his shoulder, one eye closed, following the tank's every move, his finger already beginning to curl on his trigger. Next to him, Hawkins, following the direction of his CO's gaze, concentrated his clumsy-looking anti-tank weapon on a tank in the middle of the column. Gripping the Piat's cloth-covered butt, which looked like a gout sufferer's bandaged foot, he pressed it hard against his shoulder. The weapon had one hell of a kick.

'Wolfers, ready with the signal flare!' Corrigan called, without taking his eyes off the man he was about to kill.

'Ready, sir.'

'Count to three, then fire!'

Wolfers felt a cold bead of sweat trickle down the small of his back. Then, loud and clear, he began counting, knowing that the roar of the tanks' 400-hp motors in low gear would drown any noise he would make. '*One... Two...*' His finger curled round the trigger of the ugly flare pistol. '*...Three!*'

He pressed the trigger. With startling suddenness the flare hissed into the sky, trailing grey smoke behind it, curving gracefully and seeming to halt in mid-air. Below, every eye in the German column focused on it in wonder. What was it? What did it signify? Next moment it exploded with a slight crack. In a flash the upturned faces were coloured an unnatural crimson.

Corrigan fired. The boy in the turret jumped as if someone had put a thousand volts through him, then slumped forward over the turret, dead.

In that same moment, Hawkins fired the ugly anti-tank weapon. Like an express train going all out, the ugly bottle-shaped bomb

270

sped towards its target, while Hawkins sprawled on his back in the ditch, knocked off his feet by the terrible recoil. There was an ear-splitting rending noise as metal struck metal. A ball of ugly red flame exploded at the base of the tank's turret. It reeled violently as if struck by a giant fist. Next moment it exploded, tracer ammunition from its ammo locker zig-zagging in all directions into the snow. In the momentary pause that followed, the hysterical screams of the trapped crew were all too audible. The massacre had started.

From all sides the merciless fire came pouring in. Commander after commander went down, shot by the unseen snipers. The Piats thundered. The gunners couldn't miss. Trapped as they were, the tanks hadn't a chance. In a matter of moments the whole stalled column was ablaze. Now burning tankers were running frantically for cover, trailing their flames behind them and thrashing and writhing helplessly as the greedy red tongues of fire tore at their soft flesh. Others fell screaming into the snow, rolling and flailing there frantically in an attempt to stifle the flames, only to be picked off mercilessly by the snipers.

Two tanks collided with each other as their panic-stricken drivers tried to escape the blood bath. Having somehow escaped the Piats, their stunned crews slipped out from beneath by the emergency exits. For a moment or two they lay there, panting wildly like trapped animals, wondering how to escape the merciless massacre. Then bullets started to pepper the snow all around them and the air was suddenly filled with the stink of escaping petrol. In a minute the armour above them would be on fire. They had to make a run for it. They broke from cover.

But Slim Sanders was waiting for them, his legs planted apart and his sawn-off shotgun tucked into the right hip like a western gunslinger. Seeing his victims, his face twisted in a cruel sneer. 'Come on... Come to daddy!' he called, and pulled the first trigger.

The hail of pellets caught the first man in the face. He stopped dead in his tracks as if he had just slammed into a brick wall, his face dissolving into a mass of red gore and gleaming white teeth. Blood jetted everywhere. For what seemed an age, the young German stood there tottering, scream after scream welling up from the innermost depths of his body. Carried away by the primeval blood-lust of combat, Sanders fired again. The blast lifted the man clean off his feet. When he came down again, he did so in two dripping pieces which for one awful moment writhed separately on the snow.

And then it was over at last. One by one, weary of the slaughter, the troopers ceased firing and stared with wide-open unseeing eyes at the scene of havoc and destruction all around them. Now silence hung over the scene of the great massacre, broken only by the sound of flames crackling and the soft whimpers of the dying.

Corrigan lowered his rifle. He felt unutterably weary, as if all the energy had been drained out of him; but he knew he *had* to pull himself together. They wouldn't have much time left.

'Wolfers,' he croaked.

It seemed to take a long time before the boy could answer. 'Sir?' he said dully, in a voice that Corrigan hardly recognised.

'Signal the rest ... we're moving to the top and digging in...' Corrigan's words came in short gasps, as if he hadn't the strength to utter a complete sentence. 'They'll be back – the Jerries... Back soon...'

TWO

'An Assault troop of the Iron Division has made contact with the enemy just south of Marche – *here,*' said Horrocks, and stabbed the big map pinned up on the blackboard of the little school-house in Huy which was now his headquarters. Outside, a squadron of Churchill tanks rumbled by and there was the sound of singing as the infantry made their way to the bridge. 'According to the signals which we've received from them – and they're pretty garbled, because the Huns are trying to block all our transmissions now – they've given a Hun reconnaissance unit a decidedly bloody nose and are now holding this patch of high ground.' Again, he pointed his long forefinger at the map, his normally good-humoured, skinny face unusually serious. 'But they're completely out of touch with any American unit that might be in that region.' He looked round at the assembled regimental officers of his corps. 'To be quite frank with you, gentlemen, we can assume that all organised American resistance in that area of the eastern bank of the Meuse has crumbled. As things look at the moment, all that's stopping the leading elements of the Hun Fifth Panzer Army is that single British unit. Naturally, they've no heavy weapons – just the usual infantry stuff, plus probably a few heavy machine-guns mounted on their half-tracks. Once the Hun puts in heavy tanks, they're as good as finished.' Horrocks breathed out hard. He had the look of a sorely troubled man – a man who had been asked to do the impossible once too often in these last terrible months.

'Now, the Second Tactical Air Force has promised me Tiffies and fighter cover for these chaps as soon as the weather improves, but as you can see,' he indicated the grey sky outside, 'that doesn't look very likely at the moment. So for the present, that British assault troop out there is on its own.'

Horrocks paused and once again looked around at his regimental officers. They were looking good, their tough, rough faces hardened by the months of living out in the open in all weathers. No commander could ever have asked for finer officers serving under him. And now he was about to ask some of them to risk their lives yet again. He sighed. When would the slaughter ever end?

'Now, gentlemen,' he continued, 'I'm sure that you appreciate that a corps commander simply has no alternative but to write men off sometimes. It's one of the hard facts of life in my calling. Under normal circumstances, that's what I'd be forced to do with

275

that handful of men on the hill out there. But, and it's a big but' – he raised his finger to emphasise his point – 'by sheer good luck, the chap who commands that assault troop has picked an ideal tactical position. The height on which he's located dominates the whole area and the handful of roads leading to the Meuse. If Manteuffel's Fifth is to reach the river in this area, he *has* to take that hill.'

Horrocks paused to let his words sink in, his skinny chest heaving a little from the effort of talking so much. In spite of his key position, he was far from fit. The bad wound he had suffered the previous year had taken it out of him, and he knew it. In fact, he was damned lucky to be commanding a corps at all in his physical shape.

'So,' he went on, 'that hill has suddenly become the most important piece of real estate in the worlds as far as Thirty Corps is concerned. And we're going to have to go all-out to link up with those recce chaps there and make sure they hold it.' He turned to Colonel Thomas of the Tank Corps, big, bluff and dependable. 'Tom, I'm sending you up with your Cromwells. I know they're not much good against the Huns' eighty-eights, but they're the fastest tanks we've got.'

'Yes, sir,' said Thomas, his usual capable self, not in the least bit daunted by this latest risky assignment.

'You'll be able to give those recce chaps some artillery, at least.'

Next, Horrocks turned to red-faced, red-haired Colonel MacKay, his left arm still in a sling. 'How's that flipper of yours, Mac?' he asked.

'General,' replied the Scot in the blunt fashion of the Highlander, 'dinna fash yersel about ma arm. What do ye want me and ma Jocks to do, eh?'

For the first time in an hour, Horrocks smiled. The other officers grinned too. When you had your back to the wall it was grand to have men like MacKay around. 'I must say, Mac, you're not one to beat about the bush.'

'There's been a mite too much blether in these last few months, General,' replied the Scot, unsmilingly. 'Now, gi's the word, and we're awa.'

'Righto, here it is. You mount your Jocks on Tom's tanks and off you go! How's that, Mac?'

'Fine. With your permission, General?' He turned to the big Tank Corps colonel. 'Well, Tom – dinna stand there lookin' like one o' each waitin' fer vinegar! *Let's awa!*'

Thirty minutes later, the lean, low Cromwell tanks laden with MacKay's Jocks started to roll towards the bridge. Red-capped MPs hurriedly cleared all other traffic from the road ahead, shrilling their whistles, bellowing angrily at dawdlers and now and then drawing their revolvers and waving them menacingly.

Horrocks stood at the window, gazing at the scene. As always, he was moved by the sight of the infantry. They seemed so young and vulnerable as they squatted there, laden down with equipment, laughing and joking together and making rude remarks to the harassed Red-caps. Didn't they know that they might be going to their death? That many of them would never see Christmas, 1944? And that in humble homes all over Scotland, black-clad, wet-eyed mothers would be staring at blurred photographs of young, smiling faces on the mantelpiece – faces they would never see again?

Sadly, Horrocks shook his head and turned from the window. He could stand the sight no longer. *God*, he prayed fervently, desperately, *make it end soon. I'm sick of sending them to their death...*

Fifty miles away, another general also despaired and also made plans. Sweating heavily, and constantly dabbing at his fat face with a lace handkerchief soaked in Eau-de-Cologne, General von Norden rapped out his orders, while outside, more and more tanks laden with white-suited panzer grenadiers rumbled towards the new trouble-spot. Suddenly his sector had become the most important one of the whole front. An hour ago, von Manteuffel had been on the phone to him, urging him to go all-out for the Meuse. Thirty minutes later, the Führer himself had called, all the way from his battle headquarters in Schloss Ziegenberg. 'Give me a bridge across the Meuse, von Norden,' he had pleaded – and even the bad line hadn't been able to disguise the note of desperation in his voice. 'It will be the best Christmas present I ever receive, General. Give me a bridge – *please!*'

'You have top priority in everything – *absolutely everything*,' von Manteuffel had promised fervently. 'Men, material, petrol – whatever you want, it's yours. To facilitate your advance, the Führer is even stopping supplies to his precious SS so that you can have them instead. I think that is proof enough of the importance we attach to your mission.'

But not even the Führer could give von Norden the cloud cover he so desperately needed. He had fought the Anglo-Americans before, in Africa and Normandy; he knew just how skilfully they played the air weapon. If the cloud cleared sufficiently and they could fly, he was sunk. That damned hill now in their hands would be a perfect observation post for the Tommies. From it, they could direct their fighter-bombers onto his tight columns; it dominated all the roads leading to the Meuse. There would be another great slaughter, just as there had been back in Normandy in the Summer.

He dismissed his tank commanders, who clicked to attention and doubled away to carry out his orders; then he turned to a waiting Hauptmann Hartung.

In spite of the urgency of the situation, von Norden made an effort to be polite, for he was by nature a courteous man. As the English said, 'A gentleman is a gentleman even with his trousers down.'

Hartung responded willingly enough to the general's enquiries about the welfare of his men: were they being well fed? Had their injuries been attended to? and so on. But von Norden could see by the big para's slightly mocking look that Hartung wasn't fooled. He knew he hadn't been called to divisional HQ to pass the time of day. Von Norden had something else in mind for him.

In the end, von Norden asked him.

Hauptmann Hartung pondered his question in silence for what seemed a long time. Von Norden was pleased by his cautious response: it showed that Hartung wasn't one of those dare-devil young hotheads who would promise anything for the sake of glory and then perhaps make a mess of the whole thing.

Outside, infantry were marching by, singing lustily, their faces happy and confident. *'Oh, du schöner Westerwald,'* they sang, faces wreathed in a fog of their own breath, their step brisk and even on the frozen snow. *'Bläht der Wind so kalt...'*

Slowly, Hartung began to speak. 'We did it once, back in May of 'forty, Herr General,' he said, selecting his words with care, as if he were still making his decision as he spoke. 'Perhaps you remember?'

Von Norden nodded. 'At Eben Emael? Yes, I remember.'

'But then, of course, we were all highly trained and rehearsed. Most of us had been in the parachute regiment since it had first been set up. And naturally, the weather was perfect for an operation of that kind... Early May.'

Again, von Norden nodded, his face revealing little. He waited.

Hartung fought a battle with himself. Dare he chance the lives of his young boys yet again? Hadn't his eighteen-year-olds done enough for Folk, Fatherland and Führer? It wouldn't make one bit of difference to the outcome of the war whether they pulled it off or not. Yet... He thought again of the great days: Crete ... Africa ... Monte Cassino... Why not have one last turn before the roundabout stopped forever? After all, for all he knew, he might spend the rest of his life as a door-to-door shoe salesman or something hopelessly boring like that.

'Herr General,' he said suddenly, the words coming out in a rush, almost as if he were afraid he might change his mind at the last moment, *'I'll do it...'*

THREE

Captain Corrigan groaned and opened his eyes. It was dawn at last, thank God: a harsh December dawn, with the fog curling around their dug-outs on the top of the hill, weaving silently between the trees like a soft-furred cat.

Hollow-eyed and heavy-headed, Corrigan lay in his blankets, shivering a little and very stiff, listening to the world slowly coming to life around him: the hoarse *caw-caw* of the crows in the trees; the rattle of a Dixie where someone was brewing up char; the hiss of urine as somebody crawled out of his slit-trench to relieve himself; the noise the look-outs made as they jerked their rifle bolts back and forth rapidly to clear away oil, grown sluggish in the freezing cold. The men were awake and ready – but ready for what?

Surprisingly enough, the Germans had broken with their usual custom and hadn't counter-attacked immediately after their reconnaissance force had been wiped out. For a while, Corrigan and his troopers had been subjected to a mortar bombardment, but it had been quite ineffective and had caused no casualties – though Slim Sanders had been caught out in the open in a somewhat exposed position and had been forced to dive into the nearest foxhole with his pants still around his ankles. Thereafter the enemy had remained dormant, save for intermittent machine-gun fire. *Why?* Corrigan asked himself, finally forcing his stiff, weary bones up and out of the hole. After all, he now knew from Horrocks' HQ that he had chanced upon a first-class tactical position. Yet as he looked out across enemy-held territory below, still shrouded by the morning fog, it was desolate and bare, with no sign of any activity. *Why?*

Corrigan dismissed the problem. Instead, he grabbed a handful of snow and rubbed his unshaven face with it for a brief moment – then wished he hadn't.

Crouching slightly in case German snipers had infiltrated during the hours of darkness, he moved about the wakening perimeter, stopping here and there to exchange a few words with his sleepy, frozen men, who he was pleased to see were still in good heart in spite of their night in the open.

A couple were following his lead and washing with snow; Sergeant Hawkins, old sweat that he was, was even dry-shaving with a little plastic razor, wincing every time the blade nicked him or dragged at his skin. 'Bit regimental this morning, I see, Sergeant

Hawkins?' barked Corrigan, and strode on. But for the most part, the men were squatting round hissing Tommy-cookers or makeshift fires fuelled by soil soaked in petrol and stirred with a bayonet to a thick porridge, boiling water for tea or frying soya link sausages on the blades of their entrenching tools. At that moment they looked for all the world like a bunch of overgrown, somewhat ragged boy scouts.

'Char, sir?' said Wolfers, his mouth full of odd-shaped Ersatz sausage. 'Real old sarnt-major's char, this is. I put in a whole tin of condensed milk. Yer could stand a spoon up in it.'

Gratefully, Corrigan accepted the square mess-tin full of dark brown tea and took a careful sip, feeling the steam thaw out the end of his nose. Meanwhile Wolfers opened another can of sausages and threw them on the glowing blade of his shovel.

'What's the news, sir?' asked Wolfers. 'Good or bad?'

'Good, on the whole,' Corrigan answered between sips. 'With a bit of luck we should be relieved by Thirty Corps before the day's out. And they're going to send fighter-bombers to give us some air cover – Tiffies and Spits. That's as soon as the weather picks up. Talk of the devil...' Suddenly Corrigan cocked his ear to one side. 'I think I can hear aircraft engines now.'

Crouching at his feet, Wolfers did the same for a few moments, then shook his head. 'I can't hear anything, sir. You must have been hearing things. Wishful thinking, like.'

Corrigan drained the rest of his tea and handed him back the canteen. 'Thanks. Yes, I suppose you're right. Nothing could fly in this pea-soup.'

But something could. Droning on steadily just above the cloud base, the antiquated three-engined Junkers 52, known to all paras as 'Auntie Ju', circled yet again as the pilot tried to find the drop zone. At his side, Hartung searched with him, straining his eyes to penetrate the grey morning gloom, a newly captured Russian triangular chute already strapped to his broad shoulders. Behind him, he could feel Sergeant Martini's baleful glare drilling into his back. Martini still hadn't forgiven him for accepting the mission.

'But sir,' he had exploded on hearing of their assignment, 'you can't *mean* it! Von Norden can't have got all his cups in his cupboard! He must have got a screw loose!' Martini's normally tough, good-humoured face had creased with a mixture of anger and complete disbelief. 'To jump over unknown terrain in this kind of weather with *that* bunch of wet-tails!' He had indicated the youthful paras lolling about the barn. 'Why... Why,' he stuttered indignantly, groping for the right words, *'it's downright suicidal!* Might as well blow yer shitting turnip off here and now and be done with it!' And he had glared at Hartung, chest heaving, face a furious red.

'You don't need to come with us if you don't want to, Martini,' Hartung had replied calmly, yet knowing that everything the angry sergeant had said was true. 'You've done enough already. One man more or less will make no difference.'

Martini had let his shoulders slump as if in defeat. 'Shit on the shingle,' he had growled, 'I'll go … I always do.'

But the resentment had remained. And Hartung knew, as he searched for the drop zone, that he had lost Sergeant Martini forever. After five years of combat together, their relationship was now finished.

'I'll take her round to port, Captain,' said the pilot, breaking into his thoughts, 'and down to, say, three hundred.' Hartung could hear him hesitate. 'It's … not too low to jump, is it?' he asked, after a moment.

Of course it *was*, and Hartung knew it – even though these new Popov chutes were supposed to be the latest thing for low-altitude drops. But what did it matter? They would all go hop sooner or later. Why not now?

'No,' he said with a bitter grin on his tough face, 'I'm getting a fat arse sitting here. Let's get out of this old crate so you can get back to your nice warm bed.'

The pilot grinned, relieved. The forecast was for better weather by noon. If the Tommy fighters caught him up here in clear weather, he would be easy meat for them – a real sitting duck. Let these young heroes in their rimless helmets die for their Führer. He wanted to live for his new boss, Franklin D Roosevelt.

'Okay, Captain,' he said, 'here we go.'

He turned the rudder, and the ancient plane banked to port. They were going down.

'Did I ever tell you how I got in with that Frog bint in Cairo, back in 'forty-two, cobbers?' Slim was saying, as the men all around him filled their clips with ammunition or prepared their grenades, laying them out on top of their foxholes. Slim's was already littered with weapons: a German Schmeisser, shotgun, grenades and a captured German bazooka, or 'stove pipe'.

'Yeah,' somebody answer. 'But yer gonna tell us it again anyhow, ain't yer?'

The little Australian ignored the comment. 'It was like this: I'd just come down from the Blue on leave–'

'You mean you *deserted*, mate! Went on the trot,' someone sneered.

'Yer'll get a knuckle-sandwich in half a mo

if you go on like that, cobber,' Slim threatened. 'Anyway, here's this bint, all silk frock and fancy sunglasses, and she comes swishing up to me and says, "How'd yer like something new, Tommy?" And I says, "Like what, Fatima? *Leprosy or summat?*"'

'Weren't you the little joker?'

'Fuck *off!*' Slim snapped crudely. 'Anyhow, it turned out she wasn't workin' the streets. She was a lady, and she and her sister, a real smashin' Sheilah–'

'Hold it Sanders!' Hawkins hissed tensely, suddenly staring to his front.

Slim stopped. As one, the troopers turned and stared down the long white slope that led down to the firs, pitted here and there with brown shell-holes that looked for all the world like the work of giant moles.

'What is it, Sarge?' asked Slim.

'Thought I saw something move in them trees at three o'clock,' Hawkins answered, and raised the field glasses he had taken off one of the dead Germans. Corrigan joined him, sprawling full length in the snow, his glasses also raised.

Now the easy, relaxed mood of a moment before had vanished. Everywhere the assault troopers had grabbed their weapons and crouched lower in their holes, faces tense and expectant.

Methodically, in total silence, Corrigan and Hawkins searched the terrain to their front. It seemed as empty as the surface of the moon, but Corrigan knew his Germans: they were masters of camouflage – they had learned a lot from the Russians.

Hawkins nudged him, then, keeping his voice low in case he was overheard, he whispered: 'That clump of firs, sir, left of the twisted oak... At two o'clock. Something just moved!'

Corrigan swung his glasses in the direction indicated. Yes – there it was: a bush swaying, followed by a small fall of snow. *Someone was down there!* He adjusted the glasses for better definition. There they were – two men in white camouflaged suits.

In the same instant that Corrigan spotted the Germans, the whole horizon seemed to turn a bright cherry-red. It was as if an enormous blast furnace had just burst into life. There was a hellish howl. Black trails of smoke shot high into the grey sky, followed by showers of fiery-red sparks. An obscene moan split the air. Next instant, six rockets started to shriek down out of the sky right onto their positions.

In a paroxysm of fear, Corrigan screamed, '*Moaning minnies! Hit the dirt! Here they come!*' as a terrible wave of fire submerged them.

'*Helmets on!*' cried Hartung, above the roar of the icy wind which was howling in now through the open door of the fuselage.

As one, his boys did as they were commanded.

'*Stand up!*'

They rose and shuffled into a long line between the canvas seats.

'*Check!*'

Each man turned and patted the other's equipment, paying special attention to their new Russian chutes, while Hartung stared out a little helplessly at the grey fog drifting by below, through which he could occasionally glimpse little stretches of snow-covered fields.

Finally he turned back to his paras. '*Hook up!*' he yelled, and clipped the cable that would release his chute to the overhead wire. Behind him, his men followed suit. Satisfied, Hartung turned and looked at Sergeant Martini, who was positioned at the end of the stick. Martini lowered his gaze and avoided his eyes. Hartung frowned. '*Sound off!*' he ordered, as the pilot brought the Junkers ever lower.

Below the fog had cleared a little, giving him a vague view of the drop zone. It didn't look good: a steeply sloped hillside, flanked on both sides by woods. God only knew what might lie under the snow. There would be a few broken ankles in this one, thought Hartung – and under the conditions they were soon going to have to fight in, a broken ankle now could easily spell death later. Banishing the thought from his mind, he gazed at the winking red light to the side of the door, waiting.

Suddenly there it was. *Green!* He stepped forward and grabbed both sides of the exit door, the wind whipping his uniform tightly about his big body and making his eyes water.

Now the green light began to blink on and off rapidly. It was time to go – and for the last time! He would never again experience that incomparable, almost sexual thrill of launching himself into space and the unknown: '*Los!*' he cried, and flung himself out. The wind tore at him. His arms were forced upwards, as if he were trying to grab the black cross on the Junkers' corrugated side. The slipstream caught him. He hurtled through space, gasping for breath, air roaring in his ears. He felt something rip violently at his chest, knocking all the remaining breath from his body.

Suddenly all was silent, save for the engines of the Junkers. He was sinking gently to earth. He flung a look upwards. The chute had functioned perfectly. Now he felt at ease, somehow insignificant and small; it was the kind of relief he often experienced after sex. Above him, more and more of his young men came tumbling out, snatched violently by the wind for an instant before the chutes opened and stopped their crazy plunge eastwards.

Hartung laughed out loud suddenly, like a crazy man. They had pulled it off. It was going to work. 'Now what do you say to that, Sergeant shitting Martini!' he yelled, safe in the knowledge that the NCO couldn't hear him. 'We've pulled it off – just like in the great days!' Then he forgot Martini as the ground raced up to meet him...

Corrigan raised himself to his full height, ignoring the shells bursting all around their positions. Down below, the hillside was swarming with white-clad figures, labouring up the ascent in spaced-out lines, heads bent as if they were fighting their way against a high wind, while in front of them the shells howled down, churning up the earth in blazing red fury.

'Here they come!' he yelled above the barrage. '*Stand to, everybody!*'

'*You heard the officer!*' Hawkins joined in, rising as well and trying not to think of the fist-sized razor-sharp shards of metal flying everywhere as the German bombardment hit their line. In a minute the firestorm would pass, and the infantry below would make that last, desperate charge. Then they would bloody well *have* to stop them or else they would be overrun. '*Stand fast!*'

As the barrage swept by and raced down the slope behind them, the assault troopers raised their heads. '*Alles für Deutschland!*' came the hoarse cry from a hundred young throats below. The lines broke into a trot. Corrigan raised his rifle. '*Fire at will!*' he cried, slapping the Lee Enfield into his shoulder and taking aim at the blond head of the young officer leading the first wave. Next instant, the rifle spoke. The officer flung up his arms as if in despair and let out a thin, shrill scream. He flopped into the snow and was trampled into it as his men raced over his dead body. The killing had commenced...

FOUR

Now the beaten German infantry were fleeing in panic down the slope, screaming and clawing at each other in their haste to escape that hellish fire. But as they ran, stumbling over the bodies of the dead which lay everywhere, a great roar suddenly came from the woods to the right.

Almost immediately, the sixty-ton Tigers came rumbling out of their hiding-places, snapping the firs like matchwood, their huge overhanging cannons swinging from left to right like the snouts of predatory monsters seeking out their prey. Within moments they were ploughing straight through the dis- ordered remnants of the panzer grenadiers, cutting great bloody swathes through their ranks and leaving the snow behind them a mess of butchered gore. Swiftly they formed themselves in a wedge, a white-painted command tank in the lead, aerials whipping the air, and started clattering up the hill.

For a moment Corrigan's gaze was riveted on the spectacle of a severed hand jolting up and down in the tracks of the command tank, as if waving a grisly goodbye. God only knew what would happen if the monsters ever reached his line. He *had* to find something to stop them – but what?

'Piats?' gasped Hawkins, reading his mind.

'Bounce off them like bloody ping pong balls,' Corrigan snapped contemptuously. 'Frontal armour half a yard thick.'

Now the morning air was filled with a murderous roar as the metal monsters advanced ever closer, machine-guns already beginning to spit angry white tracer in their direction.

'Knock that soddin' command tank out!' Slim Sanders yelled, and carried away with frustrated rage, blasted off both barrels of his shotgun.

'Yes, but how? Bloody hell – how?' moaned Corrigan.

'We've got the Sarge's namesake, sir!' Wolfers cried above the racket.

'What?'

'Hawkins grenades, sir!'

'Of course, Wolfers, of course!' cried Corrigan excitedly. 'Quick – get them!' And Wolfers doubled away, crouched low, to *Waltzing Mathilda*.

Now Corrigan had to yell to make himself heard above the ominous roar of the huge tanks as they rumbled closer to their position. 'Lads, you know how the Hawkins works? You clamp it to the tank and then run like hell. But my guess is that those bastards down there would even survive a Hawkins –

except in one place: underneath – near the engine. You know what that means? You'll have to wait in one of those shell-holes until the bugger rolls over you and *then* clamp it on.' He licked his lips, tense now, as he realised the full enormity of what he was saying. 'I want five volunteers…'

The men didn't hesitate. 'Here, sir!… Here, sir!' The voices came from all sides.

Corrigan made his choice in a split-second. 'Hawkins, you're in charge here. No buts, we've no time to lose. I'll take Sanders, Wolfers, you and you, Thomas' – he indicated a pale-faced, yellow-haired eighteen-year-old who had joined the assault troop in Holland as a reinforcement. 'All right, grab two grenades each and follow me. *At the double now!*'

Hurriedly each man took two of the bell-shaped grenades and scuttled after Corrigan. By now, the roar of the tanks seemed to fill the whole world. Tracer zipped back and forth. Behind him, Corrigan heard Hawkins bellow, 'Well, come on, don't just squat there like spare pricks at a wedding! Give 'em all yer've got. We've got to cover the CO and the other lads!'

A wild barrage of fire erupted from the assault troop's line as they carried out Hawkins' order. Machine-guns chattered furiously, and rifles cracked. The surviving Piats boomed, but Corrigan was right: the bottle-shaped bombs whined harmlessly off the Tigers' glacis plates.

Corrigan flung himself into a shell-hole directly in the path of the oncoming command tank just as its machine-gun scythed the slope. Wolfers was too late. He was caught in mid-stride. Throwing up his hands in agony, he clawed the air for a moment, then flopped down. 'My God,' Corrigan cursed, *'not Wolfers!'* Next moment he ducked as a burst of machine-gun fire ripped across the ground in front of him, showering his face with dirt and pebbles.

He looked up again. Wolfers had disappeared from view. Thank God, he had still had strength enough to throw himself into a shell-hole! Now the great lumbering monsters were almost on top of them. Peering over the rim of his shell-hole, his breath bated, every nerve tingling electrically, Corrigan saw the command tank loom up in front of him, filling the whole sky. He could see every bolt and every rivet – and those terrible churning tracks, still red with the blood of the fleeing enemy soldiers, coming ever closer.

The world shook and trembled. The air was evil with the stink of diesel. It clogged his throat and made him want to retch. The noise of the great engine was ear-splitting. He found himself screaming, but no sound came. Soil flew from the damp edges of the hole in a steady, ever-increasing rain. He gripped the grenades tightly. *Could* he do it? The pit rocked. He looked up like a latterday David squaring up to this metal goliath, seeing it rear up in front of him, massive, terrifying, a wall of steel blotting out the sky, descending down upon him, tracks churning crazily...

Whoomp!

For an awful eternity, he knew the pit would collapse and he would be churned to pulp beneath those tracks. He retched. Urine trickled down his leg, hot and wet. '*God ... God!*' he screamed, '*make it go away! G-O-D!*'

Totally unaware of what he was doing, he raised his hands and slammed the sticky grenades to the steel underbelly of the monster. The magnets clamped home. The blackness vanished. He retched again, the vomit mingling with the dirt that covered his contorted, tear-stained face.

Then it happened. One after another, there came two soft, muffled, seemingly harmless booms. He raised his head. For some reason that his fear-paralysed brain couldn't comprehend, the monster had rumbled to a halt, its great overhanging 88mm cannon beginning to sink lower and lower, like the head of a dying animal. Little puffs of white smoke were erupting from its armoured hide. It trembled violently, then, with terrifying suddenness, disintegrated in a horrific roar, its turret sailing high into the air, followed by what looked like a gigantic smoke ring. It wasn't until then that Corrigan realised what he had done. He had pulled it off. *He had knocked out the command tank!*

He looked up. To his right, another of the Tigers was burning furiously, its paint blistering as if from some hideous skin disease, ammunition exploding with muffled pops and snaps inside it. All around were human torches, running blindly and rolling on the ground in a vain effort to stifle their flames. One collapsed on his knees, remaining there upright for a moment while the flames melted the snow all around him with a hissing sound. Noiseless screams came from the gaping hole that had once been his mouth. Then suddenly he toppled forward and lay inert, his charred head resting in a pool of blue, crackling flame.

Another tank erupted, its turret sailing gracefully into the grey sky with a great whooshing sound. Suddenly there seemed to be grotesque, crumpled figures littering the snow, filling the air with the sickening stench of singed hair and flesh.

It was too much for the rest. Leaderless now, they swung round with a furious flurry of snow. For a moment they were obscured by the whirling white wake, and then they were scurrying back the way they had come, belching smoke as they did so. Within moments they had vanished into the white fog, leaving the battlefield to the handful of battered men on the top of the hill…

Thomas was dying. They had stuffed his shattered stomach full of shell dressings, but to no avail. The blood, dark and rich like the juice of an overripe fig, was pouring from his rent belly, his anus, his penis, and trickling out of his mouth, which gaped like that of a stranded fish. There was a stench of faeces in the air.

Hawkins shook his head. Corrigan made a pumping gesture with his finger. Hawkins nodded. He knew what the CO meant: kill him with a massive dose of morhpia. In the half-track they had scores of plastic hypodermics to treat the wounded.

Suddenly the boy opened his eyes, his blond hair matted to his forehead with sweat. He pressed Corrigan's hand with surprising strength.

'Don't let me die, sir!' he said, his voice quite under control. 'You won't, will you, sir?'

Kneeling next to Corrigan, Hawkins' faded old eyes flooded with tears. Even Slim Sanders muttered, 'Oh, my Christ!'

'No,' Corrigan heard himself say, in a voice he hardly recognised as his own. 'No,

I won't let you die, son... Just put you out of your pain for a while till the MO comes up.'

The boy's eyes flicked closed again, his features waxen. 'Thank you, sir...' he breathed. Suddenly his nose looked pinched – a sure sign of approaching death. 'Sorry ... sorry to have been a bother, sir.'

Corrigan could have broken down and sobbed. Hastily, he rose to his knees, keeping his head bent so the men couldn't see the look on his face, and went over to where Wolfers lay. Already he could hear the rumble of tracks down below again, but the fog was clearing away rapidly now. Perhaps they would be lucky and the Tiffies would appear in time. One thing was for sure: they would need them if they were going to survive the day.

The burst of machine-gun fire had caught Wolfers across the upper thigh. Now he lay on a blood-soaked blanket in his hole, trousers cut away to reveal swollen, blackened legs, thick with yellow wound dressings. Somebody had given him a ration chocolate bar, but for once he wasn't hungry.

Corrigan looked down at his ugly, ashen face, marred by the spots of adolescence. 'How's it going, Wolfers?' he asked gently. Behind him, Hawkins had pressed the first of the little syringes into the dying boy's arm.

'Fair to middling, sir,' Wolfers said, trying

302

to smile. Then he lowered his voice. 'The Jerries didn't shoot me goolies off, sir, did they?' he asked apprehensively. 'I asked one of the lads to look and he did and he said they were all right. But I can't *feel* anything down there, sir...' He licked his cracked, blood-scummed lips.

'Don't you worry, Wolfers,' Corrigan said, feigning confidence, trying not to listen to the sudden, hectic gasps of the drugged boy as he started to slip into death. 'A month from now, you'll be giving half the ladies of the night in the Rue Neuve a cheap thrill.'

'I've never been with a hoor, sir,' Wolfers whispered, as if embarrassed. 'Too frightened of getting a packet.'

'Well, I'll see you get a nice clean English nursing sister when you get back to dock. How's that?'

'Champion, sir... Sir – there's one other thing...'

'Yes?'

'I know they'll send me into dock for a while; but I don't want to be put in one of them ruddy Reinforcement Holding Centres. I want to come back to the assault troop, sir. Promise me, sir...' There was a note of pleading in his voice.

'Don't you worry, Wolfers.' Corrigan touched the young giant fleetingly. 'I'll get you back when the sawbones have seen to you, even if I have to come and fetch you personally. Now let the morphia do its work. Try and sleep.' He pulled the tarpaulin over the youth, and Wolfers closed his eyes contentedly and dozed. Five yards away Thomas died. Corrigan staggered blindly to his own hole – and for the first time since he had been a little boy, wept.

FIVE

The Tigers waddled up the side of the hill like ducks towards a village pond. Now the barrage on the top of the hill had ceased, leaving behind a loud, echoing silence, and the summit was wreathed in drifting brown smoke, flecked here and there with the cherry-red of burning trees.

Von Norden flashed a look at the sky above the smoke. It was clearing rapidly – he could already see patches of blue among the grey. It was time to eradicate the damned Tommies before it was too late. Careless of his own safety, he stood upright in the open turret and gave the signal for 'advance'.

The 'V' of Tigers started to move forward, their engines roaring mightily. Von Norden drew up his heavy fur collar against the sudden wind. He was getting too old for this sort of thing – leading an attack like a twenty-year-old subaltern! But still he could hear von Manteuffel's last words to him ringing in his ears! *'Von Norden, take that damned hill today – or suffer the consequences!'* And it was no idle threat, he knew. Von Manteuffel might simply dismiss him from his command, but Hitler would do more. He could well end up in a concentration camp, or worse, for dereliction of duty. In this year of 1944, Hitler treated his generals no better than anyone else…

A strange, ugly shape came hurtling towards him out of the smoke. Instinctively von Norden ducked. Next to him, the major in the immaculate, highly decorated black uniform remained upright, grinning all over his handsome young face. The object clanged against the side of the turret and for an instant the metal glowed a dull red; then with a howl it flew off, unable to penetrate the Tiger's thick armour.

'Piat, Herr General. Tommy anti-tank bomb. Couldn't cut its way through a piss-pot.'

'So I see,' replied von Norden, a little flustered. 'They haven't spotted us, though, have they, Major?'

'No sir. Just a random shot. We're in dead ground here.'

Reassured, von Norden breathed out. 'Excellent. Just as I had planned it.'

Again the handsome young major with the gleaming Knight's Cross around his neck grinned. The divisional commander had obviously forgotten that in battle nothing *ever* went as planned. 'How far do you want me to go, sir, before we turn in on them?'

'I want you to remain parallel with their

left flank. As soon as the shit starts flying, I want you to wheel straight in on them and roll them up, one position after the other.'

'The ... er, *shit* starts flying, sir...?'

Now it was von Norden's turn to grin. '*Jawohl*, Herr Major. You see, I have a little surprise for our buck-teethed English friends. Soon they are going to be caught – as you rough soldiers are wont to say – with their knickers round their ankles. *Nun, los! Wir haben keine Zeit zu verlieren!*'

'Martini, in the name of God, get those shitting men closed up!' barked Hartung in irritation. 'What are they – a bunch of Christmas tree soldiers or something?'

Martini, his chest heaving with exertion, bit back his angry reply just in time. With the rifles of three of the young paras draped across his broad shoulders, he needed all his breath. '*Los*,' he gasped. 'Keep moving, boys! Not much further now.'

'And keep it down to a dull roar, will you?' Hartung snapped. 'The Tommies are just the other side of that hill.'

Martini bit his bottom lip until the blood came. At that moment, he could have taken down his Schmeisser from his shoulder and ripped Hartung's back to pieces with a full magazine.

They had been marching cross-country now for five hours solid, with not even the regulation five minutes' pause at the end of each hour. The going had been murderous: sheer slopes, snow waist-deep among the trees, low stone walls barring each field, even a treacherous bog hidden beneath the snowfield which had cost them thirty minutes and caused one of the boys to break down and cry like a broken-hearted child. But Hartung had allowed the callow young greenbeaks no respite. He had driven them on and on with curses, threats, contemptuous cries – even blows. He was like a man possessed, as if this was 1940 all over again and there was still a flower-pot to be won, instead of the piss-pot which was soon going to be Germany's reward.

Martini's eyes burned with rage at the treatment being handed out to his 'boys', but at least they were now almost at their destination, for Hartung was half-running, half-stumbling through the deep snow ahead of them, charging on up to the top of the hill. *Let him,* Martini told himself sourly, *and I hope some shitting Tommy sniper's waiting for him over the other side, ready to blow his officer and gentleman's arse to hell. Playing the hero in December shitting 1944 indeed!*

But no sniper did the angry NCO that particular favour. Instead, as he flopped down, gasping, beside Hartung, he could see that the Tommies only two hundred metres away hadn't the slightest idea that

Major Hartung even existed. 'Holy arse with ears,' he exclaimed, 'I didn't know they were *that* close!'

Hartung grinned, for the first time since the drop. 'Exactly. And they haven't the faintest notion that we're here. We can give them the celebrated purple shaft right up their Tommy arses any time we want.'

Martini didn't answer. Instead he stared at the Tommy position, a cluster of foxholes, with the earth all around them pounded and pitted by gunfire; here and there a body lay sprawled out in the snow in the extravagant posture of death, and beyond were the burning wrecks of at least three Tigers, their dead crews scattered around them like pygmies in the foetal position.

'What are we going to do – *sir?*' he asked, adding the 'sir' as an afterthought.

'Our role's quite simple, Martini, and relatively harmless. Soon, General von Norden's tank boys are going to come in from the flank – that dead ground over there. Naturally, the Tommies will try to react. This time they won't be able to, because we're here right behind them, giving them as much shit as we can pump at them and forcing them to keep their Tommy turnips down.' He shrugged. 'It's as simple as that. The Second Armoured will break through the Tommies' line, barrel on to the Meuse and win the war, while we loll back at the depot, toasting our toes in front of a warm fire, supping as much good suds–'

'*Sir,*' Martini interrupted, irritated by Hartung's self-satisfied manner, his voice harsh, his eyes hard. 'How are those tankers going to roll up the Tommy line? Infantry?'

Hartung shook his head. 'No – there'll be no more good German lives lost. General von Norden is going to use a little trick he learned from the Popovs in Russia in 'forty-three.' He chuckled softly, as if whatever the trick was, it gave him vast pleasure. 'It's very simple actually. You have your mechanics bend the tank's exhaust, then you position your vehicle above the particular funk-hole you're attacking. Then the driver revs the engine for all he's worth. Those four-hundred-horsepower tank engines give off a lot of fumes!' He smiled at Martini, as if pleased with himself.

'You mean the tank exhaust is pointing inside the hole, pumping in carbon monoxide?'

'Yes, that's it.'

'But, sir!' Martini protested wildly. 'That ain't legal! That's using poison gas. It's against the Geneva Convention, or whatever the shit they call it! It's...'

His words trailed away to nothing. Captain Hartung wasn't listening any more. His gaze was suddenly fixed to the right, his little smile vanished now, his face hard and tough-looking once more. A lone tank had breasted the rise, still unseen by the Tommies on the hilltop, and was waddling straight towards their position. It was them. Von Norden's Tigers had arrived.

Suddenly it was crashing straight out of the woods, smashing through the firs as if they were matchwood, its tracks churning up the snow in a wild white fury, its driver's face a white blur behind the armoured slit. The boy in the foxhole screamed and dropped his rifle. What good was it against this armoured monster advancing straight towards him, intent on the kill? '*Help me!*' he screamed. '*Please, God,*' he yelled hysterically, carried away by panic. '*Have mercy on me!*'

But this afternoon, God was looking the other way; there would be no mercy for the panic-stricken boy. Instead, the vehicle ran right over his dug-out, blotting out the grey light, hot drops of oil splashing on to his crazed, upturned face, the soil crumbling alarmingly all around him. He buried his hands in his face, feeling his bowels turn to water, his nostrils immediately assailed by the stench of fresh faeces. While he screamed, above him the unseen driver gunned the two great Maybach engines at 2,500 revs, flooding the pit which would be the young boy's grave with grey, choking gas. He smelled it for a moment – but only for a moment. Suddenly he was fighting for air, grabbing at his collar, tearing it open, his breath coming in ever shorter, more hectic gasps, eyes bulging from his head, black and silver stars exploding furiously before him as he desperately fought back the waves of red mist. Dying, he fell into the corner, eighteen years of age, his tongue cut to shreds and his face a bright crimson, as the tank rumbled on to the next foxhole...

Corrigan knew that at all costs he had to conquer, stifle, somehow choke down that sick, harrowing fury that threatened to overwhelm him, as he watched the monsters waddle ever closer, pausing regularly to carry out their murderous work. At his feet, Slim Sanders stared up at him, his face a stricken mask as he nursed his wounded arm, that overwhelming, unspoken question blazing from his pain-wet eyes: *isn't there any way to save us?*

Another burst of bullets ripped along the rim of Corrigan's foxhole, the dirt splattering his face as he ducked down hurriedly. From above came a high, hysterical scream that cut him right to the bone and made the small hairs at the back of his neck stand erect with fear. Another foxhole had been overrun, and another of his boys had been cruelly tortured to death. Next to him, Hawkins, bleeding from a deep graze in his temple, cursed and rose to clamber out of the hole. Corrigan grabbed him just in time and forced him down again! 'No use!' he gasped. 'They'd plug you before you got a yard! The buggers up there have got us taped. We're sitting ducks.'

Hawkins looked at him, eyes wild with horror, tears streaming down his dirty face. 'But we can't let ourselves be slaughtered!' he screamed. '*Not like that! We've got to do something, sir!*'

'*What for Chrissake, man?*' Corrigan screamed back at him, his lips flecked with foam, madness in his eyes. '*I can't fight the fucking things with my bare hands, can I?*'

Hawkins grabbed for his rifle. Corrigan saw it coming, saw the riot in the sergeant's eyes. He grabbed for the muzzle and pulled. Hawkins staggered backwards, false teeth bulging from his gaping mouth, still crying, his face set in a wolfish snarl. '*Let me go, I say!*' he shrieked. '*Let me go... I must stop them before it's too late!*'

Like madmen, the two of them wrestled back and forth in the tight confines of the hole, kicking and gouging, each trying to gain the advantage. Meanwhile, the roar of the lead tank seemed to fill the whole world as it advanced upon them in inexorable menace, determined not to be cheated of its prey...

Now von Norden's tank, its tracks flushed a deep crimson, waddled ever closer to the Tommy command post. Rub it out, von Norden told himself – rub it out, and it would be all over. The rest would collapse, surrender, and the hill would be his. In twenty-four hours they would be on the Meuse. Whatever happened to the great offensive after that didn't matter. He would have carried out *his* orders successfully. Pleased with himself, he beamed at the young tank major and cupping his hands around his mouth, cried, '*Ausgezeichnet! Alles in Butter, Herr Major?*'

The major nodded, forgetting the young men so cruelly gassed to death in the holes behind them like foxes in their burrows. '*Alles in Butter!*' he roared back, and pointed to the command post twenty metres ahead of them, the radio aerials giving away its position. 'There's the heart of the defence!'

Von Norden lowered himself a little inside the turret. The fire from Hartung's paras on the hilltop to their right was getting a little too close for comfort now. He intended to survive the war – at least, he didn't want to be killed by his own side.

The major noted the general's move with a sneer of contempt. It was true what the stubble-hoppers said: generals *did* die in shitting bed! He pressed his throat-mike and rasped, 'Commander to driver. Prepare to engage the–'

Suddenly the whole horizon to the front of the advancing tanks quaked. Furious red lights blinked. With a hoarse, exultant scream that drowned even the roar of the Tigers' engines, great objects came racing towards them from the sky, trailing straight lines of thick, grey smoke behind them.

For a moment the major couldn't comprehend what they signified. Then, as the first white-striped hawk came streaming in at 500 kilometres an hour, radial motor howling ear-splittingly, violet lights rippling along its wings, he screamed, 'Evasive action … *Jabos!*'

Behind the command tank, another Tiger shuddered as if caught in a sudden storm. Great chunks of gleaming silver steel flew everywhere as the rockets ripped into it. As the Typhoon dive-bomber soared over their heads, dragging its evil black shadow behind it across the snow, the Tiger disintegrated in a mass of flying armoured plates. An instant later it exploded, sending a huge cloud of thick black smoke streaming heavenwards.

Now the second dive-bomber was coming in at a tremendous lick. It seemed to be skidding across the surface of the snow, sucking it up as it roared by. Already those angry violet lights were crackling along its wings.

'*Driver!*' screamed the major through the throat-mike, in an ecstasy of fear. '*In God's name, man–'*

Down below, the driver panicked as he saw the rockets streaming straight towards him. He ripped the wheel round too sharply. The tank gave a terrifying lurch. Von Norden, his gross face suddenly ashen, clung on for dear life, meaningless sounds coming from his parched grey lips. All around them the rockets smacked home. Huge holes appeared everywhere. Great gouts of snow and mud rose high into the air. Von Norden screamed, 'Bale out! *We're finished!'* and the next instant the tank began to go over. Ripping his earphones from his shaven head, he clambered over the turret edge, heart thumping with abject terror as the sixty-ton monster teetered for an instant.

The black-clad major cursed, pulled at his own headset and was over the turret with a single agile jump, landing like a cat on his toes. In the same moment von Norden did the same, and the Tiger crashed to its side, tracks revolving helplessly. But von Norden wasn't as swift as the major. For once, a general was destined not to die in bed...

Another Typhoon came zooming in at tree-top level, filling the world with its banshee howl, rockets blazing. The major's number two tank plunged straight ahead, its driver panicked by the roar. Von Norden held up his arms in a futile attempt to stop it. To no avail. The glacis plate knocked him clean off his feet. Madly he flailed his arms. Next moment he had disappeared beneath it, swept on by the churning tracks.

The major gasped in horror as the Tiger rattled past him. The general had disappeared completely, as if he had never even existed – save for one thing: a bloody shaven head flopping back and forth in the crimson, blood-daubed tracks...

SIX

Sergeant Martini breathed a sigh of relief as the last of the Jabos zoomed high into the clouds, rolling wildly in victory, trailing a bright white snake behind it. Down below, the shattered Tigers crackled fiercely, and from far away to their rear, there could be heard the clatter of other tracks and a faint, odd wailing sound, which he had heard once before in Normandy when those strange Tommies who wore ladies' skirts and pumped at pigs' guts had attacked. The Highlanders were coming – and it was all over.

Martini grinned. 'They don't just pump air into pigs' guts and wear women's skirts like a lot of shitting warm brothers, sir – they feed on sheep shit and drink whisky for breakfast, too,' he said happily.

'What?' said Hartung, looking gloomily at the burning Tigers. 'What did you say, Martini?'

Martini repeated his words, hoping that the officer's face would break into that tough smile like in the good old days. It didn't. Instead, Hartung snapped, 'What in three devils' name are you babbling about, Martini?' and without waiting for an answer, swung round and focused his glasses.

Far down below, a long line of vehicles crowded with dark figures which Hartung knew were infantry slid into the calibrated glass circles. '*Damn, damn, damn!*' he cursed, recognising the little Tommy carriers immediately. There were at least one and a half battalions down there. The Tommies were on their way in strength. If they reached the hilltop, supported by those damned Jabos of theirs, they were finished. That would be the end of 2nd Panzer Division's attempt to take the hill and drive to the Meuse. He let the glasses fall to his chest. 'Martini, we've got to attack. The Tommies are on their way.'

'Attack?' Martini stared at him incredulously. 'Did you say *attack*, sir?'

'Of course I shitting well did, Martini! Have you been eating big beans or something, man? Come on now, *dalli, dalli!* Usual drill: you take two sections, I take the remaining two. Marching fire...' He stopped suddenly and stared at the sergeant he had known so long as if he were seeing him for the very first time. 'What is it, Martini?' he cried. 'Why aren't you carrying out my orders? What are you looking at me like that for?'

'Sir,' Martini croaked, 'this is December, nineteen forty-four, not May, nineteen forty.'

'What the shit's that supposed to mean?'

'We're finished, sir. *Finito, fini, kaput!* The Thousand-Year-Reich is in the shit-bucket! Now it's a question of saving the necks of those greenbeaks there, those smooth-faced titty-suckers. You've said as much yourself many a time.' Suddenly Martini's anger broke through and he grabbed Hartung by the jacket, as if he were about to shake him. 'Don't you understand, you madman? *You can't sacrifice their lives for a lost cause!*'

Hartung looked coldly at the NCO's contorted red face. 'Sergeant Martini, I'm giving you a clear and explicit order to remove your hands from my uniform. Or else.'

Numbly Martini let his big paws fall. 'But sir–'

'No more buts. Do as you're ordered or take the consequences.' Hartung's hand dropped to his pistol.

Martini decided to make one last effort. 'Sir,' he said fervently, 'I've said it before, but I'll say it again, straight from the liver. I've had my fun in this war – we old hares all have. The whores, the suds, the larks, the good comrades and all the rest of it. And I've helped to pay the butcher's bill often enough.' He jerked his thumb at the silver medal on his chest which indicated that he had been wounded six times in combat. 'I was lucky; I survived. But now I've had enough. We've all had enough, old hares and young greenbeaks alike. Let's stop while we still can.' There was an unmistakable note of pleading in his voice now. 'Withdraw, sir – *please!*'

Hartung gave a cynical laugh. 'Do you think that new freedom-loving, democratic Germany that the Amis will set up will be worth dying for?' he barked. 'I doubt it.'

'It might be worth *living* for, sir.'

'*Rubbish!* Those greenbeaks you're always clucking over like an old mother hen *flocked* to our regiment, crying out for the privilege of being shipped to Russia or wherever and having their turnips blown off for Folk, Fatherland and Führer.' Hartung's face flushed with sudden fury. 'Now that's enough, Sergeant Martini. Time is running out.'

Martini grabbed for his pistol. Hartung beat him to it. His pistol thundered straight from his holster. A look almost of rapture seemed to come over Hartung as his victim staggered back as if punched by a gigantic fist. A great scarlet stain suddenly started spreading across Martini's chest, and on his face there appeared a look of complete disbelief. '*Sir...*' he choked, and raised one hand, as if he were a schoolboy in class, asking for permission to speak. Then, infinitely slowly, like a fighter who has been dealt the knock-out punch but still won't give in, he went down on his knees in the snow, head hanging. A moment later, he fell face forwards without another sound.

Hartung didn't even look down. He stepped over the body writhing in the snow and stared around at the pale-faced, shocked young paras who had witnessed the scene. In the background, the clatter of the enemy vehicles and the eerie wail of their music were getting louder.

'Ready for attack,' Hartung rasped. 'Come on now *Wirds bald... Fertig zum Angriff!*'

In silence, like ghosts arising from their graves, the youngsters rose from their holes and prepared to move out.

Hartung smiled cynically and picked up a Schmeisser, automatically tapping the magazine to see if it was securely attached. 'That's a bit better,' he called encouragingly, and waited till they formed up. *One more time,* the little voices within his mind chanted crazily. *One more time and then you can rest for ever...*

Ever since the German tanks had started their attack, the assault troop's position had been constantly under fire. Now suddenly the shelling had stopped. Corrigan groaned. He knew what it meant: the Germans were grouping for an all-out infantry attack. He shook his head like a man trying to wake out of a nightmare and attempted to collect his thoughts.

'Sergeant Hawkins,' he croaked, 'how are the lads? Ammo?' He couldn't ask more; he didn't seem to have the strength. His whole body trembled and he was afraid he might fall at any moment. He knew it was sheer nervous exhaustion, but that didn't make any difference; he was out on his feet.

'Knackered, sir,' Hawkins answered, looking haggard and weary himself. 'They're down to five rounds per man.'

'Five rounds?' Corrigan echoed, like some idiot that couldn't take in the simplest of ideas. There was a loud roaring noise in his ears. The lunar landscape in front of him seemed to waver as if he were seeing it through a heat haze, like back in the desert. A hammer was clanging against his skull. He swayed violently. If he wasn't careful, he would faint any minute. He must hold on. He *must!*

'Fuckin' Jocks,' Slim groaned, lying in the mud at Corrigan's feet. Fresh blood was oozing from his wound, but no one cared. They were past caring now, all of them. 'Why are they so fuckin' slow? Jocks … Jocks – I've shat 'em!'

'Forming up,' Corrigan croaked. 'Must stand the men to… Can't let them through… Must hold…' Suddenly Corrigan sank to his knees. For some reason his rifle was falling out of his hand. Why? *Why* wouldn't it stay in his grasp? Dimly, from far, far away, he could hear hoarse commands in German and the guttural roar which he knew so well and which always heralded an attack. But try as he might, he couldn't seem to get back on his feet... Just couldn't...

'To hell with shitting pain!' whispered Martini, dully noting the strange sound his words made. It resembled that of a fractured leather bellows he remembered his father using at the smithy as a kid. He had a sucking wound; his lungs had been shot to pieces. Somehow he staggered to his feet, swaying like a drunk. What seemed like a vast expanse of snow lay before him, wreathed in a wavering grey mist; through it he could just make out dim, helmeted figures with their backs to him, wearing uniforms that seemed vaguely familiar. Then he recognised them. They were the boys, the sugar-titties.

With fingers that felt like clumsy sausages, he fumbled for the little pistol at his waist. He staggered forward a few paces, clutching it in his hand. Space seemed to be coming at him like a solid wall. Where was the bastard? Where was Hartung?

The clatter of vehicles was very loud now; so was that banshee wailing noise the Englishmen in skirts made with their pig guts. He had to find Hartung before it was too late. He *had* to! He stumbled on, trailing the steaming, pulsating grey-purple snake of his intestines with him through the snow.

There he was. *Hartung!* His face was flint-like and ferocious, his eyes tired, yet icy-blue and completely unafraid.

'Martini!' barked Hartung as he spotted him – and to the sergeant standing there, pistol in hand, swaying from side to side, the voice seemed to come from a million kilometres away. *'Die! I order you to die!'*

Martini raised the pistol as if it weighed a hundredweight. He was dying on his feet, but still driven on by a homicidal fury, an atavistic savagery that streamed through his wrecked, shattered body.

'Die, I say,' Hartung snapped, his voice full of frigid contempt. 'Have done with it! *Die, you dog!'*

Martini pulled the trigger. At that range, he simply couldn't miss. Hartung's face turned red, then black. In an instant it was transformed into a grotesque, inhuman, red-dripping mask, slowly crumpling, collapsing into a curled, shapeless lump of smoking flesh. Agonisingly slowly, he started to sink down into the snow, uttering meaningless sounds from the ragged red hole which had once been his mouth.

Martini sighed like a man about to sink into oblivion. Around him he sensed rather than saw the startled, awed young faces of the greenbeaks. In the distance, the wailing sound was growing ever louder. He felt no pain, nothing but sadness – sadness for those confused young faces. 'Go,' he breathed, in a cracked, distorted voice. 'Go, lads...' He was on his knees now, gasping, shaking his head, clenching his fists like a fighter trying to avoid a count-out. '*Go!*' Then, summoning up the last of his strength, he raised his dying head one final time, and with a tremendous effort of sheer willpower, yelled, '*Fuck off, will you!*' – and fell face forward into the snow, dead at last.

The spell broken, the greenbeaks at last fled from that terrible scene, throwing away their weapons in their haste to be gone, screaming like children in the grip of a horrifying nightmare.

On the opposite hill, the surviving members of the assault troop watched their flight in silence, no triumph on their dirty, unshaven faces, just pity and understanding. No one fired.

ENVOI

'Merry it was to laugh there,
Where death becomes absurd and life
  absurder.
For power was on us as we slashed bones
  bare
Not to feel sickness or remorse of murder.'

Wilfred Owen

Somewhere a Yorkshire voice was crooning –
very badly – the Old Groaner's latest hit,
'I'm Dreaming of a White Christmas'. A solid
line of two-and-a-half-ton US trucks driven
by the black drivers of the Red Ball Express
rumbled at a reckless speed towards the
bridge, forcing the heavily-laden infantry
into the slush-filled gutters. Bravely, they
sang on, *'She'll be wearing khaki knickers when
she comes... She'll be wearing khaki knickers
when she comes...'* Above, in the perfect, blue
December sky, the silver birds of the US
Eighth Air Force droned eastwards, dragging their bright white contrails behind
them. All was speed and confident purpose.

General Horrocks, looking thinner and
more ascetic than ever, nodded his approval

and turned from the window of his new HQ in the great rambling Belgian *château* that overlooked the Meuse.

'Well, young Corrigan,' he said, breath fogging on the icy air of the unheated hall, 'it looks as if Monty's saved the day after all.'

Corrigan, shaved, rested, his wounds dressed, but still pale and shaken from the ordeal on the hill, cleared his throat. 'I hope so, sir.'

Behind the doors, telephones jingled, typewriters rattled and staff officers dictated to the ATS women clerks in urgent, upper-class Sandhurst accents. Wolfers would have called them 'pound-notish', if he had heard them; but Wolfers had been sent to the military hospital at Louvain with the rest of the wounded.

'Oh, yes. The Yanks certainly received a rather bloody nose in the Ardennes, but Monty's managed to staunch the bleeding. Now it's up to the Yanks to give the Hun a taste of their own medicine.' He beamed at Corrigan, his thin, craggy face lighting up. 'Thanks to you and your chaps, Corrigan, in no small part. Indeed, Monty wanted Ike to give you a gong, but after Ike found out who you were – there was some business about shootings on a train or something – the idea was dropped like a hot potato. No matter, Corrigan, I'm putting you in for a bar to your MC.'

'Thank you, sir,' Corrigan said without enthusiasm. A whole bagful of gongs would not help *him* advance in the Regular Army. The train massacre would stay on his record, inaccurate as it was, until finally he either resigned his commission or the powers that be kicked him out. It didn't matter. Nothing mattered.

'Of course, we're in for a jolly hard slog now,' Horrocks said with a sigh. 'Back in the Autumn, I thought the whole bloody thing would be over by Christmas. Not now. Not by a long chalk. The old Hun is going to fight like a madman, especially when we cross into Hunland. There's no doubt about that, I'm afraid.' He sighed again.

Outside, the Yorkshire voice sang on, dreaming of Christmases past. A troop of Churchill tanks, the white paint used as Winter camouflage still dripping from them, clattered by, heading towards the bottleneck of the bridge and its cursing, harassed MPs.

'I'm going to need you, Corrigan,' said Horrocks, face suddenly hard, 'and your chaps of the assault troop. There aren't many of the veterans left.' He nodded to the fresh-faced infantry outside, their helmets set cockily on the side of their heads. 'Kids – eighteen-year-olds for the most part, straight from the reinforcement holding units. They're always the first to get hit...

Cannon-fodder.' He sighed yet again, like a man sorely troubled. 'We're scraping the barrel back in the UK, Corrigan. We're simply running out of bodies.'

Suddenly Horrocks forced a smile. 'But let's forget the gloom, Corrigan, eh?'

'Yes, sir,' Corrigan replied dutifully – but he couldn't return the smile. He felt numb, just as he had sometimes felt as a young cadet at Sandhurst, needing to go out and escape from his cares for a while, but somehow lacking the spirit to do so.

'I've talked to your divisional commander, Corrigan. He's agreed to give you and your chaps a seventy-two-hour pass to Brussels, although strictly speaking, all leave, local or UK, has been cancelled during the emergency.' Horrocks gazed at Corrigan's pale, withdrawn face, noting the dark circles under the eyes. 'Now, get yourself off to the flesh-pots there. Spend some of your pay on a good bottle of bubbly, my boy, and find yourself a lady of the night – a clean one, preferably.' Horrocks smiled encouragingly. 'Relax for a change, Corrigan. We'll be needing you and your chaps again soon.' He held out his skinny hand. 'And thank you – for everything.'

Automatically Corrigan took the hand and was surprised by the firmness of the general's grip. A second later he had saluted and was gone.

Outside it was cold. For a moment he stood there, shivering a little, watching the troops and vehicles file past and wondering what he should do next. For the first time since the Invasion six months before, he had no command. The wounded were in hospital a day's drive away; the survivors were probably already packed and on the leave-truck, bound for Brussels. What was he to do?

For a few moments he let the newsreel of the last week roll before his mind's eye. Once more he saw the hordes of Russian partisans... The Belgian prisoner with the pail on his head... Smythe blown into eternity... The massacre of the German recce... Those desperate minutes in the foxhole as the Tiger rolled over him... *Click, click...* As each fragmentary scene flickered across his mental screen, Corrigan realised just how terribly fast the assault troop was diminishing. He remembered Thomas, his guts shot away, dying at eighteen, gasping with his dying breath, '*Sorry to have been a bother, sir...*' Corrigan shook his head and the newsreel vanished, giving way to the hard realisation that not one of them would ever go home to cheering crowds, victory parades, the joyous pealing of cathedral bells. He and all the survivors of the assault troop and those callow-faced youths who would soon be filling the yawning gaps in their ranks – they would all die before it was over. As he stood outside the grey *château* with the traffic of war flowing incessantly eastwards, Corrigan knew that with the certainty of a vision.

An urgent honking of a horn roused him from his reverie. A White half-track was trying to force its way across the main street, its driver gunning the engine and sounding his horn to clear a path for the muddy, bullet-scarred vehicle. Corrigan's heart gave a great leap. It was *Waltzing Mathilda,* the assault troop's last surviving vehicle.

Suddenly it started forward with a noisy slithering of tracks, the startled infantrymen by the roadside cursing as they were splashed with frozen slush and dirty water. Looking up, an open-mouthed Corrigan saw a well-remembered, wizened face staring out of the cab at him, a sprig of mistletoe in his cap behind the silver badge, a goose and a pile of bottles on the leather seat next to him.

'Thought I'd find you here, sir,' Hawkins, cried, above the angry shouts and the honking horns of the now stalled convoy. 'Hop aboard quick before those darkies start slicing off my goolies with them cut-throat razors of theirs!'

Blindly, Corrigan reached up and did as he was bid. Down the road, the Redcaps were already blowing their whistles angrily. From somewhere, an official voice was yelling,

'Get that bloody half-track off the road! I don't care if you have to blow it up!' Hastily he slammed the steel door closed behind him. The whole of the back of the vehicle was piled high with boxes and bottles, and at the far end was a huge Christmas tree with snow on the branches, as if it had just been plucked out of the ground.

Ramming home first gear, Hawkins gunned the engine and let out the clutch. The half-track shot forward. With men shouting, whistles shrilling, horns honking furiously behind them, they raced down the one-way street, trucks and soldiers scattering wildly to get out of their way. Grinning, Hawkins hunched over the wheel of *Waltzing Mathilda* like a racing driver at Brooklands, eyes twinkling with merriment.

'But where are we going?' Corrigan cried above the racket, finding his voice at last.

'To Louvain, sir. I've nicked the petrol. We're going to visit the lads and play Father Christmas!'

'*Father Christmas?*' yelled Corrigan, as Hawkins narrowly avoided a head-on crash with a black driver, who suddenly turned a delicate shade of yellow.

'Yes, sir!' Hawkins chortled happily. 'I flogged a whole week's ration for the whole troop on the Belgie black market – that's how I got all those goodies you can see in the back. There's wine and beer, and fags and chocs, and them-there geese. Even old greedy-guts Wolfers won't have anything to complain about when he sees that little lot. By gum, sir, this is going to be a Christmas and a half for the Iron Division's assault troop!' He laughed crazily. 'I'll have the whole shower of them pissed as newts by midnight, I swear I will. And they deserve it – by God they do!'

'Christmas and a half?' Corrigan stuttered in bewilderment.

For a moment, Hawkins, his old wrinkled face animated by happiness, took his eyes off the road. 'Didn't you know, sir?'

'Know what?'

'It's Christmas Eve – Christmas Eve, nineteen bloody forty-four – *and I intend to see that our lads never forget it, sir!*' Carried away by an almost unbearable emotion, Hawkins yelled at the top of his voice, '*Bash on, recce Assault Troop!*'

Forgetting his gloomy predictions and past miseries for a moment, Corrigan, too, was carried away by the little man's infectious excitement. '*Bash on, the Assault Troop!*' he cried. And then, laughing like madmen, the two of them were gone, rattling down the dead-straight Belgian road and into the future...

The publishers hope that this book has given you enjoyable reading. Large Print Books are especially designed to be as easy to see and hold as possible. If you wish a complete list of our books please ask at your local library or write directly to:

Dales Large Print Books
Magna House, Long Preston,
Skipton, North Yorkshire.
BD23 4ND